Death at the
Beggar's Opera

Deryn Lake

NEW ENGLISH LIBRARY
Hodder and Stoughton

Copyright © 1995 by Deryn Lake

The right of Deryn Lake to be identified as the Author of the
Work has been asserted by Deryn Lake in accordance with the
Copyright, Designs and Patents Act 1988.

First published in Great Britain in 1995
by Hodder and Stoughton
A division of Hodder Headline PLC

A New English Library Paperback

10 9 8 7 6 5 4 3 2 1

All rights reserved. No part of this publication may be
reproduced, stored in a retrieval system, or transmitted,
in any form or by any means without the prior written
permission of the publisher, nor be otherwise circulated
in any form of binding or cover other than that in which
it is published and without a similar condition being
imposed on the subsequent purchaser.

British Library Cataloguing in Publication Data

Lake, Deryn
Death at the Beggar's Opera
I. Title
823. 914 [F]

ISBN 0 340 64985 2

Typeset by Phoenix Typesetting, Ilkley, West Yorkshire.

Printed and Bound in Great Britain by
Cox & Wyman Ltd, Reading, Berkshire.

Hodder and Stoughton
A division of Hodder Headline PLC
338 Euston Road
London NW1 3BH

In memory of
Shirley Russell,
friend and agent,
who once lived down Drury Lane.

Chapter One

It being an inclement day, plagued by needle-sharp rain and whipping winds, John Rawlings, after first safely locking up his shop in Shug Lane, hurried home beneath the protection of an umbrella, that useful invention from the Orient considered by many as too effeminate for a man to carry. Jumping between the puddles and avoiding the gutters, awash with indescribable and unspeakable items, John none the less considered that much as he disliked the prevailing conditions they had brought about some excellent business. As downpour after downpour had descended upon London, so had the door of his apothecary's shop swung open, a bell attached above it ringing a warning that someone was present. And though most of this flurry of custom had come in simply to gain shelter, all had gone out holding a package of some kind; a bottle of perfume, some tablets for the gout, a cure for the clap, some carmine for a lady's lips. Reflecting on the truth of the proverb ' 'Tis an ill wind that blows nobody any good', John Rawlings hastened through the rain towards his home in Nassau Street in the parish of St Ann's, Soho.

The time being shortly after four o'clock on that raw autumn afternoon, the candles of number two had already been lit, and as John turned the corner of Gerrard Street and saw the welcoming glow, he ran the last short distance to his front door. Hurrying up the steps, he closed the unfashionable umbrella, handing it to the footman who answered his knock, then bounded into the hall with one of his characteristic hare-like movements.

'John?' called a voice from the library, and only stopping to remove his dripping broadcloth coat, the Apothecary went to join his father.

This night Sir Gabriel Kent, who had adopted John Rawlings when the child had been but three years old, and was therefore a father to him in every sense but the actual, sat resplendent in a high-backed chair before a gleaming wood fire. Casually dressed, for he obviously did not intend to go forth on so foul an evening, Sir Gabriel was still wearing the black satin suit, heavily laced with silver decoration, in which he had dined. However, he had removed his high storeyed wig, an old-fashioned affair more reminiscent of the reign of the Stuarts than that of the Hanoverians, and had on his closely cropped head a black turban of particularly fine quality. As it was Sir Gabriel's habit to affect black and white during daylight hours, black and silver for evenings and festivities, the only ornament in this striking headpiece was a silver brooch bearing a Siberian zircon, which glittered in the candlelight like a pool of irridescent water. Looking up from his book as his son entered, Sir Gabriel smiled and motioned to the chair opposite his, pouring a glass of pale sherry as he did so.

'You're home early, my dear,' he said.

John took the offered glass from his father's long fingers. 'I'm going to the theatre with Serafina and Louis, had you forgotten? She has asked me to dine with them first, so I was obliged to close the shop promptly.'

'Did you do good trade today?'

'Very. The world and his wife, to say nothing of a few lovers, came in to avoid the rain and not one of them left without buying something.'

'Were you called out at all?'

'Only to attend a rakehell who had indulged too well. He lay festering in a darkened room wishing to die.'

Sir Gabriel laughed drily. 'And what did you prescribe?'

'I gave him a dose of salts fair set to glue him to his privy pan.'

'Lud, how the world goes on!' exclaimed John's father, and laughed once more. 'Now, to speak of more pleasant things. What is it you are going to see tonight? Pray remind me.'

'A new production of *The Beggar's Opera*, complete with special scenic effects, and mounted at Drury Lane no less.'

Sir Gabriel closed his eyes. 'Ah, that sweet theatre! How many happy memories I have of it. Why, it was the very first place of entertainment into which your mother ever stepped. We saw *The Way of the World* and she remarked afterwards how very disagreeable all the characters seemed.'

'A strange comment from one who once had to exist on the streets of London.'

John's father sighed reflectively. 'Despite her terrible struggles, Phyllida maintained a freshness and directness of manner which was most endearing. You have inherited something of that characteristic.'

The Apothecary smiled naughtily, half of his mouth curving upwards in what could only be described as a crooked grin. 'Except when I am forced to dissemble, that is.'

'That apart,' answered Sir Gabriel with a twinkle in his eye, and put the tips of his fingers together.

It was almost with reluctance that John Rawlings left the library, some fifteen minutes later, and made his way upstairs to change for the evening's entertainment. Anxious though he was to meet his friends and go out with them, he never tired of his father's company nor, indeed, of conversing with the handsome older man, whose golden eyes were so full of wit and intelligence and whose keen brain had not been dulled one whit by the passing of the years.

As he put on his twilight clothes, John considered that of all his weaknesses his love of fashion was paramount. Indeed, had he had any other calling he would have dressed flamboyantly at all times. But the fact was that by day he must adopt sober black, for an apothecary not only made up prescriptions for doctors and surgeons but was also called upon to give medical advice and attend the sick in their homes, and for this reason could in no manner appear dandified. Therefore, at night the young man glittered like a bird of paradise by way of compensation. And this evening, knowing that he was to be in company with the exotic Serafina and her handsome French husband, John chose a suit of mulberry satin trimmed with gold, his waistcoat a riot of golden flowers and sparkling radiants.

'Very fine,' commented Sir Gabriel as his son came to bid him goodnight.

'Too much for Drury Lane?'

'Not at all. Did you not say Louis intends to have a stage box?'

'Yes.'

'Then you will be as closely observed as the performers. Now send one of the footmen to call you a chair. You must not get so much as a drop of rain on such choice apparel. And you are most certainly not to take that terrible umbrella of yours. It would ruin the entire effect.'

John burst out laughing. 'Why are you so prejudiced against it? It is a very sensible piece of equipment.'

'Fit for nothing but to keep the sun off dusky maidens and Eastern potentates. You would never see me abroad with such a thing.'

The Apothecary kissed him on the cheek. 'You would rather get soaked I suppose. Though, on second thoughts, I doubt the rain would have the temerity to fall on you.'

And with that he made a hasty exit into the small but elegant hall of number two, Nassau Street, where he put on his cloak, before stepping outside and into the waiting sedan chair.

It was a dismal night, dark and chilly, and after a few seconds of peering out of the chair's window, John pulled the curtain across it and contented himself with thinking about the evening ahead, cheerfully contemplating the prospect of good company, an excellent repast and a fine theatrical performance. However, it was at that moment, just as he thought of Drury Lane, that the Apothecary felt a faint thrill of unease, which he instantly thrust aside. And yet, ignore this feeling as he might, it cast a shadow over him and he was glad when the chair was set down outside the gracious entrance to number twelve, Hanover Square, the home of the Comte Louis de Vignolles and his entrancing wife, Serafina.

They were waiting for him in the first floor drawing room, a beautiful couple in such harmonious surroundings that John felt a catch in his throat. Once they had been at war with one another, these two people, and it had been partly through his intervention that they had come together again. So it was with extra warmth that he kissed Serafina's hand and made his formal bow to the Comte.

'My dear John,' said the Comtesse, embracing him fondly, 'we are so very pleased to see you. What a delight this evening is going to be, with all of us old friends together once more.'

Again, unbidden, came the feeling of disquiet, something of which must have shown on the Apothecary's face. For the Comtesse continued, 'You seem anxious. What is the matter?'

John shook his head. 'Nothing, I assure you. Nobody could be looking forward to the occasion more than I.' And he squeezed her hands to emphasise the point.

A few months previously, in the summer of 1754, he had believed himself in love with her. Now he had come to his senses and simply rejoiced in the warmth of Serafina's friendship, a far more comfortable relationship all round. None the less, this did not prohibit him from appreciating her beautiful bone structure and supple physique. Indeed, the first time he had ever seen her, John had thought of the Comtesse as a delicate racehorse of a female and his opinion had not changed during the period of their acquaintanceship.

Kissing her hand once more, the Apothecary said, 'You are in fine beauty tonight, Madam. So is it your intention to conceal your face with a mask?'

Serafina touched her husband lightly on the arm. 'Louis likes me to do so, in fact it amuses him enormously. Anyway, it is considered *de rigeur* at the theatre these days.'

'A fashion started by yourself, no doubt.'

The Comtesse shrugged elegantly. 'Perhaps.'

'I'm certain of it,' her husband put in. 'Now, John, a glass of champagne?' And he motioned a hovering footman to pour.

It was at that moment that there was a knock on the front door, which opened once more. The sound of another arrival could be heard in the hall below and John knew by the very stamp of the feet and exclamations about the inclemency of the night that his old friend Samuel Swann had come to join the party. The heavy running footsteps on the curving staircase confirmed this belief, and a second or so later the great windmill of a young man burst into the room and heartily pumped the Comtesse's hand.

'Delighted to see you again, Ma'am. And you too, Sir. What an excellent notion of yours to meet like this. John, my dear fellow, how are you? It's been an age.' And he clapped the Apothecary on the shoulder with an embrace that rocked him on his feet.

'Leading a somewhat quieter life than when I last saw you,' said John, readjusting his coat, which had slipped down his back at the enthusiasm of Samuel's greeting.

'I should hope so indeed. But for all that it was an exciting summer, wasn't it?'

'A little too exciting,' answered Louis, with feeling. He slipped his arm round his wife's waist. 'Would you agree, my dear?'

She shook her head. 'There can be no such thing. I love playing dangerous games.'

'As we all know only too well. Now, Serafina, come back to earth and lead the gentlemen in to dinner.'

The Comtesse smiled at her husband. 'I can certainly obey one of your commands, but as to the other . . .'

Louis shook his head. 'I know. We shall have to wait and see.'

Much to the annoyance of the *beau monde*, the King's Theatre in the Haymarket had recently announced its intention of opening at half past seven, an hour considered very late and uncivilised and generally unacceptable. Covent Garden and Drury Lane, however, were still in favour with polite society for starting their performances at seven o'clock. It being the done thing to view the audience just as much as the play, the secret of a successful evening was to send a footman on ahead in order to obtain a box upon the stage. From this much sought after vantage point one could clearly see everyone else present and at the same time have a close-up view of the actors. Furthermore, the eyes of the rest of the world were, quite naturally, drawn to those who sat, as it were, behind the scenes, and it was a splendid opportunity to show off one's latest gown and jewellery. There were even those so vulgar as to allow their servants to remain in the box throughout the first two acts, before finally entering during the interval to display themselves and enact the pantomime of waving at and making curtseys to all their acquaintances, all the while talking and laughing at the very tops of their voices.

John had, in the period of one intermission, observed a beau cover and uncover his head twenty times, then wind his watch, set it, check it, take snuff so that his diamond ring would flash upon his finger, sneeze violently, dangle his cane and fiddle with his sword knot, all in fifteen minutes flat. Louis de Vignolles, however, was a man of sterner stuff and had only secured such a desirable position in order to exhibit his beautiful and somewhat notorious wife.

There were fourteen of these stage loges at Drury Lane theatre, arranged in two rows on either side of the stage. The rows nearer to the audience contained four boxes, the others three, with a high peephole above for those unafraid of heights. And it was to the bottom box on the left-hand side that the Comte, having paid five shillings for the privilege, led his dinner guests, sending the footman who had secured it for them up to the gallery to join his peers. In common with all the boxes, entry to the stage loges was obtained via a door at the back, through which the group now passed. This despite the fact that the parapet separating its occupants from the stage was so low as to allow the ill-mannered to step straight over, a custom much indulged in by young bloods. To the relief of Louis's party, each of them obtained a place on a little chair, there being only four present, so no one was forced to stand behind, a most uncomfortable proceeding. Drawing his seat close to the front, John looked around him.

Even though it was still ten minutes before seven, the theatre was already packed, the boxes, stage and otherwise, all being spoken for either by audience or servants. Most of the neighbouring loges, the Apothecary noted with dry amusement, were filled by ladies, obviously there to see Mr Jasper Harcross, without doubt one of the most handsome men alive, and tonight playing the part of Captain Macheath. In the front rows of the pit sat the critics, for this was a new production and as such would be written about in the newspapers. Behind them were congregated the true theatre lovers; merchants of rising eminence, barristers and students of the Inns of Court, mostly well read in plays, whose judgement was in general worth attending to. In the lower two galleries, for which an entry fee of a shilling and two shillings was charged, sat the middle classes in ascending order of status. While the top gallery itself was packed with servants and those of a similar stamp, who rained half eaten oranges and apples below and indulged in a fearsome volley of cat calls. As ever, John was amused to see that the Tories sat to the right of the theatre and the Whigs to the left, and felt that he could well hazard a guess as to the political leanings of Comte Louis de Vignolles.

'I do believe I am being observed,' said Serafina, close to his ear, breaking his train of thought.

'There is certainly a bevy of quizzing glasses turned in your direction,' the Apothecary answered, taking a quick look.

'Yet I am no longer the mysterious Masked Lady I was when first you met me. Everyone knows my identity now.'

'Ah, but you created a legend, Madam. The woman who took on the finest card and dice players in London and beat them at any game they chose to mention. Your fierce reputation will never leave you.'

And momentarily John left behind him the buzz and excitement of the theatre and flashed into his vivid memory a picture of Serafina de Vignolles, when he had not even known her identity, seated in one of the great gaming rooms at Marybone, throwing dice with Sir Gabriel Kent. Every man in the place had been staring at her, some with hatred, some with envy, but mostly with pure, unbridled admiration. She had been one of the most exciting and arresting women John had ever encountered.

'Have I grown boring?' asked Serafina, as if she could read his mind.

'You could never do that,' the Apothecary whispered truthfully, and kissed her hand.

'Well, well,' said Samuel loudly, breaking in on their shared moment, 'look at this! The part of Polly Peachum is being taken by Miss Coralie Clive.'

'Is it?' John exclaimed, and took the programme from his

9

friend's outstretched hand. There, sure enough, were written the words, WOMEN: Mrs Peachum – Mrs Martin, Polly Peachum – Miss C. Clive, Lucy Lockit – Mrs Delaney, together with a long list of other names.

John's curved smile appeared as he remembered the occasion when his path and that of the actress had crossed so dramatically. 'It will be nice to see her again,' he said.

There was a spatter of applause, and turning towards the audience the Apothecary saw that the orchestra was making its way in, led by the harpsichord player, a Mr Martin, according to the programme.

'Any relation to Mrs Peachum?' Louis asked his wife, but she shrugged her shoulders that she did not know. And as neither John nor Samuel could give an answer they fell silent as the overture began.

It was a spirited rendering of a rather long piece of music, during which the bulk of the audience conversed with or stared at one another. A masked woman, making a grand and late entrance in the loge immediately opposite, not only hit her footman with her fan but loudly called out to a blood sitting two boxes away, regardless of the fact that the musicians were giving it their all. This intensely annoyed Louis who got to his feet and told her to be quiet in no uncertain terms and a very Gallic manner. The blood took exception to such behaviour and was only restrained from jumping down onto the stage and drawing his sword by a friend slightly less drunk than he was. In view of all this it was a great relief when the curtains were finally drawn back and the performance began.

The Beggar's Opera was already a long established favourite with the audience, having been first performed at the Theatre Royal, Lincolns Inn Fields, in 1728. Conceived by the great John Gay, the work consisted of well known folk tunes with new and pithy words set to their familiar airs. Going one step further, Gay had presented his immortal comedy as a pastiche of the Italian opera styles and traditions of the day. Yet, popular though it immediately was, with its cast of thieves, whores, villains and rogues, led by the dashing highwayman Macheath, simultaneously trifling with the affections of two women, there were many who had raised their voices in criticism. The work was considered immoral for its glorification of the criminal, to say nothing of its political innuendoes. But none of these comments had affected the show's acclaim amongst theatregoers. And now the great David Garrick himself was mounting this new and exciting production at Drury Lane.

John, who had not seen the work since he was fifteen, found himself in that happy state of remembering much, yet still being delighted by the freshness and bite of the dialogue, to say nothing of the wicked wit of the songs. In company with the rest of the house, he laughed till he wept when Mr and Mrs Peachum, wonderfully well played by two extremely rotund people with splendid voices, flew into a passion to hear that their daughter Polly had actually married Macheath, rather than becoming his mistress. No wonder, he thought, that the opera is disapproved of when such unconventional sentiments are so volubly expressed.

> 'Our Polly is a sad slut! Nor heeds what we have taught her.
> I wonder any man alive will ever rear a daughter!
> For she must have both hoods and gowns, and hoops to swell her pride,
> With scarves and stays, and gloves and lace; and she will have men beside,'

sang the large Mrs Martin, rolling her comely and expressive eyes at the audience, who guffawed all the more. And with that both actors set about their stage daughter, played by the gorgeous Coralie Clive, looking so appealing in her costume that John found himself leaning forward on the parapet to get a better view.

'I'd swear she's grown better looking,' whispered Samuel enthusiastically.

And John, raising his quizzing glass, as was every true male in the house, could only agree with him. For Miss Clive's hair, dark and lustrous as midnight, glowed beneath her pretty white lace pinner. While the colour of her sparkling green eyes, something that John had remembered very clearly, was enhanced and beautified further by her ice blue costume.

'Your mouth is open,' murmured Serafina, with a smile in her voice.

'Er, yes,' answered John, and closed it.

Yet lovely though Coralie was, and however warm the audience's reaction to her, it was as nothing compared to the moment when Captain Macheath bounded on to the stage singing the words, 'Pretty Polly say, when I was away, did your fancy never stray, to some newer lover?'

It seemed to John that every woman in the theatre simultaneously stood up and cheered, for never had he heard such a rapturous greeting, so many sighs and moans and shouts, as when the handsome Jasper Harcross strode across the planking of the stage and posed for a moment, quite still, in the fullness of the lights. And this regardless of the fact that he was in the middle of his duet with Miss Clive, who took the situation very tolerantly, the Apothecary thought, and merely smiled at her fellow actor indulgently.

'The man's a posturing ass,' commented the Comte succinctly.

'Shush,' said Serafina, and they concentrated on the show once more.

As soon as the tumult died down, the duet continued but when, at the end of it, Mr Harcross swept Coralie into his arms and kissed her full-bloodedly upon the lips, another riot broke out. The more vulgar amongst the females present let forth a series of cat calls, whilst others offered to change places with Miss Clive and pay for the privilege. Meanwhile a susceptible virgin in one of the more prestigious boxes fainted clean away and had to be revived by her relatives. John and Samuel exchanged a glance of envious astonishment, wondering at the power of any one man to so move the fairer sex.

Eventually, the hubbub faded and the opera continued. Polly and Macheath, as played by Coralie and Mr Harcross, decided that for safety's sake they had better part company and the actors, wringing the emotions of the audience pitilessly, indulged in a sad duet and an extremely tender farewell. Then the curtains closed and those with the strength left to do so made their way to the theatre saloon, a somewhat dubious meeting place for the sexes with a reputation for resembling a brothel as much as it did a tavern. Unable to face the thought of such a noisesome crush as would gather there, the occupants of the box remained where they were, awaiting the arrival of the various vendors who walked about the theatre during the interval.

'Well,' said Serafina thoughtfully, 'I am glad I'm not in Miss Clive's shoes.'

'Glad?' repeated her husband, laughing. 'I thought every woman in the place would like to fill them.'

'Au contraire,' the Comtesse answered, showing that she had lost none of her individualism. 'He is a scene stealer, that pretty peacock. When he marries I am sure he will pick an ugly wife.'

'Why so?'

'Because he could not possibly allow anyone to compete with him. Have you not noticed how Coralie is having to struggle to make an impact?'

'I think she's charming,' put in John, leaping to the actress's defence. 'I can't take my eyes off her.'

Serafina's glance glinted at him from behind her mask. 'None the less, you will have spent quite a lot of time watching Macheath, now admit it.'

'Well . . .'

'John, I know you of old, you are dissembling. The truth is that Mr Harcross is one of those people who, admire him or otherwise, commands attention. And you gave it, just like the rest of us.'

'Do you think Coralie is aware that he upstages her?'

'She must be, she's no newcomer to the theatre.'

'She showed no annoyance, none the less.'

'Then she's either very good tempered or a very good actress.'

'Or both.'

'Indeed,' said the Comtesse, and turned her attention to her husband, who was buying fruit and wine from a vendor and wanted his wife's advice.

Samuel called across the space between himself and John, 'What say we go and pay our respects to Miss Clive?'

'A splendid idea,' answered the Apothecary, getting to his feet. And leaving the box, the two friends sauntered towards the door that led behind the scenes, it being quite the done thing to go backstage between the acts and talk to the performers.

Beyond the closed curtains the stage swarmed with shirt-sleeved men, all in a fine muck sweat as they dragged scenery and furniture to and fro, changing the set for the next act. Of the actors there was no sign, but a straggle of determined women climbing a staircase that led to the right of the stage gave John the clue that above might lie the dressing rooms, and that these were the pilgrims heading for the Mecca of Mr Harcross.

'This way,' he said to Samuel, then wondered why he felt a sudden thrill of nervousness at the thought of seeing Coralie Clive again.

But at that moment his mind was completely taken off any such emotion by the sound of raised voices coming from the landing. Looking upwards, John saw that the route was blocked, almost completely, by the actress playing Mrs Peachum, who was currently pouring scorn on the rivulet of eager females attempting to make their way to Jasper Harcross.

'It's no use, ladies. He ain't receiving and that's it. And it's no good looking at me like that. Mr Harcross does not meet the public until after the performance. I thought every theatregoer knew that.'

'But I'm Lady Dukes,' boomed one of them.

Mrs Clarice Martin bobbed a curtsey that ill concealed her contempt. 'I'm sorry, Madam, were you the Queen herself, Mr Harcross would not break his rule.'

'And who are you to speak for him?' commanded Lady Dukes, undaunted.

'I am his colleague and friend. And now I'll ask you kindly to step down and return to your seats. The performance is about to begin.'

Her eyes, very large and blue and obviously once very lovely, froze the women admirers with a stare so icy that John caught himself thinking that he most certainly wouldn't like to get on the wrong side of her.

'And you, Sir,' Mrs Martin continued, not quite so coldly, 'where might you be going?'

John returned her gaze and beheld an extraordinary phenomenon that he had witnessed only once or twice before. The expression in the speaker's eyes changed rapidly without her altering her facial muscles at all. First, came a look of calculation, followed almost immediately by a sparkling flirtatiousness. The actress was one of those women who reserved her contempt and dislike entirely for her own sex and warmed at once to a male.

'I was going to see my friend, Miss Clive,' the Apothecary

answered, hoping he sounded as irritated as he felt, 'but as you say the interval is nearly over . . .'

He got no further. On the landing a door banged and there was the noise of booted feet in the corridor.

'Clarrie,' called a voice, 'where the devil's that wretched boy? Did he not get me some cordial? Go and find him, there's my good girl.'

There was a shriek from the women wending their way back downstairs and they turned in a body to peer upwards, as did John and Samuel. And there, resplendent in a scarlet coat, his black hair tied back in a queue by a matching satin bow, his beautiful eyes dancing at the extraordinary sight beneath him, his arm round the waist of Miss Coralie Clive, stood Jasper Harcross himself. Unreasonably annoyed, John attempted to turn away but not before the actress had seen him. A light of recognition slowly stirred in her eyes.

'Gracious heavens,' she called out, 'is it not Mr Rawlings?'

'It is,' John answered grimly and, hemmed in as he was, made her a polite and very formal bow.

Chapter Two

Fortunately, Act Two of *The Beggar's Opera* commenced with a rousing drinking song, given boisterous voice by the actors playing the various members of Macheath's gang of thieves, all seated round a table loaded with bottles of wine and brandy, to say nothing of jars of tobacco, the scene realistically representing a tavern near Newgate. This merry sight and sound gave a lift to the spirits of those members of the audience who had become disgruntled during the interval, of whose number John Rawlings was most certainly one. Though he would have been loath to admit this fact to anyone other than Samuel, who fully shared John's view that Jasper Harcross had an almost uncanny and quite unjustified hold over women.

'Did you see the arrogant creature preening at the sight of those eager females wanting to meet him?' he said as they had walked back to the box.

'Talk about the cock by hens attended,' John answered irritably. 'Why, the song could have been written about him.'

'Do you think Miss Clive is enamoured of the fellow?'

John had nodded glumly. 'It would certainly appear so.'

'Oh dear,' Samuel sighed. 'Why do women always fall in love with rogues?'

'I imagine,' John had observed, 'that the combination of a libertine's charm and the desire to transform the wretch into a model husband might be the answer.'

'You're right, of course. Perhaps we should adopt a more profligate approach.'

17

The Apothecary had chuckled audibly at the thought of so transparent and good-natured a creature as Samuel Swann doing any such thing.

'I would stay exactly as you are if I were you. You have an appeal that is entirely your own. And to hell with Jasper Harcross.'

'Hear, hear,' Samuel had responded as they re-entered the box.

Serafina and Comte Louis had been exchanging a kiss as their guests returned, a sight which had warmed both their hearts. But instead of jumping apart guiltily, this splendid couple had welcomed their friends with enthusiasm, and embraced one another a second time before once more assuming their role of host and hostess. Then with their wine glasses charged they had all settled down to watch the performance, Serafina much amused by the faces of her husband and companions as Jasper Harcross made more than a meal of his scene with the ladies of the town, each purporting to rival the others for his affections so realistically that it was hard to believe they were only acting.

'*Mon Dieu*, art mirrors life I believe,' Louis muttered.

'You're not envious surely?' she asked with apparent astonishment.

'How could I be? I have you.'

'Ah, gallant indeed.'

They smiled at one another and continued to watch Mr Harcross, who kissed and fondled his leading ladies with great panache and enjoyment.

'And to think he gets paid for it,' said Samuel morosely, and there was a ripple of laughter from the box which the actor obviously heard, for his head, very briefly, moved in their direction.

The Newgate prison scene began and with it the first glimpse of the amazing effects promised by Mr Garrick for this new production. In full view of the audience, the stagehands heaved off the furniture used in the tavern and then, lowered on ropes at some considerable speed, a barred window was flown down and settled on the stage to act as the backdrop. Simultaneously, two flats were pushed forward from either wing and these were hooked on to it, still in full public gaze, to form a gloomy gaol cell. There was a cheer from the gallery, which was taken up by the rest of the house, and during it Mr Harcross strode back on wearing his serious face.

'Now we're going to see some tearing tragedy,' said John with a groan.

'Yes, I truly believe he'll spare us nothing,' Serafina answered.

Spirits were raised a few moments later, however, by the arrival of Lucy Lockit, played by Mrs Delaney, a mettlesome little redhead who buzzed round Jasper like an angry wasp.

'You base man you,' she shouted, obviously putting her heart and soul into her performance. 'How can you look me in the face after what hath passed between us? See here, perfidious wretch, how I am forced to bear about the load of infamy you have laid upon me . . .'

And Mrs Delaney placed her hand upon her body, neatly padded out, to make quite sure that the audience did not miss the point that the fearless highwayman had enjoyed his wicked way with Lucy and left her in an interesting condition. There was a roar of laughter at this, loudest of all from the gallery, slightly embarrassed from the tender young females. Samuel, never a one to disguise his feelings, guffawed, whilst John, running his professional eye over Mrs Delaney's rounding, thought how genuine it looked.

The opera proceeded with the inevitable meeting between Polly Peachum and Lucy Lockit, spitting like cats over Macheath, then singing a spirited duet in which one vied with the other as to who could produce the most trills and cadenzas. Here, John Gay had parodied the Italian opera to his heart's content and the audience, understanding this yet appreciating the singing for all that, clapped wildly. Just as if it were a true vocal contest, as each girl stepped forward and sang they were rewarded with boisterous applause and, finally, cheers. Macheath, meanwhile, made quite sure that nobody forgot him by pulling the most amusing series of faces.

'Couldn't he let them have their moment of glory?' John whispered to Serafina.

'Obviously not. I told you he was a peacock.'

The act ended with Mrs Delaney alone on the stage, Lucy having given Macheath the keys to Newgate gaol in order that he might escape. Sinking down on the bare boards, the actress sang one of the most moving arias in the entire piece. There was absolute silence in the theatre, even the gallery quiet, as her beautiful voice soared out with the words:

> *'I like the Fox shall grieve,*
> *Whose mate hath left her side,*
> *Whom Hounds, from morn to eve*
> *Chase o'er the country wide.'*

'Oh dear,' said Serafina, and slipped her hand beneath her mask to wipe away a tear.

'One would almost think she meant it,' remarked the Comte, obviously also affected.

'She probably does,' John answered, and smiled to himself at the way of the world.

It was time for the interval again, but on this occasion nobody left the box except to answer the calls of nature in the Office Houses provided for that purpose. Instead, the Comte de Vignolles and his guests surveyed the audience and in turn were surveyed.

'There's David Garrick,' said Samuel, pointing.

'Where?'

'In that stage box high up.'

'Is that his wife with him or his mistress?'

'It's Madame Violetta, of course. He would hardly flaunt his light-o-love in public.'

'But she's most certainly here,' put in Serafina, and gestured towards a box in which the celebrated actress Peg Woffington sat alone.

John, staring from one lovely woman to the other, came to the conclusion that actors must be greedy when it came to matters of love and lust. The company of the dancer, Madame Violetta, Garrick's lawful wife, would have been quite enough for him without throwing the charming black-haired Miss Woffington in for good measure. Then he took himself to task for being too sober and dull and decided that it was in the nature of mankind to flirt. With this in mind he took Serafina's hand and gave it a squeeze.

'Neither of them is as exquisite as you.'

'Oh come now,' she answered, but the Comtesse was smiling behind her mask and he knew that he had pleased her.

'Are you dallying with my wife?' asked Louis.

'Of course.'

'I'm pleased to hear it, you are sometimes far too serious for your own good.' And with that the Comte refilled everyone's wine glass. 'Here, we're going to need this. Mr Harcross is about to wring our withers.'

'Oh dear!' said John, and then, just for the briefest second, the strange feeling of fear swept over him once more. Determined to ignore it, the Apothecary concentrated hard as the curtains parted for the last act.

Once again the dismal scene of Newgate revealed itself, but it was not long before there was another of Mr Garrick's wonders. As the action changed to a gaming house, the barred window was hauled up out of sight and an elegant velvet curtain dropped in its place. The two flats, meanwhile, were unhooked and turned on their casters to reveal a painted representation of a grand saloon with chandeliers. At the same moment the stagehands dashed on at speed carrying with them card tables, cards and dice. A thunderous cheer broke out and Mr Garrick, in his box, winked at his wife. Jasper Harcross appeared in a fine tarnished coat and threw himself into a rendering of *Lillibulero*, which John considered far too long drawn out.

Greatly to his relief, the scene changed to Peachum's Lock, a cant word for a warehouse in which stolen goods are received. Unable to do much with such a quick change, David Garrick had merely loaded the set with properties representing booty and directed the actors playing Peachum and Lockit to examine them as they discussed the goods lifted at the coronation of George II in 1727.

It was at this juncture that Mr Garrick dispensed with a theatrical tradition which the Apothecary, having an extremely neat and logical mind, had always thought quite ridiculous. The scene between the two men was interrupted by the arrival of Mrs Diana Trapes, the tally woman, a part played at the original performance and ever since by the actress who had taken the role of Mrs Peachum. When he had first heard the opera, John had wondered for a second why Peachum's wife had come on dressed as someone else, then had seen through the device. But tonight, mercifully, a different woman appeared, a tall thin creature with auburn hair swept up beneath a saucy hat.

'Why have they done that?' asked Samuel.

'Because Mrs Martin is too damned fat,' answered Louis with Gallic honesty. 'Nobody could mistake her, were they a mile off.'

'I wonder if the harpsichordist *is* her husband,' John said thoughtfully. 'Because, if so, he looks mighty small for the job to me.'

This amused the Comte who gave a snort of laughter which fortunately was drowned by the trio singing, 'In the days of my youth I could bill like a Dove', during which he recovered himself.

The opera had one more highlight, Lucy's attempted murder of Polly. In a very funny scene, the wronged and pregnant girl gives her rival a drink laced with ratsbane which, in true theatrical lore, the intended victim refuses to touch. After this the mood became extremely solemn as both young women begged Peachum and Lockit, their respective fathers, to spare Macheath's life, the highwayman being behind bars yet again, recaptured in bed with one of the whores.

The setting changed once more, this time to the Condemned Hold, where Mr Harcross was discovered in a melancholy posture. To achieve a truly dismal effect, David Garrick had ordered the side flats to be pushed in even further, thus giving the impression of a dark hellhole. As Jasper bemoaned his fate there were cries of sympathy and sobs from the ladies. Well aware of this, the actor turned his best profile to the audience as he brokenly sang the words of his farewell to the world.

For no reason John, who considered Jasper a conceited popinjay, was intensely moved by them and felt his throat constrict. The actor had succeeded in convincing him that, arrogant poser though he might be, he really was staring death in the face and was consequently filled with grief. And this emotion persisted to haunt the Apothecary throughout the scene in which Macheath bade farewell to his friends and his two sweethearts. Then came the last of Mr Garrick's spectacular effects. The Condemned Hold was rolled outwards and backwards and vanished, whilst wheeled forward, amidst tumultuous applause, came a wooden gallows. This consisted of a box-like shape into which had been built a staircase with a platform above it. Standing on this platform was a post with a noose attached, looking very sinister as its dark outline reared against the lights. There was an audible shudder from the audience. Macheath was to be hanged in full view, it would seem.

In the original production the actual execution had been omitted, probably because of the difficulty of staging such a thing. The condemned highwayman had simply marched out to suffer his fate, then had reappeared triumphantly as the cry of 'Reprieve' had gone up. But tonight the onlookers were to get their money's worth. Every head craned forward as Macheath cried, 'Tell the Sheriff's officers I am ready,' and mounted the wooden steps, accompanied by two gaolers, Lockit, and a priest, to where the hangman awaited him on the platform above, a black mask concealing his face.

Mr Garrick was not stinting with the crowd either. Every character in the piece, including Mrs Peachum, who had not reappeared after the first act, stood at the foot of the gallows to watch the hero die. The actors playing the Player and the Beggar entered surreptitiously from the wings, for it was on their command that the reprieve was called. Then, dramatically, there was a roll of drums from the orchestra. Jasper Harcross, in true heroic style, refused to have his eyes bandaged by the hangman and stood unflinchingly while the rope was put about his neck. Then he stepped forward as the drums continued to roll. Just for a moment the actor appeared frozen in time, or so it seemed to John, and then there was the sickening sound of splintering wood. With a sudden rush, the rope extended to its full length as Jasper Harcross crashed through the planking of the platform and dropped into the centre of the wooden box, his feet kicking wildly. In the terrified and terrible silence that followed, the Apothecary could have sworn he heard the sound of his breaking neck.

Pandemonium broke out. Half the audience, particularly those furthest away, took this dramatic turn of events to be Mr Garrick's ultimate and greatest theatrical effect and applauded wildly. This encouraged some in the stage boxes, who had seen what had happened distinctly and yet still could not comprehend it, to do likewise. Then, above the cheers, rose the sound of a thin high scream as the masked woman in the box opposite the Comte's got to her feet then swooned, her limp body falling to the floor like a broken toy.

Almost without knowing what he was doing, John rose from his chair and vaulted over the loge's parapet onto the stage. Rushing to the wooden contraption inside which Jasper Harcross was hanging, his head and shoulders still visible, swaying slackly from side to side, the Apothecary shouted, 'Lower him down! For God's sake lower him down! There might still be a chance.' Then looking up at the high stage box from which a white-faced David Garrick was staring downwards in horror, John added, 'You must order the curtains closed, Sir. This event is not for public display.'

Another voice cut in, that of the actor playing the hangman. He had whipped off his mask, beneath which the poor fellow had blanched the colour of chalk. 'We can't lower him. There isn't the mechanism.'

'Then cut the rope for pity's sake. Let me tend to him. I am an apothecary.'

Mr Garrick's famous tones came from above. 'Do what the fellow says for the love of God. Dick? Where's Dick?'

'Here, Sir,' said one of the shirt-sleeved men whom John had noticed earlier helping to change the set.

'Get the curtains closed and the poor soul cut down. And clear the stage and send everyone home while you're about it.'

'Wait, Sir,' John called out to Garrick. 'I don't think the actors should go, not just yet.'

'Why not?' asked Clarice Martin belligerently, between heaving sobs.

'Just in case,' answered the Apothecary enigmatically.

And with that warning he hurled his shoulder against the

box bearing the gallows and was pleased to hear the planking give. It was hollow inside, constructed round wooden scaffold poles, the whole thing running on concealed casters so that it could be pushed easily round the stage. As he tore at the wood with his bare hands, trying to make a hole big enough to step through, John could glimpse Jasper Harcross's dangling legs in their high boots, and the very limpness of the way they hung told him the actor was dead. Yet still he strove, until at last the Apothecary was able to squeeze inside and stand within the wooden shell. With a desperate move, he grasped Jasper round the knees in order to take the weight off the poor man's neck.

Looking up, John could see through the broken platform that Dick was now standing on what was left of it, held by the Hangman so that he did not topple forward. With his left hand he held the rope and in his right a knife, which he was using to hack through the rigging.

'Is he dead?' he called down to John, seeing his upturned face.

'I'm sure he is,' the Apothecary answered quietly.

'But how could it have happened? The scene worked perfectly at the dress rehearsal.'

'Perhaps the boards have rotted since.'

'No, there's no chance of that. We always use new planking at Drury Lane. Particularly with an effect as dangerous as this one.' His voice became business-like. 'The rope's almost cut through. Do you want someone to help you catch him as he drops?'

'There's no room in here. I'll have to manage on my own. But once he's down can you get this thing lifted off us? I daren't move him, you see.'

'I'll tell the stagehands to stand by. Now, are you ready?'

'Yes,' said John, but he wasn't, not at all.

He had only been freed from his indentures during the summer of 1754, just past, and all the teachings of his old

Master were fresh in his mind. Therefore John Rawlings knew well that to fear the dead was ridiculous, for only the living could harm a mortal man. Yet there was something about the way in which Jasper Harcross crashed into his arms, so heavily and so dead a weight that it sent him flying, that made the Apothecary's flesh seethe upon his bones. Lying flat on the stage with the dead man on top of him, his blind eyes gazing into John's own, it was all he could do, trained apothecary or no, to stop himself letting out a cry of pure terror. Yet old instincts die hard. Longing as he was to push the corpse away, John slid out from underneath it as gently as he could, knowing that to disturb the evidence was the very last thing that anyone investigating the death would wish.

There was a great sound of heaving and the box was suddenly lifted up and away. John blinked in the glare of the lights, then began his examination, able to see clearly at last. Very gently turning Jasper Harcross over, he put his hand on the actor's heart, simultaneously bending low to listen for any sign of breath. Much as he had expected, there was nothing. Steadfastly ignoring the crowd of actors and backstage staff who had gathered round to watch, John delicately eased the noose from the dead man's neck.

In cases of hanging there were two ways in which an individual could die, the most common being by strangulation. Criminals who met their end at Tyburn all perished by this relatively slow means, having first kicked out the dance of death at the end of the rope. However, it was not unknown for a victim to overcome such an ordeal. Occasionally, when the crowd had dispersed and they were alone, friends of the villain would cut him down and save his life. John had heard of one such highwayman who, only recently, had survived hanging with little more than permanent damage to his vocal cords. Yet, when the victim fell several feet with the noose around his throat, it was an entirely different matter. Such a drop would dislocate the neck and crush the vital centres in the medulla, putting a swift end to life.

Knowing this, the Apothecary, his fingers light as a bird, examined the bones of Jasper Harcross's neck to gauge their condition. Sure enough, the mass at the base of the skull had broken through its ligament. The actor had died at the moment of his fall through the shattered platform.

John glanced up to see that David Garrick had come onto the stage and was angrily waving away the crowd of onlookers. The great actor-manager crouched down beside him as the Apothecary turned his attention once more to the corpse, closing the staring eyes and looking round for some kind of cloth to put over him.

'Is he dead?'

'Yes, I'm afraid so.'

'But how did it happen?' asked Garrick, repeating an earlier question of Dick's.

'I don't know,' John answered grimly. 'But I intend to find out.'

Straightening up, he walked towards the box bearing the gallows, now standing innocently at the back of the stage. Then before anyone could question his actions he ducked his head and once more stepped inside. The wooden planks which had formed the platform were directly above him, hanging down where they had broken beneath Jasper Harcross's feet. Carefully, John raised his quizzing glass to examine them. At the top of the break the wood was rough and jagged, like a smashed spar, but underneath, most curiously, it was neat and orderly. Standing on tip-toe, John brought his magnifier to within an inch of the broken planking. Then he gave an exclamation as everything became horribly clear. Very sombre now, he stepped out of the box and addressed himself to the actor-manager.

'Mr Garrick, can you tell me what has happened to the rest of my party please?'

'The Comte and Comtesse have returned home, but your friend Mr Swann insisted upon remaining. He said he might be required to help.' David Garrick assumed a stern and somewhat officious face. 'Now, if you'd be so good, I'd be obliged if you would kindly tell me what you are doing, Sir. I would have thought you to have stepped outside your province as an apothecary, if I may say so.'

'You are right of course,' John answered shortly. 'But the fact of the matter is I have now adopted my other role.'

'Which is?'

'To act from time to time as one of Mr Fielding's Runners. And in that capacity, Mr Garrick, I would indeed like to call upon the assistance of Samuel Swann.'

'To do what?'

'To go to Bow Street and ask for one of their representatives to come here immediately.'

'Are you saying that Mr Harcross has met with foul play?' asked Garrick, bolt-eyed.

John nodded solemnly. 'Yes, I believe so. As far as I can see, and I am certain Dick will confirm this, the platform upon which the poor wretch tried to stand was deliberately sawn through. In short, Mr Garrick, we are not dealing with a case of accidental death after all.'

'You can't mean Jasper was murdered!' said an unidentifiable female voice.

'I'm afraid,' answered John, turning to face the group of actors, who still stood huddled upon the stage, 'that that is precisely what I do mean.'

Chapter Three

It was the proud boast of Mr John Fielding, Principal Magistrate of the lawless town of London, that he could despatch a set of Brave Fellows in pursuit of a criminal to any part of the metropolis, or even the kingdom, at a quarter of an hour's notice. Indeed, so confident had he been of this claim that a month earlier, on 17 October, 1754, the Blind Beak had promoted this service in the *Public Advertiser*, ending with the words, 'It is to be hoped, that the late success of this plan will make all persons for the future industrious to give the earliest notice possible of all robberies and robbers whatever'. His November advertisement had amended the wording to 'crimes and criminals'. More aware than most of John Fielding's power, Samuel Swann, at John Rawlings's behest, had gladly sprinted the short distance between Drury Lane and Bow Street to seek the great man's help.

Just before his friend left the theatre, the Apothecary had scribbled a note. It simply said, 'It seems that our paths are fated to cross once more, my very dear Sir. Last night, it being past midnight as I write this, there was a fatality on stage during a performance of *The Beggar's Opera*. Jasper Harcross, playing the part of Macheath, met his death in highly suspicious circumstances. I will guard the evidence until your Runners come. Meanwhile, I have been forced to indulge in the small falsehood that I, too, am one of your men, though on an *ad hoc* basis. This was to silence David Garrick who had the air about him that he might throw me out on my ear. Your servant . . .' And he had appended his signature.

'Do you think the Beak will come himself?' Samuel had asked as he set forth.

'I hope so,' John answered. 'I can't see anyone else being able to keep order amongst this torrent of temperaments.'

Samuel had rolled his eyes. 'I don't know which is worse, those in hysterics, those weeping, or those in the sullens.'

'Neither do I,' the Apothecary had answered gloomily.

For, truth to tell, the near riot that had broken out after he had given his opinion that Jasper Harcross had been done to death, beggared belief. First to react had been Clarice Martin, who had crashed down so heavily on the stage in a dead faint that one of the boards had cracked in ghastly parody of the fate that had befallen her fellow actor. At this, Mrs Delaney had given a shrill scream of hysterical laughter before collapsing into a veritable tide of tears, while Miss Clive had gone as white as her lace pinner, her eyes glittering in the most unnerving manner. John had gone forward with his bottle of smelling salts, hoping to attend her, but had been plucked to one side by the harpsichordist who had begged him to give succour to his wife. As John had knelt over the abundant curves of Mrs Martin he had again thought about the difference in their respective sizes and had found his mind going down some extremely naughty avenues, quite unsuitable for the occasion.

Meanwhile, the actor playing Lockit, a craggy-faced individual with alert blue eyes, decided that he would light a pipe to soothe his nerves. This upset Mr Peachum, who declared that smoke was bad for his throat and instantly indulged in an extremely forced fit of coughing. At this Mrs Vine, who had taken the role of Diana Trapes, told him forcefully to be quiet, and an argument erupted between them.

'Can't we get rid of them into the dressing rooms?' begged

Dick, who had revealed himself as the stage manager and a stalwart character.

John looked doubtful. 'As long as none of them tries to leave I suppose it would be all right.'

'Can they change out of their costumes?'

'I think not. I am sure Mr Fielding would like to see them exactly as they were at the time of the hanging.'

'But surely he can't see, so what is the point?'

'If he comes in person he will bring his eyes with him, namely his clerk, Joe Jago. Not a thing will pass his keen gaze, I assure you.'

'Then I hope they hurry. There is nothing worse than a stageful of irritable actors.'

'Perhaps Mr Garrick could make an announcement.'

'Mr Garrick is in a worse mood than the rest of them put together.'

'Oh dear,' sighed John, and was just about to take responsibility for sending the actors to the dressing rooms when there was a sound from the stage door. Listening intently, the Apothecary smiled to himself. Slowly and inexorably came the steady beat of a tapping cane. The Blind Beak, the great John Fielding, had not only arrived but was approaching the scene of the murder.

John could not resist it. He cleared his throat and said importantly, 'Pray silence, ladies and gentlemen, for the Principal Magistrate.'

Instantly there was quiet, and into that stillness the rapping of the stick grew ever louder. And then there was a rustle in the wings and suddenly John Fielding was there, his vast frame filling the dark space, the curls of his wig brushing against his strong features as he turned his bandaged eyes in the direction of the assembled company.

'David?' he called in his powerful voice, and instantly Garrick got to his feet and crossed the space between them.

'My dear friend,' said the actor, embracing the Magistrate as if they were long lost brothers. 'How very good of you to come in person.'

'It was the least I could do in view of our old acquaintance-ship,' the Blind Beak answered, and John felt faintly astonished until he remembered Mr Fielding's half brother, Henry, and his lengthy association with Drury Lane.

As if picking up the Apothecary's train of thought, Garrick continued, 'I was so distressed to hear of Henry's death last month. We have lost a fine author and playwright alas.'

The Beak nodded solemnly. 'What saddens me is that he is buried in Lisbon, whence he had travelled for the sake of his health. I would rather that such a great Englishman was laid to rest at home.'

Garrick's mobile features adopted such a grave expression that John, in any other circumstance, would have found it difficult not to smile at the theatricality of his response.

'I fear Henry's passing has heralded disaster,' the actor said, sighing gustily. 'Poor Jasper was killed on stage last night and a young apothecary who claims to be your assistant – I trust he is, by the way – says that his death was not accidental.'

'I take it Mr Garrick is referring to you, Mr Rawlings?' the Blind Beak asked, turning his head in John's direction just as if he could see him.

'He is, Sir.'

'Then be assured, my dear friend, that the Apothecary and I have indeed worked together before. Now then, Mr Rawlings, be so good as to tell me exactly why you believe what you do.'

'The planking beneath the man's feet had been sawn through to the point where it only needed his weight upon them for them to break. Consequently, Mr Harcross fell through the holes in the gallows' platform.'

'And . . . ?'

'As he had a noose round his neck at the time, acting out the hanging of Macheath, that fall proved fatal.'

'I see. Where is the body now?'

'More or less where it landed after it was cut down. I had to turn the victim over in order to examine him but he hasn't been moved since.'

'And where are the rest of the actors?'

'Still on stage. And in mighty high stirrup, most of them.'

'I'll speak to them.' Mr Fielding raised his voice. 'Ladies and gentlemen, I greatly regret that you have been kept waiting after such a very shocking experience, but I do hope that you will understand the reason. In a case of wilful murder, as the death of your colleague certainly would appear to be, it is essential that we question everyone as soon as possible before their memory of the event fades. Therefore, if Mr Garrick can put some rooms at my disposal, we shall get that task over quickly. Then you may all change and return to your homes.' He turned his head. 'Joe, are you there?'

'Indeed I am, Sir,' answered his clerk, stepping forward smartly.

'Has the physician arrived?'

'Yes, Sir.'

'Then, for the record, let him confirm the cause of death. After that the body can be removed. Meanwhile, I'd be grateful if these good people left the stage.'

'There is just one person I think you should speak to first, Sir,' said John in an undertone.

'And who is that?'

'Dick, the stage manager, a very helpful fellow. He swears that the platform through which Jasper Harcross fell was in perfect working order at the dress rehearsal.'

Mr Fielding nodded. 'Bring him over. By the way, is that platform under guard?'

'I posted Will, the theatre boy, to stand by it, with strict instructions to allow nobody near.'

The Blind Beak smiled. 'You have done well, Mr Rawlings. How very fortunate that you were here. Now, let us get rid of the onlookers.'

But this time the actors had no wish to watch as the body was uncovered and examined by a doctor, who confirmed John's diagnosis, much to his satisfaction. Instead, all looking very subdued, they returned to their dressing rooms, awaiting the summons to questioning.

'Mr Fielding would rather you remained in your costumes for the moment,' Joe Jago called after them.

'Why?' asked Mrs Martin, rounding on him, her old spirit obviously returning.

'Material evidence,' he answered obscurely, and with that she had to be content.

'But why really?' John asked the clerk in an undertone, not wishing to appear ignorant before either the Blind Beak or the actors.

'Because they wore them at the dress rehearsal, Mr Rawlings.'

'So?'

'So if whoever sawed through the planking was wearing their costume when they did so, there might still be some telltale sign upon it.'

'Oh, I see. Then what should I be looking for?'

'Anything. A dirty mark, a tear, a missing button, anything. Just keep your eyes sharp, Mr Rawlings.' And Joe Jago tapped the side of his nose with his finger.

Within a quarter of an hour, indeed as two in the morning struck, the mortal remains of poor Jasper Harcross were removed to the mortuary, awaiting claim by his immediate family, to whom it was planned to send a Runner bearing the ill tidings.

'Was he a married man?' the Blind Beak asked David Garrick as the corpse set out on its dismal journey.

'Yes and no,' came the answer, accompanied by a laugh. 'The fact is that Jasper kept a wife that nobody knew about, residing in the country. In Kensington to be precise. He would go there and serve her occasionally, so I believe.'

'And between times?'

'He loved the ladies and they loved him. He played true to type when he took the part of Macheath, believe me.'

'Was there anyone in particular?'

'All of 'em,' Garrick said with relish. 'There's not a woman in this cast he's not had some kind of dalliance with.'

'Zounds!' the Apothecary exclaimed. 'Even Mrs Martin?'

'Even she,' replied the actor, and laughed once more.

The Blind Beak turned to John. 'Now, my young friend, I wonder if you would be so kind as to let me enlist your help once more.'

'Of course.'

'If I question all these people myself we will be here till dawn and tempers will fray. I wonder if we might divide the number in half and if you would quiz some of them on my account.'

The hare-like quality in John, the part of him that could not resist adventure, responded, 'I will do that gladly, Sir. What are the kinds of thing you want to know?'

'Basically, their relationship with the deceased, for good or ill. And secondly, if they can account for themselves between the dress rehearsal and tonight's performance.'

'I don't quite understand.'

'Joe has examined the wooden box with the stage manager. Both of them agree that the planking has been sawn through, just as you thought. However, Dick assures me that it was in good order when he closed the theatre down after the final rehearsal. That means that someone came in here, probably during the hours of darkness, and sawed through the planks, knowing that the platform would not be used again until Mr Harcross stood on it in the course of the actual performance.'

'Surely that would point to someone in this troupe of actors.'

'Indeed it might well. Now, let us get a man on horseback sent to Kensington to discover the whereabouts of the wretched widow.' Mr Fielding paused, then added, 'No, on second thoughts he can go in the morning and you, Mr Rawlings, might possibly keep him company.'

'I would hate such a task, Sir.'

'I am certain of that. But for all your reticence a sharp pair of eyes will be needed to note her reaction.'

'You mean that *she* might be responsible for the crime?'

'A jealous wife, a husband with mistresses, a knowledge of the play, for surely she must have had one. What might that add up to in your opinion?'

'It could mean murder,' said Samuel, speaking for the first time since his return to the theatre. 'I'll go, Sir, if John will not.'

'Perhaps you could make the visit together?'

The Apothecary nodded. 'Samuel puts me to shame. I'll certainly accompany him.'

The Blind Beak smiled. 'You see how lucky I am, David, to have such an able and willing set of Brave Fellows in these two young people.'

'Lucky indeed,' Garrick answered drily, obviously considering John and Samuel a couple of upstarts and not worth the time of day.

'And now we must begin the questioning. Joe, have you made a list?'

The clerk, who was famous for that very thing, promptly produced one from his pocket. 'Yes, Sir.'

'And who is first?'

'Mrs Delaney for Mr Rawlings and Mrs Martin for you. One is pleading her belly as a need to get home, the other an attack of the vapours.'

The Blind Beak rumbled with laughter. 'Well, Mr Rawlings, what a fine pair to commence with. There's little to choose between 'em, so Mr Garrick tells me.'

But John was not listening, his attention caught by something entirely different. He turned to David Garrick. 'Pleading her belly? Do you mean Mrs Delaney really *is* pregnant? I thought she was just cleverly padded.'

The actor-manager winked and suddenly looked extremely human. 'Bless you, no. She's Lord Delaney's wife, that doddery old chap with a fortune and great house to boot. She married him only recently, and now she's carrying his child – or so it's said.'

Mr Fielding's bandaged gaze veered in Garrick's direction. 'So it's said?'

'Perhaps it's as well,' his friend replied succinctly, 'that dead men tell no tales,' and he winked once more.

Chapter Four

David Garrick had allocated two rooms for the purpose of questioning Jasper Harcross's fellow actors. But whereas Mr Fielding was able to sit in the relative comfort of the Green Room, John and Samuel, who was acting as John's clerk and note-taker, found themselves in an area no bigger than a large cupboard. And when three chairs and a table were brought into this confined place there was literally no space to move at all. In fact so bad was the overcrowding, John could only feel grateful that he had not been given the task of interviewing Mrs Martin. Even Mrs Delaney, dainty as a figurine though she normally was, had difficulty in squeezing her rounding shape into the seat opposite his.

Scowling slightly, the actress said by way of opening grumble, 'I do hope you are not going to keep me long. I should have been home an hour ago and my husband will be distressed and anxious beyond measure by now. Furthermore, I am with child and it is not wise for me to be out so late.'

'Indeed not,' John answered, adopting a look of grave concern. 'In fact, if you will forgive my frankness, I am somewhat surprised that you are still working in the theatre. Surely you must find it very exhausting?'

'I shall be retiring next month,' the actress answered shortly. 'By that time I will be in the fifth month of my term. That is quite soon enough to quit work in my opinion. I am an active woman, Mr Rawlings, and detest nothing more than sitting at home with nothing to divert me.'

'But surely Lord Delaney . . .'

'I don't see that my husband has anything to do with the matter. I thought I was here to answer questions about the events of tonight.'

'And so you are,' John replied, putting on his contrite face. 'You must forgive me. I have this terrible tendency to wander off the point. So let us get down to business. Tell me, what was your relationship with the dead man? You were friends, I presume?'

'The dead . . . ? Oh, you mean poor Jasper.' For the first time Mrs Delaney's lips quivered and her cheeks bleached of colour, showing how very pale she was beneath the highly coloured paint she wore for the stage. 'Well, of course, we had acted together many, many times. We were true working colleagues.'

'And nothing more?'

She blazed with sudden anger. 'I'm afraid I don't understand you.'

'Mrs Delaney, forgive me,' John said firmly. 'I have already heard that Mr Harcross was a man for the ladies, and you, if you will allow me to say so, are a very beautiful woman. Did he flirt with you?'

'I am married, Sir.'

'Yes, but surely that marriage was only recent. What was your relationship with him before you wed?'

The actress's cheeks went from snow to fire. 'As you said yourself, we were friends.'

'And that is all?'

This time there was a very long pause and John found himself being regarded by a pair of vivacious eyes, bright as bluebells but presently dark with thought.

Eventually Mrs Delaney said, 'Are you entitled to ask that?'

'In as much as I am officially acting for Mr Fielding, yes.'

'Well, then, here's the truth, before you hear some distorted version of it from someone who wishes me ill. Jasper Harcross and I had been sweethearts, that was until I met Lord Delaney. Then I ended the affair. But you are right about his weakness for women. He could not resist them, particularly those who threw themselves at him headlong.'

'And were there many like that?'

'Oh yes,' she said bitterly. 'Many.'

'Fellow actresses?'

'Of course.'

'Surely his wife could not have approved of such behaviour?'

There was a stunned silence followed by a rapid intake of breath, then Mrs Delaney controlled herself. 'I think your information is incorrect, Sir. Jasper Harcross was not a married man.'

'I'm afraid he was,' John answered sombrely. 'Mr Fielding was given that information by Mr Garrick himself. Apparently the lady was kept hidden away in Kensington but, for all that, exists.'

Before his eyes, the actress cracked. 'The bastard!' she screamed. 'The monstrous bastard! If that is the case he deserved to die! How could he have done that to me?' And she melted into a rainstorm of hysterical tears.

With enormous difficulty John rose from his chair, breathing in in order to move. Squeezing his way from behind the table, he put his arm round Mrs Delaney's shoulders, raising his bottle of smelling salts to her nose.

'Steady now! Breathe deeply. Whatever he did is not worth upsetting yourself about to this extent,' he said gently.

Once again, the actress fought for restraint and found it somewhere in the depths of her being. Wiping away tears with the back of her hand, she stood up, her face ravaged and streaked.

'Can I go now?'

'I'm afraid there are still one or two questions I have to

ask – but they can wait. I think you should return home and rest. Do you have a carriage?'

'My husband's coach has been here for the last hour.'

'Then with your permission I will call on you within the next day or two so that we can go over the last few points.'

'Come in the afternoon when my husband is out. I do not want him to be drawn into this tragic business.'

'I quite understand. I shall visit you shortly, Lady Delaney.'

'I prefer to be called Mrs when I am in the theatre.' She gave the Apothecary a sudden, sad smile which made her look extremely vulnerable, then headed for the door. 'Good night to you, gentlemen.'

John bowed courteously, Samuel attempting to do likewise in the small area at his disposal. As soon as the actress was out of earshot, however, the two friends turned to one another.

'Is it possible that Jasper Harcross kept the fact of his marriage a secret from all of them?'

'It would certainly appear so.'

'And David Garrick said nothing about it?'

'Why should he? He is the great actor-manager, beyond gossiping with his company of players.'

'None the less,' said Samuel, 'it strikes me as odd.'

'No doubt we will learn more as the evening proceeds. By the way, did you notice anything missing from Mrs Delaney's costume?'

'The red bow on her left cuff had gone.'

'Yes, though I could have sworn it was there during tonight's performance.' The Apothecary frowned as his pictorial memory came into play. 'Yes, it was, for sure.'

'Then it doesn't count, does it?'

'Everything . . .' But John got no further as there was a knock on the door and Joe Jago put his head through the opening.

'Ready for the next one, Mr Rawlings?'

'Who is it?'

'Jack Masters, who played Lockit.'

'Please send him through.'

In a swirl of pipe smoke, the granite-faced actor took his place on the other side of the table and the interview started.

A pattern began to emerge, the basis of which had come from Mrs Delaney. Jack Masters, craggy and imperturbable individual though he might be, appeared equally surprised that his erstwhile friend had been married, though once he had got used to the idea it certainly seemed to strike him as amusing.

'What a cool customer,' he said, slapping his thigh. 'There he was, with half the women in London in love with him, yet secretly having a wife all along.'

One of John's mobile brows rose. 'Ah, but look where that cool customer ended. Obviously the game that he played was a highly dangerous one.'

Jack nodded, suddenly serious. 'You're right of course. There must have been several who would like to have seen him dead.'

'Do you include men amongst that number?'

'Jealous husbands, do you mean?'

'That, or lovers.'

Jack stroked his chin. 'Well, it's known that Sarah Delaney, Seaton as she used to be, was close to Jasper at one time.'

'Are you saying that Lord Delaney had a motive for murdering him?'

The ragged face became uneasy. 'I'm not one for common gossip, Mr Rawlings.'

The Apothecary nodded. 'I respect that. So can you answer me something else, Mr Masters?'

'That depends.'

'It *is* rather important, I fear. As you are no doubt aware by now, the platform on which Mr Harcross stood had been sawn through so that the very next person to walk on it would fall. As no one else used that section of the planking but the victim,

I think we are safe in presuming the trap was set for him.'

'Yes? Well?'

'Dick has assured us that the device worked perfectly at dress rehearsal. Therefore, it seems obvious that the gallows were tampered with after that time. Because of this I must know, Sir, where you were last night.'

Jack Masters looked decidedly ill at ease. 'I think that's my affair, don't you?'

John sighed. 'As you wish. In the end you will have to answer, one way or t'other.' His face changed. 'My dear Sir, I have been asked by Mr Fielding to help him out tonight, the reason being that I assisted him, quite successfully, on another occasion. Believe me, I do not enjoy prying into the lives of others, their business is their own. But surely we all have a common interest in finding the murderer of Jasper Harcross.'

The actor nodded, somewhat reluctantly. 'You're right, of course. Well, the truth is that I was visiting a lady.'

'And she will verify this?'

'I would rather you did not approach her.'

John sighed once more. 'Sir, I will most certainly not do so. That remains with Mr Fielding. He is in overall charge of us all.'

'Oh dear!' said Samuel spontaneously, obviously perturbed by Jack Masters's attitude, and both friends were relieved to hear Joe Jago tap on the door once more.

'Mr Rawlings, Mr Fielding presents his compliments and asks that you meet him on the stage. It seems that there has been a new development in this matter.'

John stood up, extremely glad to remove himself from the stuffy confines of the little room.

'Tell him that I will attend him in just a few moments.'

The actor got to his feet. 'Are you finished with me?'

'Only one word more,' answered John. 'Whatever further information Mr Fielding might ask you to give him will be treated in the utmost confidence, I can assure you of that.'

Masters gave him a penetrating glance. 'You think a great deal of that man, don't you?'

'Yes. He is as honest and true an individual as I have ever come across.'

Jack drew on his pipe. 'That's as well with all the dark secrets this killing is going to lay bare.' And with those words he withdrew, leaving a cloud of blue smoke behind him.

A strange scene awaited John on the stage. The Blind Beak and Joe Jago were sitting on two chests, specially brought in for that purpose. Behind them stood one of Mr Fielding's Fellows, a sketch pad in his hand and an important look on his face. At the back of the stage, stretched out fast asleep, was Will the theatre boy, the wooden gallows that he was meant to have been guarding, quite unattended. All three of the adults had a conspiratorial air about them and John guessed at once that something had been discovered.

'Ah, Mr Rawlings,' said the Blind Beak, hearing John approach and obviously recognising his tread. 'I'm glad you're here. Would you mind entering the wooden contraption with my Brave Fellow? There's something he would like you to see.'

'What's going on?' asked the Apothecary, as he stepped once more into the claustrophobic confines of the box in which Jasper Harcross had met his death.

'Mr Fielding asked me to sketch the cuts made by the saw so that we could have a record of them. And it was while I was doing so that I noticed this.'

And he produced from his pocket a scarlet bow which he handed to John with a flourish.

'Um, from Sarah Delaney's costume, I imagine. Where was this?'

'Snagged on a piece of wood lower down, hardly visible in fact.'

'Strange that I did not notice it.'

'It could easily have been missed in the hurly burly.'

'There was certainly a great deal going on,' answered John, and had a cruelly vivid recollection of Jasper Harcross's dangling legs in their high leather boots, and how he had held them tightly to his chest.

'So what do you think, Sir?' the Runner went on.

'A most interesting find.'

But he would be drawn no further and said nothing more until the Blind Beak asked him the same question. Then John gave his honest opinion.

'I don't quite see how, Sir, but I believe that bow has been put there recently in order to incriminate Mrs Delaney.'

The black bandage hiding John Fielding's blind eyes turned sharply in the Apothecary's direction. 'And why do you say this?'

'For two different reasons. One is that I didn't see the bow when I was inside the gallows, though I admit that is easily explicable. The other is that Mrs Delaney's costume was intact during tonight's performance, yet the bow was missing when I questioned her.'

'You're sure of this?'

'Absolutely positive.'

'Then that means it was planted after the murder.'

John motioned towards the sleeping child. 'How long has he been like that?'

'At least half an hour. And during that time most of the actors were either being questioned or were in their dressing rooms. There must have been several periods when the stage was completely deserted, leaving anyone with a strong nerve free to tamper with the gallows.'

'Then we have a murderer who is trying to implicate another.'

'It would indeed seem so, yes.' The Blind Beak stood up, his commanding height dominating the group around him. 'Mr

Rawlings, I suggest that we bring tonight's questioning to a close. I shall see the rest of the players in the morning while you go to visit Mr Harcross's widow. Then perhaps we could meet at Bow Street in the evening in order to compare notes, if you and Sir Gabriel would care to dine.' Mr Fielding cleared his throat. 'My young friend, I do realise that I am imposing on you by asking you to be away from your shop, the source of your livelihood. It weighs heavily upon my conscience.'

John nodded. 'It does create certain difficulties, I must admit. Perhaps we could come to a compromise, whereby I work for the Public Office on alternate days, or something of that sort.'

'I think that might well be the answer,' said the Blind Beak. He turned to his clerk. 'And now, Jago, if you would tell the actors that we are done with them for the night and to be back here in costume at ten o'clock.' He called out to Dick, who had just reappeared on stage and whose footsteps he clearly recalled. 'Is Mr Garrick still in the theatre?'

'No, Sir, he's gone home. But the orchestra and stagehands want to know what to do. They have stayed on.'

'I'll see them in the morning as well. Now what about that boy? Where does he live?'

Dick stared at the Blind Beak in obvious surprise. 'Why here, Mr Fielding. He's the theatre boy, a foundling, he lives on the premises.'

'Does he sleep here?' asked John, with quickened interest.

'Yes.'

'Then he will be well worth talking to.'

The Blind Beak interrupted. 'Joe, put that on your list of things for Mr Rawlings to do. The child will be far less frightened of him than he will of me.'

'Very good, Sir. Then I'll go and get those rum cove actors shifted.'

'And I'll arrange for one of the Runners to stay here overnight,' the Magistrate added in an undertone. 'If one attempt has been made to distort vital evidence, who knows what might happen next.'

The empty theatre began to echo with the noise of footsteps descending the stairs leading from the dressing rooms, and then came the sound of people bidding each other farewell. Voices were hushed out of respect for the newly dead, and the occasional sob added its mournful note to the palpable air of gloom. Mr Fielding, sombre in a dark cloak, left for the stage door, guided by Joe Jago, while John watched the last of the players make their way out. It was only then that he heard his name called and spun round to see that Coralie Clive still prowled in the shadows. Motioning Samuel to go ahead of him and call a hackney, John went up to her.

'Miss Clive! Is anything wrong?'

'I just wanted a private word, that's all.'

Staring at her closely, the Apothecary saw that she was as pale as glass, her skin blanched and stretched so tightly over her cheekbones that her face looked almost mask-like.

'You're ill,' he said quietly. 'Come and sit down.'

She shook her head violently. 'What I have to say can be said as well standing.'

'Then how can I assist you?'

'Once, long ago, in a very clumsy way, I helped to save your life. Now it is my turn to ask a favour.'

'What is it?'

'I know that Mr Fielding admires and respects you . . .'

'Yes?'

'So I want you to persuade him that I did not kill my lover.'

John's heart lurched wretchedly. 'I take it you mean Jasper Harcross?'

A tear trickled from one of Coralie's glorious eyes. 'Oh yes. You see I was fatally attracted to him at one point. Indeed it was he who took away my innocence, more's the pity. But my only reward was to be discarded cruelly. To him I was a toy, a trifle, a mere bagatelle. You can well imagine that I wished him dead, Mr Rawlings.'

'I would rather not hear this.'

'Why, are you afraid of what I might be about to tell you?'

'Yes,' said John simply, 'I think I could be very afraid indeed.'

'None the less . . .' started Coralie, and then in the darkness of the stage something moved behind them.

'Who's there?' called the Apothecary, wild with fright.

But there was only the sound of the theatre boy sighing as he turned in his sleep, and the closing of the stage door as somebody unseen went quietly out.

Chapter Five

The villages of Chelsea and Kensington, lying only a few miles from the City of London, yet both being places of unequalled rural splendour, had a simple charm about them which John Rawlings had always found utterly captivating. With the river lapping against its shores, Chelsea had once been a fishing village and nothing more pretentious than that. Yet nowadays, with the building of the great Ranelagh Gardens, the most exclusive of all the pleasure gardens with its exorbitant entry fee of 2/6d., the *beau monde* came to Chelsea in droves, mainly for the somewhat boring delight of walking round and round Ranelagh's Rotunda in order to see and be seen. Kensington, however, could boast no such grand entertainment, not lying on the river and therefore not having the easy access provided by the waterway. Instead it lay, small and unassuming, in the midst of sweet green meadowland, geographically near to the metropolis but a million miles from its noise and strife.

The rich and famous had long since discovered these idyllic retreats. Sir Thomas More had moved to Chelsea whilst still Chancellor of the Exchequer; King Charles II had built The Hospital of Maymed Soldiers there; Jonathan Swift had taken lodgings near the river because he enjoyed the stroll into London. Kensington, in turn, could boast a palace, built by Wren for King William, who had shared a crown with his wife, Mary. Also situated outside the village was Holland House, owned by the politician Henry Fox, one of the most impressive buildings for miles around. But it was to a much smaller residence, standing just a little way from the cart track running through the centre of Kensington, that John, together with Samuel and a Beak Runner, now made their way, their unpleasant duty to inform Jasper Harcross's wife that she had only a short while ago become a widow.

They had left London early after very little sleep, returning to Nassau Street in the small hours, then being too excited to rest. Over and over again, John had thought of Coralie Clive and her urgent, whispered words, and had shuddered to think of their implications. That she had been the dead man's mistress was alarming enough, but the idea that the actress was guilty of murder and might be using her scant acquaintanceship with the Apothecary to attempt to clear herself, frankly appalled him.

'God dammit,' he had exclaimed angrily over a hastily snatched breakfast, causing Sir Gabriel Kent, up early to find out what was going on, to look at him quizzically, while Samuel raised his jolly eyebrows until they almost met his wig.

In the carriage sent by the Principal Magistrate to take them to Kensington, John's mood had not improved a great deal. Staring out of the window, he soon relapsed into silence and left it to Samuel and Benjamin Rudge, the Runner, to exchange pleasantries. Even the journey through countryside that grew ever more pastoral and remote, failed to excite him, enthusiastic traveller though the Apothecary normally was. In short, he felt worried and depressed and could hardly wait to see Coralie Clive again, to ask her to explain herself more fully.

'Well,' said Samuel, rubbing his hands together in somewhat nervous anticipation and dragging John's attention back to the ordeal that lay before them. 'I wonder what Mrs Harcross is going to be like.'

'I wonder if she's going to be our killer,' added Benjamin cheerfully.

John shook his head. 'I doubt it, somehow. It would be quite a feat to come across country during the night, then make one's way to the theatre in order to saw the gallows floorboards through.'

'But think of her motive, or motives!' Samuel replied. 'Why, her husband seems to have been sleeping with everybody.'

'I don't know where some people get the energy,' said the Runner, roaring and slapping his thigh at this fairly unfunny remark.

'I expect he took pills,' answered Samuel earnestly. 'There are tablets for that sort of thing, aren't there, John?'

'Indeed there are. I should say a good third of my income comes from mixing compounds to keep the ageing male population of London performing lustily in the boudoir.'

'What a depressing thought.'

'Yes, isn't it.'

'Now, gentlemen,' said the Runner, grinning broadly. 'There's no need to be upsetting yourselves. You've time on your side, which is more than those old goats have. And as for Mr Harcross, well, his time ran out, didn't it?'

'I wonder what his wife's going to be like?' Samuel repeated, sounding bewildered and slightly nervous.

'We'll know in a minute,' John answered grimly. 'Isn't that the house described to us over there?'

'Yes, that's it, Mr Rawlings. Just where Mr Garrick said it would be.'

'I still think it strange that he kept the fact of the marriage secret,' Samuel continued in much the same tone of voice.

'David Garrick, d'you mean? Or Jasper Harcross?'

'Well, both really. It seems so odd that none of the other actors appeared to know about it.'

'In my view, there might lie the motive,' put in Benjamin Rudge.

'What do you mean?'

'That somebody happened on the fact that her lover was already married and therefore merely trifling with her

55

affections. And, as a result, love turned to hate – with fatal consequences.'

Remembering the tightly stretched skin of Coralie's face, almost as if it were frozen, John audibly drew in his breath.

'We must not rule out the male sex from this affair. Any one of them might well have loathed Jasper Harcross enough to do away with him.'

The Runner nodded. 'That's true enough. Now, gentlemen, shall I undertake the task of breaking the news? Then you can stand by to give medical aid if need be.' He looked at the Apothecary.

'Very tactfully put,' John answered. 'I'd rather you than me.'

'Hear, hear,' said Samuel, as the carriage drew to a halt before a small, neat house of pleasing proportions.

Swiftly checking his bag for the correct remedies to treat shock, John alighted with the others and mounted the two steps that raised the front door from the level of the street. Then he stood, staring in anticipation, as the Runner gave a loud and portentous knock.

'Who's there?' called a voice. 'Jasper, is that you?'

'No, Ma'am,' Benjamin Rudge shouted back. 'I've come from the Public Office at Bow Street. Would it be possible to speak to you for a moment?'

'Of course,' the voice replied, and John heard the sound of bolts being drawn back and a key turning in the lock. Then the front door opened.

The Apothecary did not know what he had been expecting, though he had harboured vague notions of a fresh-faced country girl, a bucolic milkmaid, as the only sort of person who could be married to Jasper and not be aware of his philandering. But the woman who stood in the doorway was most certainly none of those things, indeed it was an intelligent, humourous and sophisticated face he found himself regarding.

Framed by a cloud of silver hair which she wore swept up beneath a lace cap, were a pair of shrewd eyes, crystal grey, the lines of experience and worldliness round them revealing that this woman was far from young, indeed had probably seen her fiftieth birthday some while ago. Her nose, too, strong and aquiline as it was, had grooves running beneath it. While her lips, sensuous still, were surrounded by that faint tracery of lines which denotes the passing of the years.

It shot through John's head that this could only be Jasper's mother-in-law, and before he could stop himself he found he was saying, 'We are sorry to trouble you, Ma'am, but we wondered if we might have a word with your daughter.'

The woman frowned. 'My daughter?'

'Yes,' John blundered on. 'For she is Mrs Harcross, is she not?'

She shot him a glance of amused contempt, as if she were thoroughly used to this kind of remark. 'No, *I* am Mrs Harcross.'

'Mrs Jasper Harcross?' asked the Runner incredulously, compounding John's terrible gaffe.

She cut across him impatiently. 'What is all this? You said you came from the Public Office. Kindly state your business.'

'May we step inside?' asked Benjamin.

'No you may not. How do I know who you are? You could be any kind of thief or blackguard.'

'Then I am afraid you must prepare yourself to receive some bad news where you stand, Madam.'

John found himself automatically opening his bag and slipping his hand in for salts as the voice of authority continued, 'I am sorry to have to inform you that Mr Harcross met with an accident in the theatre last night.'

Her skin went the colour of her hair but she did not falter otherwise. 'An accident?'

'Yes, Mrs Harcross. I am grieved to say that your husband died as a result of a misadventure on stage.'

Now she clung to the door for support and John automatically ran to help her, administering the salts as he led her inside and sat her in a low chair. Close to Jasper's widow like that, he could feel the grace with which she moved and sense the power of her charm. It occurred to him in that split second that she had once been an actress, and in that fact lay the key to the extraordinary relationship she and her husband shared.

'This misadventure,' she asked, in a low beautifully modulated voice which only served to confirm John's theory. 'What was it exactly?'

The Apothecary decided to tell the truth, knowing that to protect her further was only going to delay and worsen the shock.

'I'm afraid he was hanged during the gallows scene. The planking beneath his feet had been tampered with so that he fell through. The fall broke his neck.'

Mrs Harcross's hands flew to her throat. 'Oh how terrible! Who could have done such a thing?' Then her face changed and a worldly-wise expression crossed her features. 'But how silly of me to ask. Jasper played with fire and has done so for years. One cannot treat women as if they are gloves to be picked up, used, and then tossed aside. I suppose one could say that retribution has finally caught up with him.'

There was a noise from the doorway as Benjamin and Samuel, tired of waiting, entered the small hall. Mrs Harcross drew John's head down so that she could murmur in his ear and, seeing her so closely, he was struck by the fact that she had once been a great beauty.

'Listen to me,' she said urgently. 'Return here tomorrow and bring the Blind Beak with you – yes, I know all about him, I do visit town you know. I am prepared to tell him everything I can to help him find Jasper's killer but I refuse to bare my soul in front of those two. Now I shall play faint so please to tend me.' And Mrs Harcross swiftly rose from her chair, flung herself down on the sofa, and closed her eyes. John could not help it, his curved smile appeared before his expression grew serious and he went to fetch a damp cloth for his patient's brow.

'Is she fit to answer questions?' asked Benjamin anxiously.

John shook his head, keeping his face very straight. 'I'm afraid not. She is weak with shock and should rest for a while. I think it might be better if someone came back tomorrow.'

Samuel groaned. 'Well, I can't for a start. My father and I are going to look at possible premises for the goldsmith's business I hope to open soon. I must devote some time to my own affairs.'

The Runner scratched his head. 'This is very awkward. I shall have to consult with Mr Fielding.'

The Apothecary nodded, adding in an undertone, 'That would be the best plan. Being the extraordinary sort of woman she is, it occurs to me that the Beak might like to question Mrs Harcross himself.'

Benjamin Rudge looked relieved. 'I reckon you're right there, Mr Rawlings.' He turned his attention to the figure on the sofa. 'Now, Ma'am, do you have a neighbour who can keep an eye on you? For the fact of the matter is that these gentlemen and I will have to return to town. But that won't be the last of it I'm afraid. The Public Office is duty bound to ask you some questions about your late husband, and to that end someone will return here tomorrow when you are more in control of yourself.'

Mrs Harcross smiled faintly. 'It is kind of you to be so considerate. And, yes, I shall be perfectly all right. This is only a small village and everyone is very friendly.'

'Then I shall leave you some compound,' John said solemnly. 'Swallow a spoonful every hour to help you keep calm. And tonight I would like you to take some of these tablets so that you will get a good night's sleep.'

'I will do as you say,' she answered, then added in a softer voice, 'Until tomorrow, Sir.'

'Until then,' John answered as he made his departure.

The carriage arrived in Bow Street shortly after one o'clock, but John, knowing that he was to dine with the Blind Beak that evening, resisted the temptation to call on Mr Fielding. Instead he directed the driver to Nassau Street, where the Apothecary enjoyed a luxurious soak in his bath tub before changing into twilight clothes and going to seek out his father in the library. By the time these preparations were done it was dark, there being little light after three o'clock on such bleak November days, and John, as always, felt a glow of almost sensual pleasure as he walked into the exquisite room to see the rich floor-length curtains drawn against the night, the candles lit and the fire gleaming in the hearth. These were the feelings he always associated with his father, comfort and companionship coupled with two rather oddly related attributes, style and rare intelligence.

'Well,' said Sir Gabriel, looking up from his newspaper, 'there has obviously been much going on since we spoke last.'

'You know the bare bones of it?'

'Yes. Serafina called on me today to play cards. She told me everything that happened up to the moment when she had to leave the theatre. She also added that the talk is of murder rather than accident.'

'Yes, that's true enough. The planking of the gallows had been sawn through to breaking point. All it needed was Jasper's weight before they splintered.'

'And they were all right prior to the performance?'

'According to Dick Weatherby, the stage manager, the whole contraption was in perfect working order at the dress rehearsal.'

'I see. So it would appear to point to another member of the company. How much do you know about them?'

And Sir Gabriel listened intently as John described Mrs Delaney, Jack Masters, and all the others of whom he had taken particular note, ending with a brilliant word picture of Mrs Martin and her little husband. The description of Coralie Clive his son kept to a minimum, however, omitting the conversation they had had together in the darkness of the empty theatre.

Sir Gabriel must have sensed this reticence and with his unerring instinct for any of John's attempts at deception, said, 'And Miss Clive? What about her? Could she possibly be implicated?'

The Apothecary sighed and helped himself to another glass of sherry. 'I'm afraid that she must be, in a way. She was having some sort of liaison with Jasper Harcross, more's the pity.'

'But so were half a dozen other women, by the sound of it.'

'Yes, but . . .'

'They can't all have killed him so why should she be more involved than anyone else?'

John laughed out loud. 'Father, you are so refreshing. The truth is that she is walking about looking guilty as a thieving child and it is decidedly unnerving.'

'Why?' asked Sir Gabriel mildly.

'Why what?'

'Why should it unnerve you?'

'Because I like her. Because she saved my life once. I don't want her to be a murderess, she is too agreeable.'

'Ah!' replied his parent, and said no more.

Nor was the subject of the killing raised again until both Sir Gabriel and John were sitting in the pleasant salon which

Deryn Lake

stood directly above the Public Office in Bow Street. Since
the time of Sir Thomas de Veil in the late 1730s, it had
become the tradition for the Principal Justice of the Peace
to live in the Bow Street house, occupying the four floors
situated over those rooms devoted to the law. John Fielding
had moved in there when his half-brother Henry had sought to
restore his shattered health by sailing for warmer climes. But,
sadly, it was to be the great writer's last voyage, and now his
younger sibling not only ran the Public Office but also bore
the entire responsibility for policing the capital.

'I was so sorry to read of the death of your remarkable
brother,' said Sir Gabriel now, echoing a remark of David
Garrick's.

'He was broken by overwork,' answered the Magistrate
sadly. 'Do you know, he was only in his forty-eighth year.'

'What a terrible waste,' Sir Gabriel commented softly. 'Why
is it that so many with something to offer to the world are taken
from it? While others live on and on, contributing nothing?'

'Blind justice,' answered John Fielding, and laughed just a
tinge bitterly. He turned to John. 'Now tell me of Mrs Harcross.
I gather from Rudge that the lady is old enough to be the dead
man's mother. Is that correct?'

'It certainly is. It was really quite extraordinary to meet
her. She is a woman who has once been beautiful and is also
extremely sharp witted in my estimation. What she was doing
with a rascal like Jasper Harcross is beyond comprehension.
Incidentally, Sir, she says she will speak to no one but you
and requests that you visit her tomorrow.'

'So Rudge informed me. He also said that she seemed to
trust *you*, which makes things damnably awkward.'

'In what way?' asked Sir Gabriel, slightly irritated on his
son's behalf.

The Blind Beak rumbled his deep and melodious chuckle.
'Because Mr Rawlings and I have come to an arrangement.

62

Namely, that he would work in his shop on alternate days in order to keep his business thriving. If I honour this agreement, as indeed I must, then he will not be free to accompany me when Mrs Harcross reveals the secrets of her past.'

Sir Gabriel thoughtfully adjusted the white lace cuffs of his jet satin coat. 'Perhaps I could be of help in this regard. An apprentice apothecary in need of some practical experience might well be released by his Master in return for a consideration. I shall go searching for one first thing in the morning. Meanwhile, could the lady not be visited tomorrow night?'

'A splendid notion,' John Fielding answered, so rapidly that the Apothecary wondered whether he had had it in mind all along. 'Then that is settled. And now for some refreshment,' he continued as a servant came in bearing an excellent selection of drinks. 'What will you have, Sir Gabriel?'

The conversation turned to who desired what beverage and was further diverted by the entry of Elizabeth Fielding and Mary Ann, who was in fact Mrs Fielding's niece though being brought up by the couple as a daughter.

'Mr Rawlings,' said the pretty child, 'how nice to see you. Are you working with my uncle again?'

'Yes. This time we are hunting down the murderer of Mr Jasper Harcross, the actor.' John said the words slowly and deliberately, knowing how much the little girl relished the details of what was going on, but all the while with a decided twinkle in his eye. 'And now may I present my father to you?' And with great solemnity he went through the rituals of introduction.

The child adored it, miniature adult that she already was, and curtsied and extended her hand as neatly as any woman of society.

'I hope one day to have the honour of your close acquaintance,' Sir Gabriel said very seriously, and was rewarded with a swift kiss on the cheek.

'Shall I take her away?' said Elizabeth. 'Do you gentlemen want to discuss the case?'

'Oh, let her stay,' answered her husband affably. 'I only want to talk about the characters involved in the affair, one of the most interesting of whom is a child.'

'Who? Who?' asked Mary Ann excitedly.

'Will, the theatre boy. As I told you, Mr Rawlings, I am leaving you to interview him directly. But I have in the meantime found out a great deal about him. It appears that he is indeed a foundling but was taken from the Hospital by Jasper Harcross himself, after which David Garrick gave him the job of dogsbody. Drury Lane is the boy's home, he knows no other. When I expressed surprise at this I was told that it is not the first time such a thing has happened. Adam Verity, the young man who plays Filch, also began his theatre career in that way, after having run away from his foster mother.'

'Tell me about the others you questioned,' said John. 'Is there anybody who cannot answer for themselves?'

'Several,' answered the Blind Beak, almost with an air of triumph. 'And for that reason I have asked Joe Jago to make a list so that you might quiz them further, Mr Rawlings.'

'But why me? Wouldn't one of your regular Runners do it better?'

'I trust your eyes, Sir. I trust your eyes.'

'Oh don't be sad, Uncle,' said Mary Ann, suddenly throwing herself into John Fielding's arms and looking very tearful. 'It doesn't matter that you can't see, truly it doesn't. Mr Rawlings will help you. Won't you, Sir?'

The Blind Beak picked the child up and placed her on his knee, planting a kiss on her cheek, which turned the colour of a wild strawberry.

'There now, I'm not miserable. I was just telling our friend what great faith I have in him.'

Sir Gabriel laughed, a golden sound. 'D'you know, John, I always thought that marvellous memory of yours would stand you in good stead.'

'But only on alternate days it would seem,' the Apothecary answered, and slowly smiled his crooked smile.

Chapter Six

The next morning dawning very bright and fair, a crisp and sparkling autumn day, John set off for his shop in Shug Lane with his spirits much revived by the sunshine. Meanwhile, Sir Gabriel, creature of the night though this outward appearance might suggest him to be, had risen early and, having breakfasted lightly, set forth in a sedan chair to find John an assistant.

'It's a pity that I haven't my own apprentice,' the Apothecary had said as they had parted company.

'Well, you won't get one until you're made Free and there's an end to it.'

'Free!' John had exclaimed sarcastically. 'I vow and declare there's some kind of spell on me and the Court.'

And it was true that he had been most unfortunate with his application to be made Free of the Worshipful Society of Apothecaries. The after effects resulting from his first involvement with a case of murder had ruled out his attending the June Private Court Day. However, in August he had finally managed to attend the Court, but it had broken up just before his application to be admitted to his Freedom had been heard. Then, in October, urgent attendance at the site of a street accident had once more stopped him from going. And now it was dangerously near the December meeting and he had no idea when he would be finished with this particular investigation.

'I'll never get there,' John muttered to himself as he walked out of Rupert Street, named after Charles I's heroic nephew, then into Coventry Street and right into Shug Lane. 'I shall

spend the rest of my days as the only apothecary in London
not to be a Yeoman of the Society.'

But he wasn't serious and whistled as he sought the shop key
in his pocket. It was just as he located it and headed for his front
door, that a sedan chair coming from the direction of Marybone
Street came into his line of vision, and John stared in amazement as the chairmen set it down before his entrance. Hurrying
forward, he was just in time to see Miss Coralie Clive set her
foot upon the cobbles and search in her reticule for the fare.

'Miss Clive,' he said, and bowed so low that his springing
cinnamon hair briefly swept the ground.

'You're not wearing a wig,' she answered, obviously faintly
astonished.

'I don't when I'm in the shop, though I carry one with me
in case I am called out.'

'Your hair suits you, though. It's such a wonderful colour.'

If I go pink, John thought grimly, I shall never speak to
myself again. And in order to make such a terrible occurrence
appear as if it were caused by natural exertion he whirled round
and opened the door with a flourish.

'And to what do I owe the honour of this visit?' he asked,
still with his back turned.

'To the terrible events at Drury Lane, alas,' the actress
answered quietly.

'You want to continue our conversation of the other night,
I take it.'

'Yes, yes, I do.'

'Then come in. I have quite a comfortable room at the back
where I do my compounding. I also have a kettle and some
very good tea in there. Would you like some?'

'I would like it more than anything.'

'Then please take a seat while I get the shop ready for the
day. I'll only be a few minutes and then we can talk.'

'Can I help in any way?'

'You can take the covers off those shelves if you like. But mind not to spill anything. Some of the physics could stain your dress.'

'I'll be careful,' she said, and smiled.

John's heart gave an exuberant bound and he was vividly reminded of how he used to feel in the company of the Masked Lady, as Serafina had once been known. He coughed a little. 'You can borrow one of my aprons if you wish,' he said, hoping that he didn't sound utterly pompous.

Coralie smiled again. 'I have an even better idea. Why don't you organise the shop while I brew the tea? In that way I can keep clean and the work will be done in half the time.'

'A good idea,' answered John and put on one of the long coveralls that he always wore for preparing his potions.

As he worked swiftly round the place, removing the covers from the shelves and dusting the various bottles and jars beneath, it occurred to him that Miss Clive seemed in comparatively good spirits, and he wondered just how saddened by Jasper's death she had been. Her words came back to him. 'I wished him dead, Mr Rawlings,' and again the icy hand of fear clutched at his heart as the Apothecary reiterated to himself what he had said to his father about her being guilty.

Quite spontaneously and without stopping to think about what he was doing, he called out, 'Did you hate your lover enough to kill him?'

Equally spontaneously and with a speed that was to convince John that she was entirely free of blame, Coralie called back, 'Oh yes, but I didn't do it. However much I detested him, however badly he had treated me, I could never have struck him down. It is not in my capability.'

John appeared in the doorway of his compounding room, watching her where she bent over the kettle and teapot, the water heating on a little oil stove that he used in his experiments. 'Are you going to tell me everything?'

'I am indeed.'

'Omitting nothing?'

'I promise you.'

'Then start,' he said.

He must have given her an unreadable look, for Coralie stared at him for a second before she took her cup of tea and sat down on one of the stools. 'Where should I begin?'

'Perhaps with when you met him. Was it at Drury Lane?'

'Yes. My sister, Kitty, was playing Isabella in *The Old Debauchees* written by the Magistrate's brother, Henry. I had a very small part, a mere few lines, while Jasper had one of the main roles.' Coralie finished her tea and looked straight at John. 'Mr Rawlings, how old are you?'

'Twenty-three. I only finished my apprenticeship earlier this year. Why?'

'Your juvenescence appeals to me. It makes me feel that you will understand the follies of youth. I was sixteen when I met Jasper and I fell madly in love with him on sight. Do you follow?'

'Only too well,' answered John, remembering how Serafina had haunted his days and nights.

'He did not pay me any attention for two years, other than for the pleasure of flirting with a child who adored him. Then, having tired of his current favourite, he took me for his mistress, and so I remained until Sarah Seaton came upon the scene.'

'Mrs Delaney?'

'One and the same. Then he secretly dallied with us both and I, like a fool, believed his denials, that is until a few months ago.'

'What happened then?'

'Sarah became pregnant and when Jasper refused to marry her, saying most cruelly that he did not believe the child was his, she panicked and married Lord Delaney in great haste. He, poor soul, is only too delighted to think that he is potent enough to impregnate a young woman.'

'And this turned you against him?'

'I thought it unspeakable behaviour and was just about to tell him so when a very strange thing happened.'

'Go on.'

'A woman called on me, a woman who declared she was Jasper's wife, though I had never heard that such a being existed. Anyway, she warned me off. Said that I was to leave her husband alone or she would not be responsible for the consequences.'

'What did you do?'

'I showed her the door, though I was mightily upset afterwards, you can believe. Mr Rawlings, do you think she was what she said she was? Does – did – Jasper have a wife?'

The Apothecary sighed. 'I'm afraid so. Mr Garrick was party to the secret and I went to see the lady yesterday. She was very much older than her husband, quite astonishingly so. But then you must have noticed that.'

Coralie frowned. 'No, I can't say that I did.'

John's lively eyebrows rose. 'Really? How incredible! Did you meet her by candlelight?'

'Yes, but . . .'

'What?'

'I could have sworn that the woman in question was not a great deal older than I am.'

'Which is?' asked John, thinking himself mightily clever to find out Coralie's age in so subtle a way.

'I was twenty last June.'

'Um,' said the Apothecary, and fingered his chin thoughtfully. 'How very strange that his wife should call on you.' He changed his tack. 'Miss Clive, what did you mean when you asked me to convince Mr Fielding that you did not kill Jasper Harcross?'

'Simply what I said. I believe that, as the wronged mistress, I must be the principal suspect.'

'What about Mrs Delaney?'

'She has married her lord and has too much to lose. She may have hated Jasper, but I assure you she is no fool. She wouldn't give up a fortune even for revenge.'

'Then, if you did not kill him and neither did she, who do you think is responsible?'

Coralie sighed deeply and the Apothecary realised that the atmosphere between them had changed, much to his disappointment. Even while he had been asking her questions, she had gone on the defensive again. John made one last effort to put things right. Leaning forward, he took the actress's hands in his, enjoying the sensation of her cool fingers lying amongst his own.

'Miss Clive,' he said seriously, 'please accept that I believe you completely. I am absolutely certain that though you may have had every reason to kill Jasper Harcross, you did not do so. Because of this I will do everything in my power to convince the Magistrate of your innocence.'

Her emerald eyes glistened. 'Is it not dangerous for anyone solving a crime to like and trust a suspect?'

'Highly,' answered John, and very lightly kissed the fingers that he held.

Half an hour later the actress left him to go to the theatre where, so she said, David Garrick had called a meeting to discuss the possible cancellation of further performances of *The Beggar's Opera*. Left alone, John would have liked time to collect his thoughts, particularly with regard to Coralie's strange assertion that Mrs Harcross was not a great deal older than herself. But this was not to be. There was a rush of custom from the streets, culminating in a frantic husband sending for

John to come and examine his wife who appeared to be in the early stages of labour. Fortunately for all concerned a physician was found who had studied with William Hunter, the great obstetrician. Having prescribed raspberry leaf tea and juice of the white poppy, the Apothecary felt quite justified in leaving the mother in the doctor's care, thankful that the midwife she had originally asked to deliver her was away from home. By this time darkness had fallen over London and it was the hour for him to go home and change.

Sir Gabriel being out of the house, having already left for an evening of cards, John hurried over his toilette, then took a chair to Bow Street where John Fielding awaited him. There the two men boarded a carriage and set off west, an armed guard sitting beside the coachman for the rural route to Kensington was infested with highwaymen. Turning down The Strand, the conveyance made its way to Hyde Park Corner in order to traverse the park itself, waiting by the gates where bells were being rung so that travellers could gather together in numbers. Then several coaches went off in convoy down the King's Old Road to Kensington, His Majesty having given permission only recently for this thoroughfare to be used by the public.

'Having built himself a grand New Road,' Mr Fielding commented succinctly.

'In view of the hazards of the journey, do you think Mrs Harcross could have made her way to the theatre and tampered with the gallows?' John asked his companion, who sat in the semi-darkness, his bandaged eyes seeming to stare straight in front of him.

'Why do you use that tone of voice, my friend?'

'I wasn't aware that I had altered it.'

'Oh yes. Last night you spoke of the lady in quite a different way. What has happened to change your opinion of her?'

'Well, to tell the truth I had a call from Miss Clive this morning,' John answered, feeling the usual surge of reluctance to say anything against the actress. 'It seems that Mrs Harcross recently sought her out and they had some kind of disagreement.'

The Blind Beak cleared his throat but said nothing.

'But what was extremely odd was the fact that Coralie swore the lady who visited her was young. In fact she believed her about the same age as herself.'

'Strange indeed! For Rudge confirmed your impression that Jasper's wife was old enough to be his mother.'

'Samuel thought so too.'

'Surely there can't be *two* Mrs Harcrosses,' the Magistrate said thoughtfully.

'Bigamy!' John exclaimed. 'Well, I suppose I wouldn't put anything past him.'

'I take it then,' Mr Fielding said quietly, 'that all the rumours are true? That art held the mirror to life and he was having affairs with all and sundry, particularly his two leading ladies?'

'I'm afraid so, though there is no way that Miss Clive can possibly be implicated in the crime. She told me so herself. It is not in her nature to take the life of another human being.'

'Admittedly, murder is only in the nature of those who are deranged in some way, whether it be through hatred, greed, maliciousness or cruelty. Yet, let any of us be faced by a man wielding an axe when we hold a pistol and I swear there is not one incapable of firing.'

'But . . .'

'There are no buts, Mr Rawlings. If Miss Clive felt sufficiently threatened even she would defend herself.'

'I suppose so.'

'Yet,' the Magistrate continued in a more kindly tone, 'I can well appreciate how difficult it must be for you to equate her beauty and charm with such an ugly thing as murder.'

John rallied. 'Mr Fielding, I do not find it difficult but impossible! Despite the fact that Coralie had every reason to do away with the wretched man I vow that I shall prove to you she did not.'

'Good,' said the Blind Beak, 'that is the very thing I like to hear.'

And he changed the subject, talking to John about his impressions of those members of the company the Apothecary was due to see the following morning.

'I have called them into the theatre for ten, if that is convenient to you. There are seven of them, eight if you include the stage manager, nine with the boy.'

'And the reason why you have picked these particular people?'

'Everyone else could account for their movements on the night before the murder, the night when the planking was sawn through. Yet all of these others either had flimsy excuses or, so it seemed to me, were telling downright lies.'

'What about Jack Masters?'

'He still wouldn't give me the name of the woman with whom he is supposed to have spent the night. I thought you should have one final try.'

'And if he won't reveal it?'

'Then I shall charge him with impeding the course of justice.'

John would have commented that the Magistrate was obviously running out of patience, but at that moment the coach began to slow down and the Apothecary saw dim lights through the window and realised that they were coming towards civilisation, if such a term could be used for Kensington at night. Lying among green fields, rushing brooks and farmhouses as it was, the hamlet appeared to be utterly without signs of life. Had it not been for the dull and distant glow of candles coming from the various homesteads, the place would have appeared totally deserted.

'You'll have to help me to the door and beyond,' said John Fielding into the darkness. 'I have learnt every inch of my home

and the Public Office, but when I am on strange territory it is
something of a different matter.'

For the first time in their acquaintanceship, the vulnerability
of the Blind Beak came home to the younger man and he felt
a moment of tremendous closeness to one who was so mighty
and yet at the same time so powerless. 'I'll be delighted to lend
you my arm, Sir,' he said, with the merest catch in his voice.

'And I want you to watch the woman with a falcon's eye. I
shall mention Miss Clive and then it is for you to see how she
reacts. Now, let us go to business.' So saying, the Magistrate
rose from his seat and let John help him down the precarious
steps which led from the carriage to the ground below.

Mrs Harcross was clearly expecting them for her little house
shone with light, the only one in the entire village to do so.
And on this occasion she had obviously had more than enough
time in which to prepare herself for, just for a moment as she
answered the door, the gentle candlelight worked its charm
and John could have sworn that it was indeed a young woman
who stood there. Beautifully dressed, lightly enamelled, with
beauty spots positioned cunningly about her lips and cheeks, he
understood immediately how Jasper Harcross must have been
attracted to such a handsome creature. But as the Apothecary
led the Blind Beak through her tiny hall and into the small but
exquisitely furnished salon where she politely bade them sit
down, the lines on Mrs Harcross's face and her world-weary
expression became apparent once more.

'Before I take a seat,' put in the Magistrate, his melodious
voice echoing round the walls of the little room, 'will you not
introduce me to our hostess, Mr Rawlings?'

'Certainly.' The Apothecary bowed. 'Mrs Harcross, may I
present the Principal Magistrate of London, Mr John Fielding.'

'Delighted, Sir,' she answered, putting her hand into that of
the Beak as she dropped a polite curtsey.

'Mr Fielding, Mrs Jasper Harcross,' John continued.

'A pleasure, Madam,' he answered, making a polite bow.

'It was good of you to come to my house,' the actor's widow went on. 'I felt I should tell you all that I know in order to help you track down my poor husband's killer. Yet there are certain things that I would rather not say before the gentlemen who called the other day.'

'Of course,' answered Mr Fielding, removing his hat and cloak which he handed to John. 'I quite understand.' He felt for the chair behind him and carefully lowered his great frame. 'If I may make so bold, Madam,' he went on almost as if the Apothecary were not there and he was speaking *à deux*, 'you have the most beautiful voice. When I lost my sight at the age of nineteen certain delightful compensations became mine, the arts of contemplation and conversation being but two of them. Yet another was the charm of listening to voices – and identifying their owners. Surely, if I am not mistaken, I have heard yours somewhere before.'

There was a long pause interrupted by a very small maid, obviously a girl from the village, coming in with a tray of bottles and glasses. 'Shall I pour, Mam?' she asked nervously, very flustered by the grand company.

'Yes,' answered Mrs Harcross, obviously also much confused. 'Do so.'

There was another strained silence during which the girl gave John a gin so strong that it made him sneeze. Mr Fielding, meanwhile, accepted a glass of claret and sat with a benevolent smile on his face, waiting for his hostess to make the next move. Eventually, when the girl had gone, she said, 'I think you must be mistaken, Sir.'

'Quite possibly,' the Magistrate answered. 'None of us is infallible. Yet I could have sworn that I am speaking to Mrs Egleton, the great actress, who, if my memory serves me correctly, took the part of Lucy Lockit at the very first performance of *The Beggar's Opera*, then went on to retire into obscurity after playing the finest Lady Macbeth of her day.'

The white make-up concealed any pallor that might have swept Mrs Harcross's cheeks, but there could be no denying the frantic glint in her eye, nor the fact that her breathing increased to such an alarming rate she was almost panting.

'I hear that you are startled,' Mr Fielding went on inexorably. 'Why is that, Mrs Harcross?'

She drained her glass in one draught, then stood up. 'Damn you,' she exclaimed violently. 'I wish I had never invited you over the threshold.'

The Magistrate also rose to his feet and his vast height loomed over the angry woman. 'I think it would be better,' he said, his voice as soft as satin, 'if you put your trust in me. All will come out in the end, be assured of it. Remember, if you are innocent of your husband's murder then you have nothing to fear. Now Madam, answer me true. Did you kill Jasper Harcross?'

'No,' she answered, her lovely voice breaking on a sob. 'I didn't kill the wretched man. You see, the tragedy of it was that I loved him. And in that lay the cause of all that was to follow.'

Chapter Seven

There was a profound silence during which the blind man stood so still that just for a moment John had the ridiculous notion he might have dropped off to sleep. Then the Principal Magistrate spoke.

'Mrs Harcross, I trust you will believe me when I assure you that the last thing I desire is to cause you distress. As I have already said, I was not born blind, and one of the final things I was privileged to see was your performance as Lady Macbeth opposite James Quin. I thought you one of the greatest and most beautiful actresses of the day. I could hardly believe it when I was informed by my brother Henry that you had disappeared to the country at the very pinnacle of your career.'

The former Mrs Egleton gave a harsh laugh. 'At the time I had little choice in the matter.'

'Why was that?' asked the Blind Beak in such a conversational manner that John felt rather than saw her attitude to the Magistrate soften.

'Because I was in love, Sir. So crazily, I made that sacrifice. For that was what Jasper required of me. That I give up my career in order to concentrate entirely on his.'

'What a terrible thing to do,' John exclaimed thoughtlessly. 'To ask that of anyone is monstrous, but to demand it of your wife, a celebrated actress, is beyond forgiveness.'

Mrs Harcross laughed again. 'That is the sort of man Jasper was. He was, without doubt, the most selfish individual I have ever encountered.'

'Perhaps,' said John Fielding, 'we should talk the whole matter through. Mr Rawlings, pour Mrs Harcross a glass of wine. Asking questions is an ordeal for everyone concerned, so let us at least act in a companionable manner.'

The Apothecary rose to his feet with alacrity, marvelling at the ease with which the older man was placating the unhappy woman.

'A little claret, if you please,' she said, turning her handsome eyes in John's direction.

'Certainly.' And he gave an unreciprocated smile.

There was another moment of quiet during which the Blind Beak listened for the sound of pouring and his hostess settling herself in her chair, as did he. Then he spoke again.

'It would be of great help to me if you could relate your story from the start. Going back to the time before you met Jasper Harcross.'

'But surely that is not relevant to this enquiry?'

Mr Fielding sipped his wine. 'In a case of murder, I fear, it is often the smallest detail, a fact from the past that might be considered unimportant, that betrays the identity of the killer. A strange point but for all that true.'

Mrs Harcross nodded half-heartedly. 'I suppose you are right.'

'Perhaps you could tell me something of your youth. Did you live in London as a child? Or are you originally from the country?'

'No, I was born and brought up in Spitalfields. My father was a Hugenot, a weaver, my mother was English. I was baptised in St Mary's, Whitechapel.'

'And what was your given name?'

'Elizabeth Tessier.'

'So how did you become an actress from that non-theatrical start?'

'My father wove materials for John Rich, manager of the

Theatre Royal in Lincolns Inn Fields. Finally won over by my insistence that I wanted to go on the stage, Papa asked the great man if I might go to him for training.'

'So small wonder that you played Lucy Lockit in the very first production of *The Beggar's Opera*?'

'Yes, it was staged at the Theatre Royal, as you know.'

'I have heard it said that the play made Mr Gay rich and Mr Rich gay. Is it true?'

Mrs Harcross smiled for the first time. 'Oh yes. The show was an instant success. The whole of London flocked to see it.'

The Blind Beak frowned. 'But by this time you were Mrs Egleton, surely?'

Observing Jasper's widow closely, John saw that she had gone as still as death, and the fingers clasped round the stem of the wine glass were unnaturally white.

'Yes, you are perfectly right. I met my first husband when I was just sixteen and had been training with Mr Rich a mere few months. Mr Egleton was considerably older than I was and at first I simply laughed at him. But eventually his constant showering of gifts wore me down and I married him four years later, on condition that he would let me pursue my chosen vocation.' Perhaps realising that the last remark had made her sound heartless, Mrs Harcross added, 'I was very fond of him, of course. He was a thoroughly decent man.'

'Indeed,' the Blind Beak said softly. 'Pray, continue.'

The former actress gave a humourless chuckle. 'Of course being so young, and with a head full of feathers, I did not fully understand the possible consequences of married life.'

'Surely you are not referring to children?' asked the Apothecary, slightly shocked.

She shot him a look full of bitterness. 'Of course I am. Nine months after my wedding I gave birth to a son. Mr Rich was so furious that he nearly dismissed me and it took all my pleading to make him keep me on. Then, in 1728, when I created the role of Lucy Lockit, I found that I was expecting another child.'

'You played the part pregnant?'

'Yes.'

'What a strange coincidence.'

Mrs Harcross grew even more rigid. 'What are you saying?'

'That Mrs Delaney, playing Lucy in the present ill-fated production, is also *enceinte*.'

'Really?' said the widow, her voice a rasp.

'Mrs Delaney is married to Lord Delaney,' the Blind Beak interposed. 'Enough said, I believe.'

She shrugged, her whole manner defeated. 'Perhaps, perhaps. Anyway, I gave birth to a girl whom I named Lucy, more for a joke than anything else. Then I handed the infant into the charge of a maid and returned to the stage. But when my first husband died in 1733, I placed my children in the care of a good woman in Chelsea and paid her to raise them. Mr Egleton spent more time with them than I did, you see. I felt I had no other alternative.'

Mrs Harcross held her glass out to John for him to refill. 'And then I met Jasper and was repaid in full for all my indifference to my young. It was in 1739, when he was twenty and I thirty-seven. Of course I still had my good looks and was considered to be at the peak of my career, while he was a nothing, a nobody, a stage-struck young upstart with not a penny to his name.' She paused and drank deeply. 'I can tell you, gentlemen, that there is nothing more obscene than the kind of love Jasper Harcross engendered in me. It was like a sickness, a vile craving. It was almost as if I fed off him.'

Involuntarily John gave a shudder and the former actress glanced at him.

'Yes, it is a revolting picture, I know. Even I, in the moments when I faced my soul, saw the ugliness of it. But there was nothing I could do. I was caught up in a trap created by lust and passion. A young girl who had entered a loveless marriage, deeply smitten at last. That is why, over all the years, he has been able to do exactly what he liked with me. I gave up my career, my children, everything, all so that I could keep him at my side.'

'Even to letting him pretend he was not married?' the Blind Beak asked, his voice betraying his astonishment. 'Or did you not know about that?'

'I knew about it full well. Jasper told me that to ingratiate himself with the women of London society, his principal patrons, it was better that he was thought single. And I, fool that I was, believed him. It was not for some while that I discovered my husband was behaving as a bachelor, surrounding himself with whores and doxies, spending his time in town and rarely coming to my side – or my bed.' Mrs Harcross began to weep silently. 'Oh, Mr Fielding, if only you could understand what a sickness this love of mine was. I put up with his liaisons, tolerated his flagrant infidelity, just to be thrown an occasional crumb of affection. Dear God, when I think about how low I sank I could die of shame.'

'I do not sit in judgement,' the Magistrate continued quietly, 'you must remember that. My one purpose is to find your late husband's killer.'

Elizabeth Harcross gave a wretched laugh. 'It will be like looking for a wolf in the midst of a pack. He treated women like dirt, while men despised and envied him. The child that Sarah Delaney carries, it's his, he told me so. As for that silly girl Clive, she surrendered her virginity to him and even played my role for a while, allowing him to deceive her.'

'Until you warned her to be off, of course,' John said, wondering why he suddenly felt so heartily sick of the entire conversation.

Mrs Harcross gave him a look of total astonishment. 'I don't know what you mean. I've never met the wretched girl, let alone given her a warning about Jasper. She is an adult and capable of looking after herself, as are they all.'

'And at that point we shall leave the matter,' said the Beak, standing up. 'You have been of enormous help, Madam.' He held out his arm for John to guide him. 'There is just one last thing, though. I take it you were at home on the night before Jasper was killed and that someone can vouch for you?'

'Yes and no,' answered Mrs Harcross, sounding surprised. 'I was indeed here but I spent my time alone.'

'Did the maid not see you?'

'I sent her away after she had cleared dinner. She lives locally, you see.'

Mr Fielding nodded gravely. 'Of course. It is of no consequence.' He turned to the Apothecary. 'Is there anything you would like to ask Mrs Harcross, my friend?'

'Yes,' said John, as he helped the Magistrate into his cloak. 'You said that you gave up your children for Jasper Harcross. Yet I could have sworn you also told us that, following the death of your first husband, you fostered them out in order to continue in your profession. Which is the truth?'

The enamelled face set itself into a mask. 'When I retired from the stage I decided that at long last I should be a proper mother to the poor creatures. So I wrote and invited them home. But Jasper would have none of it. I suppose he thought a boy of sixteen, as George was by then, would be too critical of the brash young buck his mother had married. My husband told me he would not tolerate my children under his roof and that was the end of it.'

'How did they react to that?'

'I don't know. When I next went to see them they had gone.'

'Gone?' asked the Blind Beak, obviously startled.

'Yes, George had disappeared from the home of the carpenter to whom he was apprenticed and taken Lucy with him. Their foster mother had no idea where they were, except that she thought they had made their way to London.'

'There to vanish amongst the hordes of others, no doubt.'

Mrs Harcross wept again. 'No doubt. For that crime alone, Jasper deserved to die.'

'Be careful what you say, Madam.'

'No, I have already told you that mine was not the hand that struck him. The hideous love I felt for him possesses me still, even though my brain finally admits that he is dead.' She gave the most distressing laugh that John had ever heard. 'After all, a parasite does not kill its host, does it?'

'It is time we left,' said the Magistrate, feeling his companion give another shudder of revulsion. 'I thank you for your frankness. Good night to you Mrs Harcross. Should you think of anything relevant to the case, however trifling you might believe it, please contact me at the Public Office.' And with that he allowed John Rawlings to lead him out into the cold night air.

Travelling back in the carriage, neither man spoke a great deal, John thinking that despite his medical training, nothing had prepared him for quite such a terrible confession as Mrs Harcross had just made. He tried to imagine being in the grip of a devouring obsession and shied away from the very idea. Almost thinking aloud, he said, 'God's wounds, I hope I never become so besotted with another that I sacrifice everything else in life.'

'Nor,' answered Mr Fielding solemnly, 'to allow someone else to cloud one's judgement so greatly that one goes beyond the point of rational thinking.'

In the darkness the Apothecary felt himself grow hot. An idea that he had been pushing away for some time came back to him and he reluctantly faced it. Despite all Coralie's protestations that her liaison with Jasper Harcross was at an end, that her love, indeed, had turned to hatred, she had still stood close to the actor on the night of the killing. Casting his vivid memory back he saw again how Jasper had held his leading lady tightly, his arm around her waist, and they had smiled at one another.

'Damn,' said John under his breath. 'They say there's no fool like an old fool – but as far as I can see there's no fool like a young one either.'

'You spoke?' asked the Magistrate.

'Thinking aloud, Sir, that is all.'

'Ah. Well, I hope you have good hunting in the theatre to-morrow. Let us see what you make of the rapscalion bunch.'

'Is Coralie Clive amongst them?' John enquired, then immediately regretted it.

'Most certainly. Her excuses for the night before the murder are amongst the flimsiest I heard. Why do you ask?'

The Apothecary gritted his teeth. It would appear that despite all his earlier hopes that Coralie was not involved he was going to have to think again about her.

'Only because, as I have already said, it is hard to believe her capable of killing.'

'Remember Mrs Harcross and beware of sentiment, my friend.'

'Yes,' John answered grimly, 'I most certainly will.'

And he stared out of the window into the darkness as the coach made its way through the silent fields towards the city of London.

Chapter Eight

He slept very uneasily, waking almost hourly with two unresolved questions repeating themselves again and again in his brain. What had become of the Egleton children, who by now must be fully grown adults? And if Mrs Harcross had not called on Coralie in order to warn her off, who had? A nasty thought crept, unbidden, into John's brain and he had sat up in bed, feeling very depressed. Could Coralie have made the whole story up in order, perhaps, to detract from her own guilt?

Thoroughly confused, the Apothecary had wandered downstairs to sit by the library fire, kept burning all night in this wintry weather, and there he had finally fallen asleep, curled up in Sir Gabriel's chair, only to wake again as a sullen dawn made its reluctant appearance in the London skies. Knowing that further rest was out of the question, John had gone upstairs to shave and dress.

Staring into the mirror in the harsh early light, he thought that he looked only one step removed from a savage. His eyes, normally the deep bright blue of flowers, were dull, and there were bags beneath them in spite of the fact he had drunk very little wine the night before. His lively eyebrows were currently set in two harsh lines, while his skin appeared to have a greenish tinge. His mouth, famed for its crooked grin, a characteristic over which he had no control, was positively turning downwards, and sticking out his tongue, John saw that it looked coated and unhealthy. Sighing, he mixed himself a potion, vile to the taste but wondrous in its effects.

'Stop thinking that Coralie's a liar,' he told himself firmly. 'She might well be speaking the truth.'

His reflection pulled a sardonic face. 'She had her arm round him, didn't she?'

'Perhaps it was for a reason.'

'Are you talking to yourself?' called Sir Gabriel, sweeping past the door in his nightrail and turban, a sight to inspire fearful admiration in the minds of all who beheld it.

'Of course,' John replied promptly. 'I am such a fine conversationalist I cannot resist. But tell me seriously, should I leave my shop unopened today or have you found someone to deputise for me?'

'I have succeeded superbly, my dear. Come and join me for breakfast and I shall tell you all about it.'

As always Sir Gabriel ate lightly, a connoisseur in all things, but John, much to his own surprise, suddenly found himself excessively hungry and consumed large amounts of ham and eggs and pickled herring, just as if he were a hearty country squire.

'I observe that the pressure of finding a murderer has not diminished your appetite in any way,' said John's father, with a certain dry amusement.

'On the contrary, after a really bad night I now feel half starved.'

'You did not sleep well?'

'No, I kept thinking about Mrs Harcross and her mysterious missing children.'

'Surely not by the handsome Jasper?'

'No, she was married before. In fact she was Mrs Egleton, the celebrated actress.'

'Really? How extraordinary! I remember her as Lucy Lockit in the original production of *The Beggar's Opera*.'

'Even more extraordinary is the power her second husband exerted over her, a power which led her to leave the stage and disappear into obscurity.'

And John described in detail all that the former actress had given up for Jasper Harcross, and the outrageous situations to which she had been forced to turn a blind eye.

'He sounds highly unpleasant to me,' Sir Gabriel commented, spreading a delicate helping of marmalade onto a thin slice of toast.

'He certainly seems to have done his share of wrecking other people's lives.'

'And you say his widow's children have vanished off the face of the earth?'

'Apparently so.'

John's father looked thoughtful. 'But supposing they are near at hand? Supposing they tracked Jasper Harcross down and are somewhere close by?'

'Waiting to wreak revenge? But surely if he had seen them he would have recognised them at once.'

'From what you say I doubt he ever met them. All they would need to do was change their names and their true identities would remain hidden.'

John sighed. 'Father, do not complicate the issue further. Everyone had a motive for killing the man, or so it seems to me. He was a ruthless philanderer and a selfish cheat. His destroyer could be anybody.'

Sir Gabriel nodded. 'You are quite right about that, of course. Still, missing children are always fascinating. How old would they be by now?'

'She said that the boy was born in the year of her marriage, which was 1723. And she was carrying the girl when she played the part of Lucy. That was a real pregnancy you were looking at.'

'You astonish me!' Sir Gabriel stared at the ceiling. 'Now, that would make the boy thirty or thereabouts, and the girl twenty-six, though obviously they don't have to tell the truth about their ages.'

'What do you mean?'

'That if the Egletons wished to conceal who they really were they could say they were any age, provided their looks did not belie them.'

Coralie immediately came into John's mind and he stopped with a forkful of food halfway to his mouth.

'You look troubled. Why?' asked his father.

'Because everything is so complex. What with spurned wives and mistresses, jealous husbands and lovers, and now runaway children. It is like weaving one's way though a maze.'

'But there's the challenge,' said Sir Gabriel, 'and that is what you enjoy. Now to other things. I have found you an apprentice lad in the last year of his studies. His Master said he is a fine pupil and in exchange for a remuneration, some of which the lad himself will get, he is quite happy to release him on alternate days, indeed at any time that you might need him. His name is Edward Holby, known as Ned, and he will be here within the hour to get the keys of the shop.'

'You shouldn't have spent your money,' said John contritely. 'I shall ask Mr Fielding if he will reimburse you.'

'The Public Office is underfunded enough. Let this be my small way of making a contribution.'

'I shall mention it to him all the same.'

'You must do as you think best,' answered his father, and poured himself another cup of coffee from the delicate silver Gurnsey pot which the footman had thoughtfully placed upon the table.

An hour later, John was on his way to Drury Lane theatre, walking through Leicester Fields, past the painter William Hogarth's home, with the sign of The Golden Head hanging outside the door, and steadfastly ignoring the house of ill-repute which stood discreetly hidden amongst the trees. From there the Apothecary cut through Bear Street, named after some wretched performing animal, then turned left into Castle Street, through the narrow confines of Newport Street, emerging in Long Acre, from where he made his way to Drury Lane. Going straight to the stage door, John stated the fact that he was on Mr Fielding's business and, feeling somewhat self-important, was granted admittance and directed towards the stage. Here, any idea of glory vanished, however, for all was uproar and not a solitary soul glanced in his direction.

It seemed that the meeting to decide the future of *The Beggar's Opera* had come down against continuing with the production, for a frantic rehearsal for *Love's Last Shift*, a sentimental and mawkish play by Colley Cibber, a former manager of Drury Lane, was in progress. Costumes which had obviously been hanging up for some while were being altered on the actresses even while they rehearsed, and David Garrick was using his magnificent voice to order everybody about, simultaneously addressing three different sets of people. John received the strong impression that the play had been in storage, as it were, and had hastily been brought out to fill the gap. Almost reluctantly, his eyes were drawn to Coralie who this morning looked so utterly charming, a little seamstress at her feet turning up the hem of her dress, that John felt that strange leap of his heart which meant he was becoming sentimentally attached.

Seeing him, she called out, 'Good morning, Mr Rawlings,' and at that Dick Weatherby, gallantly in charge of all those on stage, left his crew of scenery makers and picked his path through pots of paint to the Apothecary's side.

'Mr Jago's been and gone,' he informed the new arrival. 'He said to tell you that he had made a list.'

John grinned crookedly at the news. 'Excellent. Now where am I to do the interviewing?'

'In the Green Room. Everyone's here that you need to see,

but as some of them are involved in the rehearsal Mr Garrick is not best pleased.'

'I am sure that he regards the whole affair as a thorough nuisance.'

Dick smiled ruefully. 'He certainly does. I think you had better talk to me last when, with any luck, the rehearsal will be over and his temper less frayed.'

'I'll do that gladly. Now, who's to be first?'

'I'd be obliged if you could see Mrs Martin. She's walking round looking as if she's dined on poison, and the sooner she leaves, the better.'

'Is it really true that she once had a liaison with Jasper Harcross?'

'About twelve years ago, yes, so it's said.'

'Was she as big then?'

'I don't know. I wasn't working at Drury Lane at the time. I am only repeating hearsay, I'm afraid.'

'Never the less, it is very interesting,' John answered, as he struggled across the cluttered acting area and went into the room that Dick had pointed out, only to find that the subject of their recent conversation had arrived in advance of him.

'Good morning,' said Mrs Martin frostily, and the look in her pale blue eyes could quite easily have frozen the Apothecary into a solid block of ice.

He bowed politely. 'Madam, please forgive me for keeping you waiting.'

'I find the whole thing extremely inconvenient, your lateness included,' she replied. 'I have already given an account of myself to Mr Fielding and I fail to see what good can be achieved by going over it again.'

'Then let me ask you some different questions,' John answered, as he took his seat behind the table that he was to use as a desk. 'First, tell me about your relationship with the late Mr Harcross. It was one of great friendship, was it not?'

'Well . . .'

He decided to be ruthlessly forthright. 'Madam, I was back-stage on the night of the murder and saw for myself the rapport between you. It seemed to me that you treated him with motherly affection. Yet it has been said to me that your fondness for Mr Harcross replaced something much stronger, in other words you and he were at once stage in your lives, lovers.'

'How dare you,' she answered, heaving herself to her feet.

'I dare because I believe what I say to be accurate. Mrs Martin, knowing that you will have to answer for yourself at the Public Office if you lie to me, I ask you to tell the truth. Were you and Jasper Harcross intimate?'

She burst into spectacular and noisy tears. 'Yes, yes,' she sobbed, 'and I never stopped loving him, never. It was simply that I could not hold onto him without agreeing to become merely a friend. He would have abandoned me long ago if I had refused.'

'What about your husband, did he know?' John asked directly.

Mrs Martin poured tears afresh. 'Indeed he did, pour innocent soul. Oh, what a life I have led that man. I tremble to think of it. Strangely, he found out when it was all over, after . . .' She stopped abruptly and blew her nose. 'Anyway, he challenged me with infidelity and I, like a fool, confessed, burdening him with my guilt.'

'But as you are still together I presume he forgave you?'

The actress let out a sob that bounded against the walls of the room. 'The tragedy of it is that he still loves me, with all his heart and soul. In my husband's eyes I am a goddess.'

John had enormous difficulty in suppressing a smile. 'How very touching.'

Mrs Martin shot him a suspicious glare. 'And I love him too. It is simply that Jasper and I found a rare fulfilment which very few couples experience.'

Even though the remark was horribly similar to the words spoken by Mrs Harcross, this statement was said archly, in a revoltingly cloying manner, almost like a boast. John found an expression of distaste crossing his features.

'Yet even though you saw other, younger, women take your place, you never felt any hatred towards the victim?'

'Indeed not. I was his mother confessor, there to soothe his brow whenever he needed me.'

'Did you know that Jasper was married and that there was a lady in Kensington who also soothed that very brow?'

Mrs Martin shot him a look of such pure astonishment that if it were feigned it could only mean she was one of the greatest actresses in the world. 'I beg your pardon?'

'I said that he was married and had been for many years, since he was twenty, in fact.'

She rose to her feet again. 'Is this true?'

'Yes.'

Mrs Martin exploded. 'Oh the deceiving wretch! How dare he? Why, he deserves to die.'

'He has,' John answered drily. 'Had you forgotten?'

Looking much chastened, Mrs Martin wept once more. 'I don't know what I'm saying. You must forgive me.'

The Apothecary shook his head. 'You are not the first to make such a statement. It seems to me that Jasper Harcross caused havoc wherever he went. You can believe that I feel a certain sympathy for all his ladies. So, remembering that, is there anything further you would like to tell me?'

She hesitated, right on the brink of confession, and John could see the thoughts going through her eyes like swimmers in a lake.

'Well?'

Caution must have won, for Mrs Martin lowered her lids and said, 'No, there's nothing.'

'Then, for the sake of formality, could you repeat what

you have already told Mr Fielding, namely where you were on the night before the murder.'

'I was at home with my husband. We left the dress rehearsal together and returned to our house by Hackney. We live in Portugal Street, overlooking St Clement's Churchyard. We spent the rest of the night there and did not go out again until morning.'

It sounded plausible enough and John wondered why Mr Fielding had doubts about the story.

'I see. Well, thank you for being so honest with me.' The Apothecary stood up, his face adopting a look of bewildered sincerity. 'Mrs Martin, you are a woman of the world. Who do you think is responsible for this crime?'

She drew in her breath gustily. 'It could be anyone. Probably this wife of his that nobody knew about.'

'Quite so,' answered John, aware that he was going to get no further with that particular ploy. 'Now, if you would be kind enough to ask your husband to step this way.'

Mrs Martin appeared to swell, an awesome sight. 'You are not to upset him, d'ye hear? He has had enough to bear, poor being. When he found out about myself and Jasper I thought his heart would break. He sobbed clean through one night. Why, it causes me to weep at the very memory.' And she did, all over again, her bosom heaving with emotion.

'Pray calm yourself,' said John hastily, going to her, salts at the ready.

'Calm?' she repeated indignantly. 'I doubt you and those of your stamp know the meaning of the word!' And with that she swept from the room, trembling like a blancmanger.

The Apothecary sank back into his seat, dabbing his brow with his handkerchief, and was thus caught unawares as Mr Martin, seemingly the total antithesis of his wife in every way imaginable, came silently through the door and stood hovering.

'Mr Rawlings?' the newcomer enquired nervously.

'Please be seated,' John answered, recovering himself. He put on his beaming countenance. 'It is a pleasure to make your acquaintance at last, Sir. I cannot tell you how much I admire your musicianship.'

Mr Martin looked delighted. 'Really? Well, that is most kind. I had not thought in the midst of all this turmoil that you would have remembered who I am.'

'I am a regular theatregoer,' John answered smoothly, 'and always look forward to an occasion when James Martin will be playing the harpsichord.'

'How very civil.'

'Sincerely meant, I assure you.' And the Apothecary smiled even more broadly.

It was a neat figure that he was surveying, a tidy little parcel of a person, sprucely dressed and trimly wigged. Even the features of the face seemed to have been snugly put together, so that there was no jarring note anywhere. Where everything concerning Mrs Martin was large and expansive, in her husband there was only miniaturisation and economy. Where she was fat, he was slim; where her eyes were blue saucers, his were brown and small; where she fluttered like a great vapid moth, he moved briskly like a creature of the riverbank. If these were the two halves of a married whole, John thought, then Cupid had an outrageous sense of humour.

He cleared his throat. 'Mr Martin, I shall come straight to the point. As you are probably aware, Mr Fielding has requested me to ask a few more questions which might be relevant to the death of Jasper Harcross. So, with this in mind, I wonder if you could give me your opinion of the dead man.'

The musician's beady brown eyes grew even beadier. 'Well, I . . . er . . . I admired him as an actor.'

'But not as a person?'

'Well . . .'

* * *

The Apothecary decided to put the poor man out of his misery. 'I know all about the liaison that Harcross had with your wife. She has told me everything. So let us converse without inhibition. I would rather suspect that you detested the fellow. Am I right?'

'Of course you are,' James Martin replied, with more vehemence than John would have thought him capable of expressing. 'He almost ruined my marriage with his vile, lecherous ways. Why, to desert poor Clarice when . . .' He stopped short, obviously thinking better of what he had been about to say.

'When what?' John persisted.

'He grew tired of her,' the musician went on, making the Apothecary certain that he was hiding something.

'And when exactly was that? When did their love affair end? And why?'

Mr Martin's face looked very slightly disordered. 'It was nine years ago, that is all I can tell you. I presume Jasper met someone else, but my wife did not confide in me about that. All I know is that she was in an hysteric for what seemed like months.' He sighed wearily and John's heart went out to him. Ten minutes of an hysterical Mrs Martin was quite enough for any man to put up with in his opinion.

'But they remained friends?'

'Oh yes. I think she is probably still in love with him.'

'And you were prepared to accept this?'

The musician sighed again. 'I could have left her, I realised that. But we had once been through a terrible ordeal together. We had a child that died in its cradle. It grieved poor Clarice so terribly that I do not think she ever recovered. It is my belief that she turned to Harcross for consolation.'

'Did you wish him dead?'

A ghost of a smile appeared round James Martin's trim

mouth. 'Certainly. I and a legion of others. You'll be hard put to it to catch his killer, Mr Rawlings.'

'I am growing increasingly aware of that with every passing hour. But let me ask you one final question. Where were you on the night before the murder?'

The shipshape face worked momentarily and Mr Martin looked extremely ill at ease. 'Did my wife not tell you?'

'No, I forgot to ask her,' John answered, amazing himself at the effortless way in which he lied.

The musician breathed out audibly. 'Well, the dress rehearsal done, I sent her home in a hackney.'

'Yes?'

'Then I went to visit a friend.'

'Who will vouch for you, no doubt?'

James Martin shook his head violently. 'No, I'm afraid that will not be possible. You see, he is just a child, an orphan boy in whom I take an interest. He lives – poorly. I give him gifts of clothes and food because I pity his wretched existence.'

'But surely this child can speak? Or do you not know where he is?'

The musician seized on this like a drowning man grabbing for a rope. 'No, he moves on. He is just a street urchin. I never know where I will find him next.'

It was such a patent falsehood, yet short of calling the man a downright liar there seemed little John could do about it. He decided that, for the time being at least, it would be wiser to humour Mr Martin. 'How difficult that must make things for you. Hard enough to befriend such a child without having to look for him all the time,' he said sympathetically.

'Er . . . yes.'

'But despite that, Sir, I would like to have a word with the boy when you do discover his whereabouts.'

The musician stood up, presuming that the interview had

come to an end. 'Certainly, certainly. Of course. Naturally.'

John looked at Joe Jago's list. 'Now, if you would be so kind, could you ask Will to step this way.'

The musician turned the colour of snow. 'Will?' he repeated dazedly.

John stared at him, wondering what could possibly be wrong. 'Yes, Will,' he repeated.

'But he's assisting with the rehearsal,' Mr Martin protested, still in the same extraordinary way.

'That is unfortunate, but I none the less want to speak with him.'

'Very well, I will see what I can do.'

He made for the door but John beckoned him back. 'Don't forget to bring your boy to me as soon as you can.'

'I won't,' James Martin called over his shoulder, and made a hasty exit.

After he had gone, John sat in silence for a few moments, wondering what could possibly have caused the musician's peculiar change in manner. But before he had had time to think the matter through there was a gentle tap on the door.

'Come in,' he called.

Will the theatre child stuck his head through the opening. 'You wanted to see me, Sir?'

'Certainly. Come in and sit down. There's nothing to be nervous of, you know.'

'I'm more scared than nervous if you want the truff, Sir. But I ain't done nuffing naughty – except for falling asleep when I should have been guarding the scaffold.'

'That's hardly your fault. I expect you were tired.'

'I wasn't,' Will answered instantly. 'It's my belief me milk was doped.'

John stared at him. 'What are you talking about?'

'Me milk, what was standing backstage in me beaker, I fink

it had been interfered with. I never felt so sleepy as after I drunk it. I just couldn't keep me eyes open.'

'I'll come back to that,' said the Apothecary determinedly. 'You must forgive me, Will, but I've got one of those brains that likes to do things neatly. So let me start with *your* story. How old were you when you went to the Foundling Hospital?'

'I dunno exactly, Sir. I was dumped on the steps as a baby. St Swithin's Day, it was. That's how I got me name, William Swithin.'

'But wasn't it Mr Harcross who took you from there and set you up in a job at Drury Lane?'

'Yes, Sir, it was. And wiv that kindly action he won me eternal gratitude.'

'Um,' said John reflectively. 'But why did he choose you, do you think? Had he met you before somewhere?'

'No, Sir. Never clapped his eyes on me.'

'Then why?'

Will rubbed his squat little nose and John found himself thinking what an unattractive child the boy was, pallid through being constantly indoors, his mouth lined with the grooves of early suffering, his only redeeming feature a pair of large china-blue eyes. Yet even as the Apothecary considered these things, he had a momentary flash that Will reminded him of someone, though by the time it came to the front of his mind, the connection was gone.

'I dunno, Sir,' the child continued. 'Perhaps he just liked me 'andsome face.' And he laughed heartily, obviously used to making fun of himself.

The Apothecary joined in, thinking how pathetic it all was. 'Did Mr Harcross treat you well?'

'Oh yes, Sir. Not in a doting way, you understand. He was more like a rough-and-tumble father. Whereas Mr . . .' He stopped abruptly.

'Mr . . . ?'

Will went slightly pink. 'Several people treated me like their son. I suppose they felt sorry for me. The ladies tried to mother me too.'

'But you were about to say a specific name then, weren't you?' John had a moment of inspiration and took a chance. 'Was it Mr Martin?'

The boy had obviously received no acting training as yet, for his jaw dropped and his blue eyes widened. 'How did you know?'

The Apothecary became ultra casual. 'Because he mentioned to me that he has a protégé. A boy to whom he gives clothes and food. I simply guessed that it was you.'

Will's cheeks went a raw-looking shade of red. 'Well, you're not to tell.'

'I won't. Though why is that?'

'Cos Mr Martin don't want anyone to know. But he's ever so good to me. Brought me extra clothes and food all the time I've been here.'

'I wonder why he wants it kept so secret,' John muttered to himself. Then he frowned as an unpleasant thought came to him. 'He doesn't want paying for what he does for you, does he?'

'How could I pay 'im? I ain't got no money.'

'Don't come the innocent with me. You know perfectly well what I mean. Does he make any demands on you, demands of any sort?'

'No he don't,' Will answered hotly. 'He's good and kind, so he is.'

'Tell me about the night of the dress rehearsal,' answered John, unruffled. 'Who was the last to leave the theatre?'

'Dick Weatherby. He always checks that everything is clean and tidy before he goes 'ome.'

'And did you help him?'

'I swabbed out the dressing rooms, then straightened round.

Then I come downstairs and he was just getting ready to leave.'

'What did you do then?'

'I 'ad me milk, Mr Garrick always insists I do that, then I went to bed. I've got a place where I sleep in the properties room.'

'And did Mr Martin come in once everyone had gone?'

'Yes, he did. But please don't tell on me for saying so. He wanted the meeting kept quiet.'

'It's strange that he's so secretive regarding your friendship.'

'Yes, I suppose so. I never really thought about it.'

'Ah well! So let us proceed to the night of the murder. You say that you believed your milk was tampered with.'

'Yes, I do, Mr Rawlings. You gave me the job of guarding the mobile, that's the technical term for the wheeled platform bearing the gallows. Well, I'd 'ave never let you down normally. But I was ever so thirsty, what with the shock an' all, and after I drank the stuff I just couldn't keep awake a moment longer. That proves it was doped, don't it?'

Remembering that evidence in the shape of Lucy Lockit's bow had been planted while the theatre boy slept, John considered the possibility of a sleeping draught having been slipped into his drink.

'But who could have done such a thing?'

'Anyone, Sir. Me beaker stood backstage for all to see.'

'Um,' said the Apothecary again, wondering if the boy had drunk the milk too early and was really meant to have slept deeply all night long.

'Do you want me for anything further, Sir?'

'Only to ask Miss Clive to step this way.'

'I'll go and fetch her.' Will hesitated in the doorway. 'You won't say nuffink about Mr Martin, will you?'

'I'll do my best to be discreet.'

'Gawd bless you,' the boy answered, and disappeared.

Tremendously aware that he must share all this information with the Blind Beak soon, John decided to call in at the Public Office before he paid a visit to Mrs Delaney, and was just envisaging Mr Fielding's reaction as he heard the latest strange twists in the tale when there came yet another knock on the door. Certain that it was Coralie, John straightened his wig and brushed at his coat, only to feel rather foolish when David Garrick came into the room.

Today, to John at least, the great man was the very essence of charm itself, urbane smiles flashing, eyes kind and considerate, every movement of his body exuding tolerant good humour. He made the Apothecary a courteous little bow.

'My very dear young friend, may I throw myself headlong upon your mercy?'

'By all means. How can I help you?'

Garrick gave a smile, the quintessence of the word deprecating. 'Nobody could understand more than I the necessity for the murderer of Jasper Harcross to be found, and quickly at that.'

'Yes?'

'Yet despite this, alack, the theatre must remain open. It is the great tradition of we thespians that the play continues whatever the odds.'

'Of course, I quite understand.'

'But do you? So I must ask myself.'

John saw a glimmer of light. 'My questions are getting in the way of your rehearsal, is that it, Sir?'

Garrick made a dismissive moue. 'I, you must believe me Mr Rawlings, am the very last soul alive to impede the course of justice. But the decision to abandon *The Beggar's Opera* has created its own set of difficulties. We must bring another play into the repertory with haste.'

Wishing that the actor would say what he actually meant, the Apothecary attempted to do so for him. 'You would like me to go away for a while, perhaps? To leave you in peace for a few hours?'

The great man's eyes shone with humble gratitude, assumed, the Apothecary felt certain. 'Oh how well you understand, my dear friend. For someone so young and . . .'

John stood up. 'How long would you like me to be absent?'

David Garrick seemed on the point of tears. 'Would four hours be asking too much?'

The Apothecary looked at his watch. 'Perhaps you would be good enough to tell the other people I shall return to question them at three o'clock.'

The actor-manager gave a florid bow. 'Certainly, but of course.'

'Then I will say *au revoir*,' John answered, irritated despite himself at the break in his concentration.

Striding across the stage, he gave a flamboyant bow to the rest of the company, called out, 'Goodbye everyone. I shall return,' and made his exit to an audience of startled faces, wondering exactly how he was going to spend the next few hours productively.

Chapter Nine

Once outside the theatre, John took a deep breath, but so horrid was the stink from the gutters that he did not repeat this natural response to being cooped up within the confines of Drury Lane most of the morning. Instead, he turned right into the street after which the theatre was named and strode briskly along its not inconsiderable length until he eventually bore right once more into Great Queen Street, then on to the delights of Lincoln's Inn Fields where the air was indeed much sweeter. Suddenly deciding what he was going to do, the Apothecary merely cast his eyes on the Theatre Royal which stood on the south side of the Fields, nowadays quite empty and deserted. Paradoxically, *The Beggar's Opera* had made its owner, John Rich, so very wealthy that he had opened a new playhouse at Covent Garden. Cursing the railings which had been put up some twenty years earlier, to keep out the beggars and prostitutes who were using the Fields as a place in which to both dwell and work, John made his way through a festering little alleyway into High Holbourn.

Before him lay a straight, long, piece of road, Red Lyon Street, and dimly in the distance the Apothecary could glimpse his destination lying in the very heart of Lambs Conduit Fields, which stretched away, green and fresh and fine, as far as the eye could see. With a pricking of anticipation, John Rawlings set off along the direct route to the Foundling Hospital.

It was a stately building with a curving outer wall in which was set a towered gatehouse. Beyond this wall lay the Hospital itself, as grandiose and gracious as any royal residence despite a slight smack of the institution about it. Well aware that without its presence thousands more children would have died deserted and alone, abandoned in empty rooms or dumped on the streets of London to perish, the Apothecary approached it with a great sense of respect for all the charitable good the Hospital did.

A porter in the gatehouse asked him his business in a somewhat officious manner and John, simply to avoid explanations and arguments, showed the letter of authorisation given to him by Mr Fielding for just such an occasion as this. To the Apothecary's cynical amusement there was a prompt change in attitude and the next moment he was ushered through the wicket gate and into the large carriage-sweep beyond. On either side of this great arena were walkways leading to the Hospital, which stood imposingly at the far end. Somewhat tired by now, for he had journeyed a long way, John set off on the last lap towards the offices, situated beside the chapel, a classical building running crossways immediately opposite the gatehouse.

It seemed that he was too late to see the governor who had stepped abroad about his business an hour earlier. But after a few minutes' delay a small birdlike woman with dark bootbutton eyes, entered the parlour into which John had been shown. The avine gaze appraised him rapidly, obviously indicating approval of his elegant clothes but mistrustful of his youthful appearance. The curtsey which followed summed all this up to a nicety, not too deep but respectful enough to show that she regarded him as a member of the professional classes.

'I am Mrs Carter,' she said by way of introduction. 'How may I help you?'

John gave a straightforward bow, thus indicating that her assessment of him was correct, and adopted his thoughtful face.

'Madam, I am here on behalf of Mr John Fielding, Principal Magistrate of London. Here is his letter of authorisation.'

He handed it to her and Mrs Carter read it at a glance. 'I'm afraid I don't quite understand,' was her only comment.

'I am here regarding a child who was deposited at the Hospital as a baby, then taken away some time last year to become a trainee at Drury Lane. His name is William Swithin. Do you know the boy?'

She shook her head. 'Thousands pass through our doors, Mr . . .' Mrs Carter glanced at the letter again. '. . . Rawlings. In the past the flood of mothers with their bastards was so great that we had to introduce a balloting system to permit admission. Can you tell me a little more about this particular child?'

'Apparently he was deposited here on St Swithin's Day, 1745, or round about then.'

'That was the year in which we first opened our doors . . .'

'And the year in which the Pretender marched south.'

Mrs Carter ignored this aside. 'Naturally, we have records. Would you care for me to look him up?'

'Very much.'

'Then step this way.'

In the next door office everything was tidy to the point of being clinical, not a speck of dust anywhere, not even a mote whirling in the pallid sunshine. Stacked on a shelf on one wall was a series of volumes, bound in red with gold embossing, each representing half a year in the history of the Foundling Hospital, all of them equally dust free. Mrs Carter lifted down the second and flitted through the pages.

'Let me see now. St Swithin's Day, 1745. Ah yes, here it is. Baby boy found outside gatehouse, guessed to be about six months old. Healthy. Baptised William and given the surname Swithin.'

'Is there anything else?'

'Only a list of the items he was wearing. Shawl, bonnet and so on.'

'Oh dear,' said John, suddenly deflated.

'The note attached to him has been stored, however, though

his clothes have long since been passed on to some other poor mite.'

'A note?' asked the Apothecary, a ray of hope returning.

'Yes, it will be in one of those boxes over there. Would you like to see it?'

'Indeed I would.'

Marvelling at the efficiency of their record keeping, John watched in admiration as Mrs Carter, after looking at an index of some kind, went straight to the box in question and lifted it down.

'All the notes and letters for that year are kept in here.'

'Does every abandoned creature have something with it, then?'

The snapping eyes looked at him sharply. 'Of course not, only those with a kindly heart bother about their young. Most mothers can't wait to get rid of the evidence of their shame.'

'What a depressing thought.'

'Here it is. Swithin, W. Note attached to basket and a man's handkerchief dropped nearby.'

'May I see them?' And suddenly there was a ring of excitement in the Apothecary's voice at the thought of what he might be about to discover.

'This is still with Mr Fielding's authority?'

'Certainly it is.'

'Very well.' And Mrs Carter handed him the items in question, each bearing a label with the theatre boy's name written upon it.

He looked at the letter first. It simply said, 'Care for this poor child, William. His mother cannot keep him with her. It breaks my heart.'

He handed it back to Mrs Carter. 'What do you conclude from this?'

She studied it carefully. 'Well, it sounds to me as if the mother did not write it.'

'Precisely as I thought.' John unfolded the handkerchief. 'Where was this found exactly?'

'It says on the cobbles. A foot from the basket. Someone with foresight picked it up in case it happened to be relevant.'

'Then thank God for them, for it bears a set of initials.'

The bright eyes peered. 'Why, so it does! J.M. I wonder whoever that might be.'

'I think,' the Apothecary answered slowly, 'that when the answer to that is provided we will have advanced somewhat in untangling this extraordinary web of deceit which threatens to ensnare all those who try to unravel it.'

Chapter Ten

It was only after a great deal of reassurance that John persuaded Mrs Carter to release the note and the handkerchief into his safe keeping. Furthermore, he was asked to guarantee that the items would be returned as soon as Mr Fielding had finished with them, and to promise that he would be personally responsible for taking the evidence back to the Foundling Hospital. Even so, there were receipts to be signed and a written pledge to be made. Yet finally, well pleased, John left the Hospital, the note and the handkerchief in a small parcel beneath his arm, and, tired by the long walk and lack of food, climbed with relief into a hansom carriage which was by the gate house, plying for hire. Leaning back against its somewhat uncomfortable upholstery, he sighed deeply and closed his eyes.

'Where to, Sir?' called the driver from the seat above.

'The stage door, Theatre Royal, Drury Lane,' John called back, and received an inquisitive glance from the cabman, who obviously thought he was an actor. 'I need to be there by three o'clock,' the Apothecary continued, and added mysteriously, 'rehearsals, you know.'

'I'll do my best,' the driver replied, clearly impressed, and cracked his whip.

But willing as both he and his horse obviously were, there was not much that could be done about the teeming streets, and it was a good half hour before the conveyance stopped outside the theatre. Glancing at his watch, John saw that it was almost three o'clock and congratulated himself that everything had turned out so well. And indeed, on setting foot inside, he saw that the rehearsal was still going on and tempers were getting even more frayed. In fact everyone turned towards him with a sigh of relief and there were cries of, 'Ah, Mr Rawlings, you're back with us.' Thinking that the break might actually have done good, and that sheer relief at getting away from the play could make everyone more cooperative, John hurried into the Green Room.

The response to his return was so quick that he was still sorting through his papers when the first knock came and Adam Verity entered almost with alacrity. Giving the actor an appraising glance, John saw that he was somewhat different from how he had remembered him. Whereas, taking the role of Filch, he had been dirty and tousle-headed, today, as the young male lead, Adam appeared handsome and sleek. He was also, seeing him closely, a little older than John would have thought, probably around thirty.

The Apothecary started his questioning with his usual stratagem, asking Adam's opinion of Jasper Harcross.

'I really had very little to do with him. I acted with him, of course, but never socialised.' The actor pulled a quizzical face. 'I think I was the wrong gender as far as he was concerned.'

'Am I to take it from that that you disapproved of his womanising?'

Adam shook his head, looking noncommittal. 'You may take it in any way you wish. The truth is that I neither approved nor otherwise. You see, I rarely thought about Jasper. He did not enter my consciousness.'

'Then, obviously, he was no particular friend of yours.'

Adam gave a rather charming smile. 'Yes, that statement is fair.'

The Apothecary changed the subject. 'Is it true you ran away from a foster home? It fascinates me how people start a career on the stage. Were you a theatre boy like Will?'

Adam's smile broadened. 'Well, yes and no. I was sixteen when I approached Mr Giffard for a job. I was about to sign indentures with a truly dreary artisan and, to cut a long story short, I packed my few belongings and took off to Ipswich where Henry Giffard was in charge of the theatre circuit. Mr Garrick was completing his training there at the time and when he left for Drury Lane, so did I.'

'I see,' said John, then added casually, 'by the way, does the name Egleton mean anything to you?'

Well aware that he was dealing with a professional actor, he studied Adam's face closely but not a flicker of shock passed over it. Eventually, though, the young man's eyes lit up and he said, 'Wasn't that the name of the actress who created the part of Lucy Lockit?'

'Yes, it was. You never met her I suppose?'

'Somewhat before my time, actually. I did not have the honour.'

The reply could have been utterly genuine or a brilliant performance, and there was no way of telling which. Once again, John changed tack.

'Can you tell me where you were on the night before the murder?'

'Yes, I was at home. I share an apartment with my sister, who is quite a successful milliner in New Bond Street. She can most certainly answer for me because she awaited my return from the dress rehearsal and then we shared some food and a bottle of wine.'

'A sister?' asked John, surprised. 'Was she then also a foundling?'

'Oh yes,' Adam answered, his voice relaxed. 'The only difference between us is that she stuck with her apprenticeship while I abandoned mine. She supplies hats for this theatre, incidentally, as well as running her own shop.'

'A prosperous woman indeed,' the Apothecary murmured.

More loudly he added, 'Someone will call on her regarding the matter, but meanwhile I can only thank you for your co-operation. You have been most kind.'

Adam stood up, then headed for the door. 'Who do you want to see next?'

'Perhaps Jack Masters could spare me a moment of his time.'

'I'll try and extricate him.'

The door closed behind him, leaving John in a quandry. The similarity in age between Adam Verity and the missing Mr Egleton was too close to be ignored, added to which the actor had a sister. Yet his performance when the name was mentioned had been superlative. Either he was totally innocent or brilliantly concealing something sinister.

'I wonder,' said John, speaking aloud as Jack Masters came into the room, causing the older man to stare at him and say, 'Eh?'

'Nothing of importance. Now do pray take a seat.'

'I trust you are not going to keep me long. The rehearsal is still going on, I fear.'

'I have no intention of doing so, for I have only one question to ask you. But I must warn you that if you refuse to answer it I shall keep you here until you do. Then, if you persist in that folly, Mr Fielding assures me he will have you in his court on a charge of impeding the course of justice.'

'Are you threatening me?' asked the rugged-faced actor, lighting a pipe with much deliberation.

'Certainly,' answered John succinctly. 'The time has come to stop mincing words. For the final time, where were you on the night before the murder?'

'I've already told you. With a lady friend.'

'Her name and address, if you please.'

There was a pause while the actor blew blue smoke into the air. 'If I tell you, do I have your assurance that the information will go no further?'

'It will go to Mr Fielding, obviously.'

'And what then?'

John felt his impatience rise and boil over. 'How would I know? He is the Principal Magistrate of London and can do as he pleases. But one thing is sure. If he gets you into public court you will have to answer for yourself or face a term in gaol. Now which is better, to tell me the truth in the privacy of this room or be forced to blurt it out before all the world?'

Jack Masters puffed out a perfect ring of smoke, thought a moment, then said, 'It was Melanie Vine, if you must know.'

The Apothecary stared at him. 'Are you referring to the actress who played Diana Trapes?'

'Of course I am.'

'Then why the secrecy?'

'Because I am her clandestine passion. She is actually the mistress of Tom Bowdler, who took the role of Peachum.'

'A strange situation.'

'People in the theatre are all governed by their emotions. And Melanie and I are no exceptions.'

'So that is why you were so cautious! Afraid that Mr Bowdler might seek retribution.'

'Not at all,' answered Jack surprisingly. 'He and I are the greatest friends in the world. No, it was just that I didn't want to hurt his feelings.'

'But surely you run that risk continually? He could find out the truth at any time. Aren't you playing with fire?'

'I suppose I am,' the actor said with a sigh. 'But I cannot help myself. Melanie and I are soul mates.'

'Then why doesn't she leave him and go to you?'

'Oh she couldn't do that,' Jack answered, looking shocked. 'It would cut Tom to the quick.'

John gave up, unable to comprehend this line of reasoning. And throughout the next couple of interviews, which were with the other two members of the tortuous triangle, felt a strong sense of embarrassment. From the somewhat stilted conversations, however, several facts emerged. Melanie Vine, unlike the other female members of the company, had never had time for Jasper Harcross, had not had an affair with him, and had actually heard a rumour that he was married.

'From whom?' John asked, amazed.

'From Dick Weatherby. He mentioned it to me once when he had imbibed more than his fair share of gin.'

'I wonder how he knew.'

'He is the stage manager and therefore aware of everything.'

'Oh, I see.'

Chastened, the Apothecary had delicately asked about the night before the murder and, under pressure, Mrs Vine – it appeared she had been given that title out of courtesy, for she had never been married – had admitted she had spent it in the arms of Jack Masters.

'Though I beg you say nothing to Tom. He would be made so unhappy,' she went on, virtually repeating her lover's words.

'Naturally I shall respect your confidentiality, though I must admit the entire situation is beyond my understanding.'

Melanie Vine had risen to her full height and glared down at her questioner. 'Then I see that you know little of the world. What if you fell in love with the wife of your dearest friend? So fatally that you were drawn to consummation? Would you proceed to ram the information down his throat? Or would you behave circumspectly, as we are doing?'

'I really don't know,' the Apothecary had admitted lamely.

'Well, then!' said Mrs Vine triumphantly, and had swept through the door, to be met by the deceived Tom Bowdler coming the other way.

Strangely, his account of the night before the killing seemed a mass of evasions to John. It appeared that, the dress rehearsal over, Tom had gone calling on various friends, all of whom had been out. Finally, very disappointed, he had gone home and spent the rest of the night alone.

'So there is no one who can vouch for your whereabouts?'

'I fear not. You see, my young friend, I am still a bachelor and live by myself.'

Oh dear! John had thought, and had rapidly changed the conversation to Mr Bowdler's opinion of the murdered man. It emerged that this had not been favourable. In fact Tom had despised Jasper for his cavalier treatment of Coralie Clive and Sarah Delaney. With the talk heading rapidly towards a discussion of infidelity and having two lovers at once, the Apothecary thought it wiser to draw the meeting to a close.

'And who shall I send in next?' Tom asked, his round face beaming a smile.

'Miss Coralie Clive,' John answered, and felt a shiver of apprehension even as he said the name.

'I'll do what I can but it might take a few minutes.'

'That means she's still rehearsing.'

'Yes. She grows in stature, that young woman. It won't be long before she is equalling her sister Kitty.'

'Kitty, of course,' John muttered to himself. 'I'd forgotten about her. So Coralie can't be Miss Egleton after all, thank God.'

Then realising how very prejudiced in favour of Miss Clive he was becoming, he took himself to task for not having an entirely open mind about solving the mystery of Jasper Harcross. Full of good intentions, John determined to conduct the forthcoming interview with ruthless integrity, then melted completely as she came into the room, pretty as a primrose in a milkmaid's costume, and most delightfully tremulous about the lips at the thought of the ordeal that lay before her.

'Please don't be nervous,' John said, standing up and bowing.

'Why should I be?' she answered swiftly, then gave him a delicious smile. 'After all, we are friends, are we not?'

The Apothecary's heart bounded. He was rapidly coming to the conclusion that he would far rather be a lover than a mere acquaintance.

'Of course. I told you so on the last occasion we met. Therefore, I am going to ask you very few questions, but would appreciate thoughtful answers. You have already told me how much you hated Jasper Harcross but when Samuel Swann and I came backstage to see you, you were standing in his close embrace. Further, you smiled indulgently when he stole your thunder on stage. Why was that?'

The emerald eyes were suddenly hidden by the droop of Coralie's eyelids. 'It will sound so petty when I tell you my reason.'

'Pettiness is part of human behaviour.'

Her eyes opened wide again and John was treated to a sensational glitter of green. 'You are so wise. How can you know so much at your age?'

'Because I was trained to observe. My Master believed that the mind and the body are connected, that stresses and strains can bring about actual ailments.'

'Well, in that case I'll not insult you by lying. I allowed Jasper to cuddle me in order to annoy Mrs Martin who, if rumour is correct, has allowed him to walk all over her in matters of love yet still remains his friend, a situation which I find denigrates the role of women.'

'And on stage?'

'I know . . . knew . . . Jasper of old. He would stoop to any trick to keep the audience's attention focused on him. If I had fought back he would only have redoubled his efforts.'

'What a vile creature he sounds!' John exclaimed involuntarily. 'The only person who has a good word for him is the theatre boy.'

The guarded look that he dreaded closed Coralie's features. 'Yes, he was good to Will,' she answered softly. Her expression changed again and she gave the Apothecary a cheerful smile. 'Now, what were your other questions?'

'I want to ask you about the so-called Mrs Harcross who visited you. I can definitely assure you that the real one is a lady of mature years, so can you possibly describe the person you saw?'

Coralie frowned. 'Well, I did not see her all that clearly. She wore veiling over her face, an unusual fashion to say the least. Yet she seemed to me to be aged somewhere between twenty and thirty and of small build. I don't think I can say more than that.'

'It could not possibly have been an older woman dressed to look young?'

The actress shook her head. 'I suppose it's possible, though her movements and voice appeared to denote someone youthful.' Coralie's frown deepened. 'In fact there seemed to be something familiar about the way she conducted herself.'

'Are you saying that she was someone you knew?'

'No, not really. It was just that momentarily her voice triggered a memory. But the impression was transient as a butterfly. No sooner had I caught it than it was gone.'

'Coralie,' said John, leaning forward over the table and looking earnestly into her face, 'I want you to do your best over the next few days to try and recall who the supposed Mrs Harcross reminded you of. It could be of enormous importance.'

She gave him an amused grin. 'Do you realise this is the first time you have ever called me by my Christian name?'

'I hope you will return the compliment. As you saved my life on a particular occasion, perhaps it is time we were on more friendly terms.'

'Ummm,' she said, but made no other reply.

'And now to my penultimate question. I asked you once

before who in your opinion had killed Mr Harcross and you flitted away from giving me an answer. So now I'll ask you again and hope to have better luck.'

Coralie looked serious. 'Well, anyone could have done it, particularly any female. But my money would go on the wretched wife. She seems to have had more than her fair share of grief.'

'How do you know that?'

'From what you've told me,' she answered, and smiled sweetly. 'Last question?'

'Just reiterate your actions on the night of the dress rehearsal if you would.'

'I left the theatre with everybody else. Dick was still here, cleaning up with Will. Then I walked home.'

'Alone? At that hour of the night?'

'There were plenty of people about. I did not fear ruffians because I had hired a linkman and we kept to the main streets.'

'Linkmen often work in collusion with thieves, did you know that?'

'One must trust somebody sometime,' Coralie answered simply. She stood up. 'Will that be all?'

'No, I would just like to know where you live and if anybody can answer for your whereabouts once you got to your dwelling place.'

'I live in Cecil Street, which runs down to the river from The Strand. My sister loves to be near water.'

'The famous Kitty Clive! Was she in when you got home?'

'No, she had gone out to have supper after the theatre. I had retired for the night by the time she came back. I did not come across her until the following morning. So no one can vouch for me, I'm afraid.'

'I see.' John rose to his feet. 'Thank you for being so helpful, Miss . . . Coralie. Oh, one final thing. Does the name Egleton mean anything to you?'

'Yes. Surely she was the actress who created the role of Lucy Lockit?'

'She most certainly was – and she was also Jasper Harcross's wife,' the Apothecary added softly.

Coralie looked thoroughly startled. 'Are you serious?'

'Very. And to compound the tragedy she gave up her career and her children for him.'

'Then more fool her,' Miss Clive answered with spirit. 'How any woman could make that sacrifice for a goat like Jasper cannot be credited.'

'But you let him deceive you,' John answered mildly, then knew he had made a mistake as soon as he had spoken. Coralie shot him a look of glittering malice and swept out of the room, head high, almost colliding with Dick Weatherby as she did so.

'Oh dear, she's in high dudgeon,' he commented, grinning a little.

'I have a genius for upsetting that young woman,' John answered sadly.

'Oh take no notice.' Dick's smile broadened. 'There's a lot of temperament there, I assure you.'

'What do you mean?'

'Coralie is beautiful and talented – and well aware of both.'

'Are you saying Miss Clive is spoilt?'

'I think she would have been if Jasper hadn't delivered a bitter blow to her confidence.'

'What did you think of him?' the Apothecary asked, changing the conversation's direction.

'As stage manager it is not my place to comment on the actors, though of course I do,' Dick added on a more human note.

'And your true opinion?'

'I disliked the preening poppinjay, though I never showed it, you can believe me.'

John adopted a man-to-man expression. 'Were you surprised when he was killed?'

'I was surprised that it didn't happen years ago.'

'You are very forthright!'

'There seems little point in lying.'

'How true. Now, as you are obviously a vital witness regarding the dress rehearsal, tell me what you know of it.'

'Well, as I have already informed Mr Fielding, it went through without a hitch. The hanging scene worked perfectly and the floor was sturdy. Then, the show done, the actors went home. It was about eleven o'clock by that time. I stayed on with Will to clean the dressing rooms and stage and left at about midnight. I hired a hackney to take me to Seven Dials, the somewhat seedy area in which I dwell.'

'Can anyone confirm that? A wife or sweetheart?'

Dick shook his head. 'I live alone.'

'Ah well!' said the Apothecary wistfully.

'Obviously someone must have come back to the theatre during the small hours, managed to force an entry, then sawn the planking through, or almost through.'

'Could a woman have done that?'

'By all means. It would require little strength.'

'How surprising that the noise did not awaken the theatre boy.'

'He sleeps soundly, the young rogue. But then, he works long hours.'

'Yes,' said John, considering.

There was a tap on the door and the little seamstress, whom John had seen earlier altering Coralie's costume upon her, put her head round the door.

'Sorry to interrupt, Sir, but Mr Weatherby is required on the stage urgently.'

She gave an anxious smile and bobbed a curtsey and John got the impression of rather a tragic young person, who had been much put upon by life. Dick looked at the Apothecary enquiringly.

'Will that be in order?'

'Oh certainly. We can't have Mr Garrick flying into a passion.'

'Indeed not,' Dick replied, heading briskly away. 'If you want me for anything else, please don't hesitate to contact me,' he called over his retreating shoulder. 'You know I'll do all I can to help.' The door closed behind him.

So that was it. Only Mrs Delaney left to see and John had spoken to everyone connected with the case. Yet he felt no nearer to solving the crime than when he had started. It seemed that Jasper Harcross, like a handsome but unpleasant spider, sat in the midst of a web of intrigue, the strands of which spread everywhere, often to quite the most unexpected places.

Consulting his handsome watch, a present from Sir Gabriel to celebrate his twenty-first birthday, the Apothecary realised that he just had enough time to slip into the Public Office and inform Mr Fielding of the latest developments before he made his way to visit Mrs Delaney in the early part of the evening. Picking up the notes he had made during the various interviews, together with the precious parcel, John put on his cloak and made his way out of the stage door for the second time that day.

Chapter Eleven

It being rather dark and cold by now, turned five o'clock as it was, John, unable to find a hansom yet too tired to walk after his earlier jaunt to the Foundling Hospital, called a sedan and bade the chairmen take him to the Public Office on the run. Somewhat reluctantly, they broke into an ambling jog which, for all its faults, still got John to his destination within fifteen minutes. Deposited before the tall, thin house in Bow Street, the Apothecary tipped his carriers handsomely and sent them away with a smile on their faces.

Entering briskly and going to the desk, John Rawlings enquired after the Principal Magistrate but was dismayed to hear that both the Beak and his clerk, Joe Jago, were still in court, which today was sitting late. With an exclamation of extreme disappointment, the Apothecary turned to go, still clutching his parcel and papers, tired but none the less prepared to venture forth once more and call on Mrs Delaney at her home in Berkeley Square. It was then that he was stopped by a voice that came from directly behind him.

'My dear Mr Rawlings, is that you?'

He spun on his heel to see both Elizabeth Fielding and Mary Ann standing there, each giving him a wide and utterly artless smile. Instantly falling under the spell of their charm, John bowed and said, 'Alas, it is.'

'Alas?'

'I have come to see your husband but he is still in court, which is a great pity. The fact is that I think I might have discovered something very important and can't wait to discuss it with him.'

Mrs Fielding looked housewifely, an adorable expression which John could have hugged her for.

'Then you must stay and let me give you some refreshment before dinner. For which you will be joining us, I trust.'

The Apothecary spread his hands, indicating that his time was not his own. 'Sadly, Madam, I have to call on Sarah Delaney, the actress, before the hour becomes unsociable. She is the last person in this extraordinary affair of whom I have to ask a few further questions.'

'She can wait!' said Elizabeth firmly. 'You look to me, Sir, if you will not consider this personal, as if you could do with some relaxation.'

'I must admit it has all been a little tiring. So, Mrs Fielding, I will gladly step above for a while. Do you think your husband will be engaged in court much longer?'

'No, my boy tells me that he will not be above half an hour.'

'Your boy?'

'Not our son, sadly. Nature has not blessed us so far. No, it is a child I employ to sit in the court and report back to me as to what time the meals can be served.'

John burst out laughing. 'Women are wondrous creatures, Heaven be thanked. So full of beauty and charm, yet so resourceful and cunning.'

Elizabeth looked at him narrowly. 'And would you still have this opinion once you married? Or would you want your wife tied at home, a meek housewife, only fit to do your bidding?'

'God forbid!' John answered seriously. 'A female has as much talent and splendour to offer the world as any man. If my wife wished to continue with her career, then I would encourage her to do so.'

'But what if children came?'

'That would remain to be seen.'

Mrs Fielding smiled. 'You are an advanced young man indeed. Now, no more talk. I'm sure you would appreciate a glass of cordial much more.'

'Indeed I would,' said the Apothecary with feeling, and allowed himself to be led by the arm to the light, airy room on the first floor used by the Fieldings as their parlour. Here, a potent but refreshing brew was swiftly brought and pressed into his hand and John, relaxing for the first time that day, stretched his legs in front of him, admired his silver buckled shoes, and hoped against hope that he would not fall asleep.

Fortunately, help was at hand in the shape of Mary Ann, who chattered a stream of amusing innocence which kept him laughing until, at last, he heard the familiar tap-tap of the Blind Beak's cane and the heavy footsteps which signified his arrival. Then the door opened and John Fielding was there, sniffing the atmosphere in that extraordinary way of his.

'Mr Rawlings?' he enquired, veering his blind gaze towards the exact spot in which the Apothecary was sitting.

As always, John rose and bowed politely, even though he could not be seen to do so. 'Here, Sir.'

'This is an unexpected pleasure which, I imagine, denotes a discovery of some kind.'

'Your perception is as keen as ever, Sir.'

The Blind Beak patted his niece's head, feeling for her with uncanny precision. 'Mary Ann, be so good as to fetch a jug of cordial and another glass. Though I am anxious to hear Mr Rawlings's news, I would none the less prefer to do so in comfort.'

She dropped a polite curtsey, replied, 'Yes, Uncle,' and went from the room, leaving John pondering on what it was about the Beak that made the whole world treat him as if he were sighted.

Yet again John Fielding performed one of the small miracles

that were probably the explanation for this phenomenon. 'Take a seat, my friend, do,' he said, as if he could see that the Apothecary was still courteously on his feet.

'Thank you,' John answered, but never the less waited until his host had settled his great frame in his favourite chair, his legs stuck out before him in an attitude of negligent ease.

'Now tell me,' said the Blind Beak, 'what is it you have discovered?'

While he was about it, the Apothecary gave him a resumé of all the morning's interviews, even discussing the extraordinary relationship between Melanie Vine, Jack Masters and Tom Bowdler.

The Magistrate rumbled his melodious laugh. 'Well, well, a *ménage à trois* indeed.'

'Well almost, yes.'

'Now tell me more of your theory concerning the Egleton children.'

'I just have this uncanny feeling that they are somewhere near at hand. Adam Verity and his milliner sister fit the description best, but he was so open about running away from his foster home that I can't believe it is him.'

'An honest countenance is often the best way of disguising guilt,' Mr Fielding answered drily. 'Remember that. Now tell me about the boy.'

'He was taken from the Foundling Hospital by Jasper Harcross, then he was cared for by James Martin. But, according to Will, he was picked randomly to go and work at Drury Lane. None of it made any sense to me and so, just because my thumbs pricked, I went to the Hospital this late morning.'

'And?'

'I discovered several things. The child was abandoned outside the gatehouse on St Swithin's Day, 1745. He was healthy and about six months old. Attached to his basket was a note and dropped nearby was a man's linen handkerchief bearing the embroidered initials J.M.'

'James Martin?'

'He immediately leapt to mind, Sir.'

'And the note?'

'I will read it to you if I may.'

'Please do.' And the Blind Beak sat in silence while John read the simple message once again. 'Care for this poor child, William. His mother cannot keep him with her. It breaks my heart'.

The silence continued and was only broken by Mary Ann returning with a well-filled jug and a glass, both contained on a tray which she carried with some difficulty. Seeing the two gentlemen deep in thought she behaved as her aunt had trained her to do, simply dropping another curtsey and quietly leaving the room. A child brought up in such an important place as the Public Office in Bow Street knew exactly how to conduct itself, as did all those born to parents who ranked amongst the great and the powerful.

'Well, Sir?' asked John eventually.

'Obviously the note was not written by the mother.'

'Precisely.'

'But in that case, who did write it? The father, perhaps?'

'I would have thought so. But, if we assume this to be true, why should James Martin give up the child? It would have been born in wedlock, after all.'

'Perhaps not,' said the Blind Beak.

'What do you mean, Sir?'

'Well, the way he cares for Will now, under a strict code of secrecy, suggests to me that Mr Martin is hiding something.'

'Then, if the theatre boy is his bastard why did he send Jasper Harcross, of all people, to go and fetch the child to Drury Lane, particularly as Jasper had enjoyed a long-standing affair with his wife and James had much to hate him for?'

'There you have me,' Mr Fielding answered truthfully. 'Unless, of course . . .'

'Unless what, Sir?'

But the Magistrate refused to be drawn any further, shaking his head and saying that it was an ill-formed idea and one that he would rather not air until he had more evidence. Somewhat put out, John stood up, having first hastily consumed another glass of cordial.

'Then I'll be on my way. I must fit Mrs Delaney in before seven o'clock. If she is on stage tonight she will hardly appreciate my being any later.'

'You are working very hard, my friend. I am extremely grateful for your assistance. I hope you realise that.'

'Oh I do, I do,' said the Apothecary, not mollified.

And with that he left, hastily bidding farewell to Elizabeth and Mary Ann, still hurt and upset by the fact that the Blind Beak refused to discuss his embryonic notions with him.

'I should go out this evening and enjoy myself instead of wasting time asking even more questions,' John muttered to himself as he hailed a hansom. But for all these rebellious thoughts he none the less directed the driver to number fifteen Berkeley Square, the address that Mrs Delaney had given him when he had first questioned her.

Despite his gnawing hunger, John enjoyed the drive down through the little streets towards The Strand, then on past the Charing Cross, into Cockspur Street and along Pall Mall, where stood so many beautiful houses, each of them lit by the golden glow of candles. Finally, though, the conveyance turned north up St James's Street, left into Piccadilly, then straight up Berkeley Street towards their destination.

Much as John had suspected, fifteen turned out to be a grandiose building indeed, its frontage facing directly over the large green garden round which the square was built. Yet, to his horror, as he alighted from the hansom and paid the driver off, he caught a distinct glimpse of a man's bewigged head passing through the candle-lit living rooms, presumably making his way to the library at the back. Praying that it was only a footman and that Lord Delaney was not yet home, the Apothecary knocked at the front door.

A servant answered, staring at John somewhat suspiciously. 'Yes, Sir?'

'I have come to see Mrs . . . I mean Lady Delaney. If you could tell her that it is John Rawlings, I think she will receive me.'

'Have you an appointment, Sir?'

'I promised to call on her but have had no opportunity to do so until now. Would you tell her that?'

'Certainly, Sir. Wait in here if you would,' and he ushered the Apothecary into a small, elegantly furnished ante room in which a festive fire burned brightly.

A moment or two later he came back, appearing to be in something of a hurry. 'Lady Delaney says she will see you at once in the salon, but please be quick.'

'Why, is she going out?'

'I couldn't possibly say, Sir,' the servant answered, returning to pompous vein. Scampering along the corridor behind him, John wondered if all the haste was being caused by the fact that Lord Delaney was at home.

And sure enough, as he followed the footman into a fashionable room, decorated in delicate pink and rose red, the actress got to her feet and hurried towards him, whispering, 'You must not be long. My husband has returned early. If he gets wind of this terrible tragedy I tremble to think of the consequences.'

'Do not distress yourself, Madam, please,' John replied smoothly. 'In your condition it really is not wise.'

'Well, can we keep these damnable questions to a minimum? I told you as much as I could the other night.'

'I am bound to ask you all that you did not give me time to

say on that occasion. Further, wherever I go I hear consistent rumours that it is Harcross's child you are carrying. I do realise I want for tact in phrasing the matter in that way, but I thought there was little point in beating about the mulberry bush.'

The actress hissed with rage and drew back her hand as if she were going to strike him. 'How dare you, you miserable little beast!'

'I think,' said John, with as much dignity as he could muster, 'that I had better go. I shall recommend to Mr Fielding that he interview you personally.'

'Yes, go,' answered Lady Delaney, spiritedly. 'And may the devil take you and all of your kind.'

John bowed and turned to the door, and then an extraordinary thing happened. The actress, without any warning, burst into tears as swiftly as an April shower. 'No,' she sobbed, beckoning him back. 'John Fielding would be worse, far worse, than you. 'Tis said that for a blind man he sees more of what is going on than anyone else in the kingdom.'

'That, Madam, is completely true. Furthermore, he has a remedy for those who will not speak. He holds them in contempt of court.'

'Oh merciful Heavens,' sobbed the poor creature, sinking onto the sofa. 'What shall I do?'

'Trust me,' said John, going down on one knee in front of her so that their faces were on a level. 'Tell me everything and tell it quickly, in case your husband walks in.'

'And if he does?'

'Leave that to me to deal with.'

Sarah's voice dropped to a whisper. 'This *is* Jasper's child.' And she laid her hand on her abdomen. 'Of course, as soon as he discovered I was pregnant he abandoned me, a charming habit of his. I was frightened out of my wits and rushed into marriage with Lord Delaney, an old admirer of mine who had treated me to champagne and flowers over the years. Three weeks after our wedding night I told him I suspected I was *enceinte* and the poor soul was overjoyed to imagine he had sired an heir at his age. Naturally, I feared Jasper, thinking he might tell Arthur the truth. But though he seemed to have taken great delight in informing everybody else, he kept away from here, thank God.' She paused and wept further, then said, 'Does he really have a wife?'

'Oh yes, I saw her the other night. She, too, has suffered at his hands so don't hate the poor woman too much.'

'I pity her for sacrificing her life to that wastrel.'

'Did you kill him?' John asked quietly, gazing directly into her tear-filled blue eyes.

'No, I swear it. Anyway, it would not have been easy for me in my state to have squeezed into the mobile and sawn the planking through.'

'I admit that is certainly in your favour.'

'And I didn't, I didn't,' she added, her voice growing louder and a certain hysterical note becoming audible. 'Much as I longed to do so, it wasn't me.'

There was a noise in the passageway outside and Sarah gripped John's arm in alarm. 'It's my husband. Oh, my God, how can I explain your presence?'

'Lie down,' he whispered urgently.

'What?' She stared at him in amazement.

'I said lie down,' and not waiting for her to comply, the Apothecary pushed Lady Delaney flat, simultaneously jumping to his feet and leaning over her. 'Well,' he continued in a loud professional voice, 'the baby is certainly large for four months. It would not surprise me to see you give birth prematurely.' He winked an eye at her, then proceeded to examine her rounding with an adept hand as the door flew open.

'What's all this?' asked Lord Delaney, obviously shocked.

John finished the examination and turned to bow. 'Pray

set your mind at rest, my Lord. I am John Rawlings, apothecary, of Shug Lane. Lady Delaney sent for me. She has been suffering from heartburn and wondered if my special compound might ease the pain.'

'I didn't hear you come in,' his Lordship continued suspiciously.

Sarah Delaney sat upright. 'I did not wish to alarm you, my dear. I asked the footman to show Mr Rawlings directly to me.'

'Why so secret?' Lord Delaney went on, running a narrowed eye over the Apothecary, and obviously not missing the fact that he was both young and attractive looking.

'Because I did not wish you to think I was ill, my love,' Sarah continued in the same patient voice.

'Humph,' said his Lordship.

'My Lord,' put in John, bowing again. 'I see that my presence disturbs you and I will take my leave. However, I trust that you will allow me to prescribe for Lady Delaney. So large and well grown a baby with so delicate a mother will need all the help that my physick can give them.'

He had dragged the old fellow's attention away from jealous thoughts at last. 'What's that you say?'

'I said that your son – if son it be, for I have not yet made the test – is large, while your wife is small. Therefore it is my duty as an apothecary to ease her symptoms and to treat her as best I can.'

'Test?' said Lord Delaney, his mouth opening slightly. 'Did you say test?'

John shrugged a careless shoulder. 'There is an ancient belief that the swinging of a pendulum over the abdomen of a pregnant woman will reveal the sex of the unborn child. Of course, there is probably nothing to it. However, many parents enjoy this innocuous practice, more for a joke than anything else.'

At last Lord Delaney stepped into the room from his hovering position in the doorway, revealing himself as a handsome man, probably aged about seventy, very expensively dressed and wigged and keeping a good figure for his years. His vision, though, had obviously let him down and he wore a pair of magnifying glasses upon his nose, behind which his eyes appeared as big as decorative buttons and decidedly glassy. In a way, John thought, this gave Sarah's husband a rather vulnerable look which she probably found endearing.

'Well, my dear,' he said now, rubbing his hands together in anticipation. 'Should we indulge in this harmless foolery?'

'Why not?' she answered with relief, obviously aware that he had accepted the Apothecary's presence as innocent. 'Does it really work, Mr Rawlings?'

'It is a method used in the country, I believe, to sex unborn calves and lambs.'

'So what kind of pendulum do you require?'

'Your wedding ring suspended on a piece of your hair would do well.'

Without further ado Lady Delaney pulled out a hair, grimacing as she got two rather than one, and threaded her wedding band on to it. 'There!'

'Now lie back on the sofa.'

She did so and John, leaning forward, hung the motionless ring over her rounding belly.

'What is supposed to happen?' asked Lord Delaney, whispering as if he were witnessing some magical art.

'If the ring goes in a clockwise direction, the child is a boy. If it swings counterclockwise, Lady Delaney is carrying a girl.'

'And how do I know that you will not swing it one way or t'other yourself?'

'By conducting this experiment in person,' John replied with an exasperated sigh, and handed the ring to the older man.

After a few moments of absolute stillness, the wedding band

swung clockwise, quite definitely so. 'A boy, Sir,' said the Apothecary drily. 'Congratulations.'

'Oh Arthur!' Sarah exclaimed, jumping up and putting her arms round her husband's neck.

'An heir!' he cried in triumph, and burst into tears.

'Would you like me to confirm that?' asked John, who by now was in an evil mood, partly caused by intense fatigue and hunger, and partly by irritation with the world at large.

'Oh yes, yes,' yelled Lord Delaney ecstatically.

'Very well,' said John, and leaning forward dropped a coin between Sarah's delectable breasts, of which he had a momentary enchanting glimpse. 'And which side did it fall, Madam?'

'Why, to the right.'

'Then you are most definitely expecting a son.'

Lord Delaney wept afresh while Sarah crossed to the bell rope and tugged it. 'This calls for merrymaking, I am sending for some champagne.'

'But of course,' said Arthur. He threw his arm round John's shoulders. 'My dear young friend, you have made me the happiest man in London.'

Actually, the Apothecary thought cynically, it was Jasper Harcross who did that. Aloud he said, 'I am mightily pleased to hear it, Sir.'

'I trust you will stay for supper?'

'That would be very pleasant. I have been so busy today I haven't had time to eat since breakfast.'

''Zounds, I did not know an apothecary led such a hectic life.'

'I am very popular, Sir. I have quite a reputation for my strengthening potions. In fact older gentlemen come from far and wide.'

'Really?' said Lord Delaney, looking interested.

'Really,' answered John, and took a sip of the champagne which a discreet servant had poured for him.

Five minutes later he was asleep in the chair by the fire, the combination of wine and weariness having taken their inevitable course.

'What a charming boy,' said Lord Delaney, looking down at John's slumbering form. 'What was that he was saying about our son being large for his age?'

'He thought the child may be born prematurely. I might have no more than a seven month pregnancy.'

'Well, all the Delaneys are big men,' his Lordship said proudly. 'I am the exception to the rule, alas.'

'You are the dearest husband in the world,' answered Sarah, tweaking his nose and draining her glass simultaneously. She held it out for a refill and then raised it to make a toast. 'To you, darling, and to our boy. And also to Mr Rawlings, such a very charming – and clever – young man!'

Chapter Twelve

So delighted was Lord Delaney with the young apothecary whom he now considered not only to be a genius but also his protégé, that he sent him home in one of the Delaney coaches, especially brought round from nearby Bruton Mews. After this, having slept most of the way, John fell wearily into bed. But the next morning he made up for his day without food by consuming another heroic breakfast, at which Sir Gabriel raised thin eyebrows.

'My dear child,' he commented, 'anyone would think you are starving near to death during your working hours.'

'I am,' John answered, his mouth full, and he regaled his father with a detailed description of the previous day's exploits.

Sir Gabriel listened in silence, sipping coffee from a bone china cup. 'So whose is the child?' he said eventually. 'Surely not James Martin's?'

'Why do you say that?'

'Because he would never have entrusted Jasper Harcross with the task of removing the boy from the Foundling Hospital. No, my wager would be on the victim himself as the father.'

'Then why the handkerchief initialled J.M.? And the subsequent loving care and attention?'

'Perhaps he just felt sorry for the child.'

'But that doesn't explain why it should have been Mr Martin who abandoned him at the gates.'

'*If* he did. Perhaps the handkerchief was purely coincidental and was dropped by a passer-by.'

The Apothecary frowned. 'There are too many coincidences for my liking. There has to be a thread in this somewhere.'

'I'm sure there is,' answered Sir Gabriel. 'Perhaps a surprise visit to Mrs Martin might not come amiss.'

John groaned. 'The very thought makes me shudder.'

His father clapped him on the shoulder. 'Be of stout heart, my lad. She is obliged to answer your questions or face the Beak.'

'I think even he, the great John Fielding, might quail in her presence.'

'I doubt it,' Sir Gabriel replied naughtily. 'Remember, he has the advantage of not being able to see.'

'You're incorrigible,' said John, and left the breakfast table with a smile on his face.

'By the way,' called his father, just as the Apothecary was about to leave the house. 'There is a letter for you on the hall table. It is from Serafina. She is having a few friends for supper and cards tonight and wonders if you would care to join them. I know because I dined with her and Louis yesterday. We played dice.'

'Did she win?'

'Occasionally she was kind and allowed her husband and me some good fortune.'

John popped his head back in through the front door. 'She *is* the finest gamester in England, isn't she?'

'I would say probably the entire known world.'

'Oh dear!' sighed the Apothecary, and went on his way.

The first hour in the shop produced little trade except for two beaux, their white make-up cracking and ghastly in the bright morning light, who came in for a reviver after a night out at some assembly or other. One of them was promptly sick immediately outside, and John had enormous pleasure in throwing a bucket of icy water over both the offender and the contents of his guts. For good measure he chucked a pitcher of brown disinfectant as well, managing to soil and spoil the beau's pea green frock by careful aiming.

'Mind what you're doing,' called the silly creature petulantly.

'And so do you!' John shouted back furiously. 'Next time I'll put some arsenic in it for good measure.'

They minced away angrily, stamping their high heels, while John, having checked that everything outside was fresh and clean, went within to prepare for proper custom. As he had half expected, at ten o'clock sharp Lord Delaney's coach crunched through the narrow confines of the lane and disgorged its owner at the front door bearing a list in his hand. He smiled on seeing the Apothecary, wiped his spectacles, and made his way within, leaning hard upon his great stick.

'My very dear young friend,' he began, his smile growing by the second, 'I have come on behalf of m'wife and m'self with an order as long as your arm. Everything is here from oil of Venus and eau-de-luce to potions for pregnancy and childbirth. I am, er, also interested in the strengthening compound you mentioned.'

The Apothecary looked at the list, his eyes widening. ''Zounds, my Lord, this is a purchase of considerable size. Would you prefer to go to the coffee house while I prepare it? Or would you like to step inside? I can offer you refreshment.'

'I'll stroll about a while for my health, then return and drink a cordial with you. I feel I have so much to say. With the news that Lady Delaney is to bear me a son my whole world has changed. All thanks to your good young self.'

Hoping to God that the pendulum prediction was going to prove correct, John attempted a humble expression which did not fit too well with his inner doubts.

'It was nothing, Sir. I just followed a simple country method.'

His Lordship went white. 'But it is accurate, isn't it? The future of our line is pinned on the outcome.'

'All I can say is that rural folk swear by it.'

Lord Delaney looked relieved. 'They always know best. It's the clean air they breathe. I feel much healthier on my estate in Suffolk, d'ye understand? Talking of that, is your physick truly efficacious? The one for mature gentlemen, I mean.'

'They keep coming back for it, if that is any proof of its power.'

'Ah,' said his Lordship, obviously well pleased. 'Well, I'll saunter forth, my boy, and return in an hour or so. I'm very mindful of my well-being these days. We older fathers!'

He executed a small and nimble dance step, then strode away with a cheery whistle.

'Jasper Harcross, you've done some good at last,' murmured John, then set about his task of compounding those items on the list not already made up. But there he was to be thwarted, for the doorbell rang continuously, customers pouring in off the streets, partly to avoid a sudden squall. Yet everyone bought at least one item, attracted by the Apothecary's display of exciting bottles, filled with strange blue liquid, together with his array of exotic perfumes.

'I would like a large bottle of otto of roses, and some oil of cinnamon,' said one young lady who had alighted from a sedan chair. 'I've just met Lord Delaney and he recommended you, said you were quite *bon ton* in fact.'

'D'you have some verdigris for my face paint?' asked an emasculated nothing, waving a handkerchief stiff with powder.

'I want a remedy for corpulence,' said a stout lady, flopping into the only chair available.

'Don't eat,' responded the pretty fellow instantly, and fell against the counter, laughing hysterically.

'How dare you?' responded the big woman, heaving herself to her feet and looming over him in the most menacing manner.

'Ha, ha, ha,' the beau responded, oblivious to her presence.

The smart young lady suddenly pealed with mirth. 'Never eat

again might perhaps be better.' And collapsed in the direction of the beau, at which they jigged a strange sort of ritual cackling dance together. Fighting desperately to control himself, no mean feat, the Apothecary bowed low.

'Youthful high spirits, Madam. Please forgive them. If you would care to step into my laboratory I will serve the merry-makers, then give you a private consultation.'

Slightly pacified, the object of derision moved into John's compounding room, and it was while she was doing this, accompanied by a great deal of sighing and clucking, that Will, the theatre boy, came in, colliding in the doorway with Lord Delaney.

It was an extraordinary moment, a moment that, for no par-ticular reason, the Apothecary committed to memory and would recall time and again. He saw Will gaze up at the important personage entering with him, saw Lord Delaney glance down to see who had bumped against his legs. Then he observed Will look over at him and mouth words which he could not catch.

'Do you want to tell me something?' John called over all the hubbub.

The boy nodded, then stared round the shop, taking in the beau and the girl, still giggling insanely, the rear view of the large lady disappearing into the back room, Lord Delaney's jovial smile. And it was at that second that he panicked. Without another word Will turned and ran, up the cobbles of Shug Lane and out of sight, leaving John with the impres-sion of someone very much afraid.

The Apothecary stood helplessly, longing to chase after him but quite unable to do so with a shop full of customers. The best he could manage in the circumstances was to make a mental promise to go to the theatre to see the child on his way home from Serafina's supper party, when the evening performance at Drury Lane would be over and done.

'Good trade, my young friend,' said Lord Delaney, joining

in the general air of jollity emanating from the other two customers.

'Yes, very good, thank you, Sir,' John answered automatically. But his mind was elsewhere, already conjecturing what it could have been that Will had wanted to say, and coming to the conclusion that the boy had remembered something of sufficient importance to drive him to leave the safety of the theatre and venture to Shug Lane to tell the Apothecary of it.

In a hurry as ever, John shut the shop promptly and hastened home to change into his very best clothes for the evening. How true it is, he thought, that old habits die hard. At the height of his passion for Serafina, when he had known her only as the Masked Lady and had gaped at her admiringly from afar, he had dressed to try and attract her attention. Now he was doing just the same thing, though his feelings for her had long since altered to those of friendship. Not having too much time to spend in preparation, yet finally satisfied with his appearance, unbelievably splendid in black and crimson, John set out in a sedan to Hanover Square.

It was a miserable night after a relatively fine day and John huddled in the chair, pulling his cloak around him. But when he alighted at number twelve a sense of warmth swept over him just from looking at its torchlit exterior, and it was with eager anticipation that he paid off the chairmen and hurried inside. Serafina and Louis were receiving guests in their stately upstairs salon and much to John's delight, as he climbed the curving staircase, the sound of Coralie Clive's voice could be heard. Well aware that when they had met on the previous day the actress had been furious with him, the Apothecary adjusted his features accordingly. So it was a somewhat contrite looking young man who walked into the room and kissed his hostess's hand, bowed politely to Louis, then finally went to greet the other guest.

'Mr Rawlings,' said Coralie, 'I did not think you were going to be here.'

'Would you not have come?'

'Of course I would. We cannot let this vile murder ruin all our lives.'

'What do you mean?' John asked quietly.

'That working for Mr Fielding means you will be forced to upset people sometimes.'

'So have you forgiven me for irritating you?'

'Naturally,' she answered rapidly, but John still felt that there was a certain coldness in her voice.

Serafina came to the rescue. 'My dear John, I have another pleasant surprise in store for you. Samuel is to be here at any moment, and later we are to be joined by Coralie's sister, Kitty. She is performing in *The Merchant of Venice* tonight but will join us as soon as she can.'

'It will be a great honour to meet her.'

'And she can confirm that I was at home when she arrived back on the night before the killing,' Miss Clive said acidly.

John suddenly lost patience with her and shot her an angry look, unaware that his eyes had deepened to the colour of wintry seas from their usual delphinium blue. Out of his deep affection for his hosts he remained silent, though there were many words he would like to have spoken, but his glance said it all and Coralie turned her gaze away, her back rigid. It was a great relief at that moment to hear Samuel clattering into the hall below, then pounding up the stairs with his usual noisy stride.

'Ha ha,' he said, bounding into the room. 'A gathering of all my favourite people!' And he set about effusive greetings which lifted the atmosphere enormously.

A footman poured champagne, another aid to conversation, and soon everyone was chatting freely, though Coralie directed her words mainly to Serafina and Louis, rather obviously, in John's opinion.

Finding himself alone with his friend, Samuel begged to be told all that had happened since they last met, explaining apologetically that he had been very busy with his new premises, where he was soon to set up as a goldsmith, and therefore unable to be of much help.

'I could use you tonight, however,' John answered, and Samuel's face lit into a grin bright as a full moon.

'What for?'

'At the end of the evening I must call in to Drury Lane. That pathetic boy had something to tell me and the sooner I find out what it is, the better.'

'And you want me to go with you?'

'To be honest it's an eerie place after dark.'

Samuel chuckled. 'Not afraid of Jasper Harcross's ghost, surely?'

John shook his head. 'Probably just afraid would be nearer the truth.'

At this juncture Serafina interrupted their conversation. 'Dear friends, let us go in to supper. Afterwards we shall play cards and await the arrival of Miss Kitty Clive.'

'I hope you're going to be easy on us, Comtesse,' said Samuel jovially.

Louis interposed. 'If she were not she could bankrupt us all in a night.' But he smiled fondly at his wife and briefly kissed her for all his words.

John, observing, felt enormously happy for them that all their earlier difficulties had been resolved. Then, looking up, he caught Coralie's eye upon him and studiously ignored it. It was occurring to him, ever more strongly, that the young lady was as full of temperament as every actress was reputed to be and that he, for one, had no intention of playing her silly little games of personal power.

The evening continued in this fashion, John talking to Samuel, despite the fact that he was placed next to Coralie at table, she devoting her attention to her hosts. And it was not until they had sat down to cards that she finally spoke to him once more.

'Mr Rawlings,' she whispered, close to his ear, 'I believe you are not best pleased with me.'

The Apothecary turned on her a cool look that he did not even know he possessed amongst his repertoire of differing expressions.

'That is because, Miss Clive, you continue to dig at me for the role I have been given as one of the Blind Beak's co-opted Runners. Let me assure you that from all I have learnt about the murder victim his killer deserves a medal, yet that will not detract me one whit from keeping my promise to Mr Fielding. And if this leads you to take offence, then so be it.' And he laid a negligent card.

'Bravo,' murmured Serafina, though whether she was cheering his choice of words, quietly spoken though they had been, or his method of play, he was not certain. Further speculation on this point being precluded by the arrival of Coralie's glamorous sister, John decided to forget all about the younger actress and concentrate on the elder.

She was certainly an attractive young woman, like Coralie in many ways except for the fact that she had light blue eyes. Mr Garrick considered her one of the finest actresses of the day, and it was a fact that when she played Portia, as she had been doing tonight, she invariably reduced the house to hysterics during the trial scene by her portrayal of various well-known living advocates. Her ear was sharp, her mimicry cruel, her talent undoubted; both John and Samuel thought her absolutely fascinating and made the fact quite clear.

Just as Louis de Vignolles had promised, his wife was kind to her guests and allowed them to win on several occasions. Only once did she show her true mastery, and then with such a breathtaking display of play that everyone applauded and did not resent her in the least.

'You are brilliant, Comtesse,' said Kitty in genuine admiration. 'But then, of course, you were the famous Masked Lady, were you not?'

'Until Mr Rawlings uncovered my true identity, yes.'

John was aware of Coralie's eyes upon him.

'He must be very clever,' Kitty continued, smiling. 'Are you, Mr Rawlings?'

'Sometimes I make lucky guesses, let me put it that way.'

'You are too modest,' Serafina said, then added wickedly to Coralie, 'Never try to keep a secret from him, my dear. He'll find it out for sure.'

'Why are you all talking about me as if I weren't here?' asked John. He pinched himself. 'I am still visible, aren't I?'

'Only just,' Samuel answered, and guffawed at his own joke.

From downstairs came the sound of the great hall clock striking once and Serafina cast her eyes in the Apothecary's direction. 'Are you working tomorrow?'

'No, but I have to attend the Public Office early. Mr Fielding will no doubt have some tasks for me, so unfortunately I will have to take my leave.'

'And I,' Samuel said, springing to his feet surprisingly steadily for one who had consumed a great deal of champagne, to say nothing of wine and port.

'Ladies, do not desert us please,' pleaded the hostess, but Kitty was already shaking her head.

'I have a ten o'clock rehearsal tomorrow so, sorrowfully, we too must go. Gentlemen, may I offer you a lift in my carriage? It awaits outside.'

'Actually,' said John, 'we are going to Drury Lane. I have to see Will.'

'What about?' asked Coralie, surprise in her voice.

'He came into my shop earlier, obviously wanting to speak to me. But it was very crowded and he went away again. He looked worried about something so I thought I would try and see him tonight.'

'He'll be asleep,' the actress answered.

If they had been alone together privately, John would have challenged her, asked her why she didn't want him to talk to the child, but as it was he let the matter pass.

'I shall visit you in Shug Lane very soon,' said the Comtesse as she kissed him goodbye.

John's mobile eyebrows rose in query, but Serafina merely laughed at him and turned to her other guests. And then they were outside in the bitter cold, clambering into Kitty Clive's splendid equipage and driving down Piccadilly towards The Strand.

'We're taking you out of your way,' said Samuel, not so much apologising as commenting when the driver struck out in the direction of Covent Garden.

'Not at all,' answered Kitty, 'but we won't wait for you if you don't mind.'

'Of course not,' John put in. 'Samuel and I will hire a hansom home. He can spend the rest of the night in Nassau Street.'

Coralie spoke out of the darkness. 'I haven't behaved very well recently, have I?'

'What are you talking about?' said Kitty.

'Mr Rawlings knows.'

'And Mr Rawlings forgives,' answered John, as the coach drew to a halt before the dark shape of the deserted theatre.

'Do you?' Coralie asked wistfully as the Apothecary descended the two steps down to the street, Samuel immediately preceding him.

For answer John remounted the bottom step and leant into the carriage. 'Come here,' he said.

She leant forward, imagining he had something to say to

her. But John was beyond words. Instead he kissed her, full on the mouth, letting his lips linger for several sensual seconds before he bowed, said, 'Good night,' stepped down to the street and closed the carriage door.

'Hare and hounds!' exclaimed Samuel. 'That should give her something to think about.'

'I sincerely hope so.'

'You've got your nerve, you know.'

'She drove me to it.'

Samuel chuckled. 'I rather thought you two didn't like one another.'

'That,' said John with a sigh, 'remains to be seen.'

Chapter Thirteen

It had not occurred to the Apothecary, or to Samuel Swann for that matter, that gaining entry to Drury Lane theatre might be difficult. Despite the lateness of the hour both had expected the stage door to be open and Will not yet abed. But it seemed that there they had miscalculated. Everything was locked and shuttered and the place in total darkness, not so much as the glow of a candle lighting the interior.

'Now what do we do?' Samuel asked, aware that with their conveyance gone they might well have to face the prospect of walking home through London's dangerous streets.

John frowned. 'I would say forget the visit until tomorrow were it not for a strange feeling I have. Something caused that boy to take fright and run off, though I can't for the life of me think what it could have been. Now I believe he dearly wants to speak to me.'

'Perhaps it was the sight of the fat lady,' said Samuel.

'What?'

'Perhaps he mistook the large woman for Mrs Martin.'

John gazed at him in the faint winter moonlight. 'God's wounds, but you're right! Why didn't I realise it before? He must have glimpsed her disappearing into the compounding room and made a mistake.'

The Goldsmith's honest features took on a look of concern. 'From what you say, Will must be very frightened indeed. I think we should try and effect an entry.'

'By force?'

'If necessary, yes.'

'Good,' said John, the wild side of him relishing the adventure, and beckoned his friend to walk round the theatre in order to try all the entrances.

Fortunately, one of the scenery doors had not quite caught on its latch and by careful insertion of his herb knife, the carrying of which was a patent affectation in the heart of London but one that the Apothecary refused to give up, it swung silent back on its hinges.

'It's damnably dark inside,' whispered Samuel, peering into Drury Lane's fathomless depths.

'Very,' agreed John, and a most unpleasant feeling, practically one akin to horror, crawled the length of his spine.

'I wonder if there's a candle anywhere,' Samuel went on, taking a few tentative steps into the abyss.

'We'll never find it even if there is.' John raised his voice a little. 'Will, don't be afraid. It's John Rawlings, the apothecary, come to see you. Where are you?'

There was no reply and John had the odd sensation of hearing his words come back to him through layers of muffling cloth. The curtains were obviously drawn across the stage, adding to the impenetrable dusk.

'Where can he be?' asked Samuel.

'Probably asleep. He sleeps very soundly, sometimes aided by some sort of opiate in my opinion.'

'I hope he's all right,' the Goldsmith continued, and suddenly there was a note of genuine fear in his voice.

'William,' John called again, this time more urgently, but still there was no answer, only the unnerving echo of his own disembodied tones.

They had been standing in the dark for several minutes now and slowly, as their eyes adjusted, vague shapes began to rear out of the shadows. It was apparent that they were in one of the scenery bays, those roomy areas backstage where flats and other theatrical contrivances are stored when not in use. To their left was the great expanse of the stage itself, still set for *The Merchant of Venice* and strangely haunted-looking because of the fact that the auditorium was blocked off by drapery. To the right were the scenery doors, a chink of moonlight glinting through. Beyond the stage, invisible in the blackness, lay the staircase leading to the dressing rooms and, on stage level, the properties and costume rooms, together with the Green Room and various other bits of storage space.

'The child told me he had a bed in the properties room,' John said to Samuel, finding that his voice had dropped to a nervous murmur.

'Then we had better go and look for him. It shouldn't be too difficult once we've crossed the stage,' Samuel answered, bravely striking out and instantly tripping over some furniture and falling flat, then rising again amidst a great deal of cursing.

What, when the theatre was lit and the audience assembled, was normally a haven of pleasure now seemed a pit from hell. As uncertain as blind men, the two friends stumbled and felt their way across the arena of Drury Lane Theatre until at last they entered the opposite wing. Here they were helped by a small amount of moonlight coming through a barred window next to the stairs, and it was by this pallid illumination that they crept along the corridor from which doors led off to the various rooms.

'Which is the properties room?' Samuel asked quietly.

'I don't know. I haven't been in there. This is the Green Room for sure,' John answered, opening and closing a door after staring into the dimness beyond.

'But where's the boy? Surely he should have heard us by now?'

'As I said, the poor thing sleeps deeply.'

But even as the Apothecary spoke the words, alarm plucked the strings of his heart and the spine-freezing hand of fear laid itself upon him once more.

'There's something wrong,' he exclaimed involuntarily.

'I know,' Samuel answered.

They stared at one another in the sickly moonlight and then, with one accord, began wrenching open doors and calling the child's name. As is always the way in awful situations, the properties room was the very last they came to, even though they instantly recognised the place for what it was by the ceiling-high pile of everything from Roman armour to Macbeth's great chair of state.

'Will,' called John loudly, striding in. 'Will, where are you?'

No sleepy little voice answered from the pile of bedding clearly visible beneath one of the two windows, and no ugly-faced child got to his feet, yawning and rubbing his eyes.

'Where is he?' asked Samuel, clutching the Apothecary's arm in panic.

'Not here, certainly.'

'Then what . . .' The Goldsmith's voice died away as his attention was caught by something else. 'My God, isn't that the gallows over there?' And he pointed with a broad finger, now visibly trembling.

Caught by the rays of watery moonshine, John looked across to where the mobile, the contraption on which Jasper Harcross had met his death, had been pushed into a corner. It loomed, dark and somehow threatening, in the place to which it had been removed once Mr Fielding had given permission for it to be taken from the stage.

'I would like to chop the vile thing up for firewood,' Dick Weatherby had told John in confidence. 'But, alas, the Blind Beak said it would be destroying evidence.'

'And so it would,' the Apothecary had answered.

Obviously, the fate of the murder platform had been to store it in the properties room, from whence it could be retrieved should further examination prove necessary. But none of this was in John's mind as he stared in growing horror at the evil piece of stage machinery. For it seemed to him in the blurred and imperfect light that Jasper's body still dangled from the noose, lifeless but swaying slightly in the draught created by the open door. But just as John remembered that there *was* no noose, that it had been cut down, still round the actor's neck, he saw Samuel spring into action.

''Sblud, John, there's someone hanging there! Oh God help us, there's been another murder!'

As if released from a dream, realisation came to the Apothecary at exactly the same moment, and he and Samuel sprinted forward, knocking things flying as they went.

'It's the child!' screamed the Goldsmith, more agitated than John could ever remember him. 'It's the poor, innocent boy.'

'We must cut him down!' John yelled, his voice rising to a note of hysteria. And with that came the memory that he had used virtually the same words about Jasper.

But here all similarity ceased. As Samuel, with his commanding height, slashed through the rope with Macbeth's dagger, unusually sharp for a stage weapon, and the pathetic body was lowered into John's arms, the Apothecary realised that Will and Jasper Harcross had been doomed to die in entirely different ways. Whereas the actor had been spared the agony of slow suffocation, the theatre boy had not. Wretched, tragic Will, who had started his life abandoned outside the Foundling Hospital, had met his dismal little end in pain and suffering. His callous killer had strung him up and left him there to die.

But for all that, the Apothecary tried every skill at his command to restore life. He had supported Will carefully as he was lowered, in order to put no further strain on the neck, and now that the noose was within his grasp he loosened and removed it. Then he pumped fiercely on the heart and blew into the child's mouth, a strange technique which he had been taught by his Master, and which still needed some form of perfecting in order to succeed properly. Yet though he worked for a full quarter of an hour, willing that small, sad heart to start its beat beneath his hands, poor Will remained lifeless.

'It's no use,' said John, his face white as lace in the moonlight. 'I can't save him.'

'By God,' answered Samuel fiercely, 'this man has to be caught! To kill Jasper Harcross is one thing, but to take the life of a blameless child is entirely different. Who could possibly do such a thing – and why?'

'Perhaps because the poor little wretch remembered something,' John replied slowly. 'I told him when I questioned him that if he were to recall anything further about the night before the murder, he was to tell me at once.'

'But even if he had remembered something vital, how could anybody else have known that?'

'Because he obviously confided in another, and that person was the wrong one to speak to. Will was silenced before he could get to me, don't you see?'

'I see only too clearly,' Samuel answered grimly. 'If he had spoken to you in the shop, if the fat lady hadn't frightened him off, all this could have been avoided.'

'Oh don't, don't,' John said wretchedly. 'I cannot bear even to think about it.'

'You must not take that guilt on yourself,' was Samuel's sensible reply. 'What happened, happened. The child ran away and that was that.'

John looked thoughtful. 'He must have hastened back to Drury Lane and bumped into someone and decided to tell them everything. Now who could have been in the theatre at that time?'

'Any of 'em,' his friend answered morosely. 'It seems to

me that they are always hovering round the place, rehearsing and so on.'

'Yes, you're right.' In the gloom the Apothecary stared at his watch. It was half past two in the morning. Samuel, reading his thoughts, said, 'Is it too late to rouse the Beak?'

'It is but we must. There is no way in which we can wait until later.'

'I suppose you want me to run?' asked the Goldsmith with a sigh.

'It is a straight choice between that or staying with the body.'

'I'll run,' said Samuel hastily.

Together they found the stage door which John left open, partly to let in more light, partly so as not to feel cut off from the world outside. This done, he went back to the properties room, having found a candle and tinder box on the way. There, with greater illumination and without Samuel lurking in the background, he made a more thorough examination of the mortal remains of poor Will Swithin.

He had choked to death all right, and sufficiently long ago to render John's attempts at resuscitation useless. Whoever had killed the boy had obviously waited until the theatre emptied after *The Merchant of Venice* and then returned to silence the unhappy child. Holding the cold, pale corpse in his arms, John thought what a waste everything was. Here was a young creature starting out on the adventure of life, courageously doing his best to make his way in the world. Now there was no hope for him. He had been despatched because he knew too much.

'God bless you, sad soul,' said John, and kissed the icy forehead.

It was in that moment, almost like a flash of lightning, that Will's true parentage was suddenly revealed to him. Mr Fielding had guessed at it yet had refused to commit himself, but now the time had come to prove it. As Samuel crashed back in through the stage door, John, having covered the corpse with a theatrical cloak, ran to meet him.

'Are they on their way?'

'Yes,' his friend panted. 'Mr Fielding is getting dressed, as are two of the Beak Runners.'

'What about Joe Jago?'

'He lives in the Seven Dials area. Someone has gone to fetch him.'

'Samuel,' said John earnestly. 'Do you think you could go back and divert one of the Runners to bring Mr and Mrs Martin here? Their presence is vital, I believe.'

The Goldsmith rolled his eyes in his head, still puffing. 'Must I?' he gasped.

John nodded. 'It's very important. Really.'

With a look of total resignation his friend said no more, heading out of the theatre at a strained trot, his face a picture of despondency.

'I'm sorry,' the Apothecary called after him, 'but we must find the boy's killer.'

Samuel's receding figure quickened its pace as John, his expression grave, returned to keep his vigil with the newly dead.

Within half an hour all the officers of the law were present. The physician had examined William and confirmed John's diagnosis of death by strangulation, caused by murderous hanging. But then, contrary to normal practice, the body had not been removed to the city morgue. Instead, at Mr Fielding's instruction, it had remained in the properties room, still covered by the cloak.

By now all the chandeliers that normally lit the stage and theatre had been illuminated, so it was possible for a thorough search of the gallows and the surrounding area to be made. It had not surprised John greatly when a woman's glove had been found abandoned not far from the scene of the murder. But what had shaken him to the core had been the fact that it smelled distinctly of the perfume worn by Coralie Clive.

'But that's impossible,' he exclaimed to the Blind Beak, shortly after the discovery had been made. 'I was with Miss Clive last evening. We dined with the Comte and Comtesse de Vignolles. Later we were joined by Miss Kitty who arrived at about eleven o'clock. Coralie's movements can be completely accounted for.'

John Fielding had raised the glove to his nose and sniffed it thoughtfully. 'Sarah Delaney's bow and now this. It would seem that the murderer is definitely trying to incriminate a woman.'

'He's made an error this time!' John replied triumphantly. 'I suppose he thought that the glove belonged to Sarah and by placing it in the properties room he was drawing her into the net more tightly.'

'I'm not so sure,' the Blind Beak answered. 'Think of the play, my young friend.'

'The play?' John repeated, surprised.

'Do not Polly Peachum and Lucy Lockit become united by misfortune at one stage? Surely there is a line which Polly speaks, "Let us retire, my dear Lucy, and indulge our sorrows"? Having no one else to turn to, do they not console one another?'

'Are you saying that the killer is trying to lay the blame at the feet of both Coralie and Sarah?'

'It is a possibility, you must agree. One had been his mistress, the other expects his child. These two women, as far as we know, were Jasper's most recent conquests.'

'I don't quite follow you, Sir.'

'If jealous revenge was the motive for the original crime,

then why not get rid of his two sweethearts by leaving clues that point to both of them?'

'As if the women were working in collusion?'

'Exactly.'

John sat silently, considering the idea. 'On the other hand, Sir, he – or she – could have mistaken the glove for Sarah Delaney's.'

'Indeed, they could. The entire case is surrounded by bewildering possibilities. And speaking of women, could a female have strung that poor boy up?'

'Quite easily. He weighed little and could have been subdued without difficulty. There's nothing that points directly to a man as his killer.'

'As I thought,' said Mr Fielding, and sighed deeply.

Samuel came over to join them, his expression one of dismay. 'The Martins have arrived and apparently she is creating a scene fit to burst her skin.'

And indeed, into the relative quiet of the stage area burst the most fearful commotion, Clarice Martin's voice rising to a crescendo above all other sound.

'How dare you bring me here at this hour of the night? Are honest citizens no longer allowed to sleep peacefully in their beds? What is going on? That is what I would like to know.'

In one powerful movement, the Blind Beak lunged off the stool on which he had been sitting and loomed to his full height of six feet and three inches. His vast shoulders shook, though not with suppressed mirth, and his expression was merciless. John, who had seen the Principal Magistrate gentle as a lamb with his adopted child, Mary Ann, trembled despite himself.

'Bring her to me,' roared John Fielding, drowning the din from the stage door. 'Bring that damnable woman to me and tell her if she utters one more word I'll charge her with impeding the course of justice.'

The hubbub ceased as abruptly as it had begun and across

the stage, very red in the face and accompanied by Joe Jago, foxy hair on end and minus a wig, came the perpetrator of all the din.

'Stand before me, Madam,' said the Beak commandingly, 'and utter not one word until I have finished speaking.'

'Now see here . . .' she began, though somewhat halfheartedly.

'I cannot see,' he retaliated, his voice harsh as a whip, 'that is why I wear this black bandage. But I can see in my imagination and I have built a very clear picture of you, Mrs Martin. You are a spoilt and selfish woman who has spent her entire life besotted with one ignominious creature, for whom you have sacrificed both your husband and your child. But now your deserts have come. That very child whom you ordered your poor wretched spouse to abandon at the Foundling Hospital, though it broke his heart to do so, tonight met his end at the hands of a murderer. As his natural parent I thought you should be informed, it even occurred to me that you might wish to make your farewells.'

'What are you saying?' asked the actress hoarsely, her flushed face suddenly the colour of frost.

'I am saying that William Swithin, your son sired by Jasper Harcross, whom your husband adored, having lost his own child through a tragic accident, was hanged tonight, presumably by the same hand which took the life of his father.'

'Oh my God!' she exclaimed, though John, looking for genuine signs of distress, could see few.

Yet the same could not be said for James Martin, who now came to join them, his small orderly features already contorting with grief. 'Will is dead?' he asked in a hoarse, unrecognisable voice.

'Yes, Mr Martin,' answered the Magistrate unremittingly. 'I know it is grievous news but there is no other way of breaking it.'

'Murdered, you say?'

'I fear so.'

'Oh my poor little boy,' James muttered brokenly, and started to weep silently.

Very gently, John Fielding took him by the arm. 'But he wasn't really your little boy, was he?'

Mrs Martin interrupted, her voice surprisingly subdued. 'No, he was my son by Jasper Harcross, as you correctly guessed. We had had a child, James and I, but he died in his cradle. So when I became pregnant by my lover I tried to deceive my husband into thinking this next baby was also his. But as soon as Will was born, James seemed to guess the truth. It was uncanny, for the poor creature did not resemble Jasper in the least. After the facts came out I could not and would not tolerate the situation. As James began to dote on the lad so I turned more and more against him, to the point where I could not bear the baby to be under the same roof.'

'So you insisted that your husband leave him at the Foundling Hospital?'

'Yes.'

'And what did you think about that?' the Blind Beak gently asked the sobbing musician.

'It broke my heart to abandon him. I loved him as much as if he had been my own.'

John Fielding's tones became extremely solemn as he addressed Clarice Martin once more. 'I am glad that it is you who must live with your conscience, Madam, and not I.'

The Apothecary broke in, anxious to ask a question. 'I presume that Jasper Harcross knew who the boy was and that was why he brought him to Drury Lane to work?'

Mrs Martin shot him a baleful glance. 'Naturally he knew. But I did not approve of Will coming here. I said it would make trouble and so it has.'

Her husband's tragic voice interrupted their conversation. 'May I see him please?'

John Fielding turned his head in the direction of the sound. 'My young friend Mr Rawlings will escort you in a moment, but first let me ask you one more thing.'

'Which is?'

'Did Jasper consult you about bringing the boy here or was that kindly action all his own?'

'I begged him to do it and as soon as the child was of an age, he agreed. I think it amused him to have one of his little bastards about the place.'

'Who else knew that Jasper was Will's actual father?'

'Nobody, as far as I know. The child certainly didn't.'

'But is it beyond the bounds of possibility that Jasper joked about it to someone, perhaps even boasting of his virility?'

Clarice Martin spoke up, her voice bitter. 'I am sure he mentioned the fact. I was never comfortable with Will around the place. I always felt that people were sniggering at me behind my back.'

'Well, that won't be a problem to you any more, will it?' said the Blind Beak, and his voice was like shards of ice.

She blanched beneath the power of it so that now she seemed almost as pale as her pathetic son. 'Oh poor Will!' she said brokenly.

'Too late now,' snarled her husband. 'The child was sacrificed to your enormous ego, in every sense.' He turned his back on her. 'And now, Mr Fielding, if I may say farewell to the boy.'

'Of course.' The black bandage shifted in John's direction. 'Mr Rawlings, if you would be so good.'

It was a bleak experience. John stood with his back to the room, staring out of the window at the dark street beyond, only too aware that behind him James Martin had lifted the cloak from Will's body and was at present cradling the fragile form in his arms, speaking to the boy as if he were still alive.

Through the Apothecary's mind rushed a torrent of thoughts:

what evil being could possibly murder an innocent child; were there two murderers involved in this equation or had the same bloodied hand committed both crimes; was Mr Fielding right in thinking that the killer wished to implicate Coralie and Sarah together, or had an error been made in dropping Miss Clive's glove?

He must have made some small sound or movement at this juncture, for James Martin spoke into the stillness.

'What will happen to the body?'

'I don't know. I am sure Mr Fielding will release it to you if you so wish.'

'Yes, I would like to see the lad given a decent funeral and not be put in some pauper's grave. He had little enough in life, after all.' Mr Martin paused. 'Jasper is to be buried tomorrow, so I hear.'

'I wonder where?'

'In Kensington. I believe his widow wanted it to be a quiet affair.'

'I think she will get her wish,' John replied austerely. 'I expect Mr Fielding will require everyone here for questioning.'

James Martin stood up, then gently laid the body back on the floor and covered it with the magnificent cloak. 'Jasper wore this when he played Othello and now it shrouds his tragic son. What irony, what irony!'

'Mr Martin,' John said quietly. 'Is there anything I can do to help you? Should I mix you a soothing potion of some kind?'

'Perhaps you could see to it that Mrs Martin gets home safely.'

'Will you not be accompanying her?' the Apothecary asked, astonished.

James shook his head sadly. 'I simply cannot continue with her after this.'

'What do you mean?'

'That our marriage is at an end. I shall seek lodgings elsewhere.'

'Isn't that a little extreme?'

'If I had done it years ago, Will might still be alive today.'

John froze with horror. 'Exactly what are you saying, Sir?'

Mr Martin gave a tragic smile. 'If you think I am accusing my wife of murder you would not be far off the mark.'

'*Did* she kill him?' John asked, thunderstruck. 'Surely no mother, however harsh, would take the life of her own child?'

'I don't suppose that, in the sense you mean, Clarice murdered William. But she set the wheels in motion by sending him from our house.'

The Apothecary shook his head. 'Don't go down that twisted path, I beg you. Life is nothing but a series of "If onlys" and there is no point in torturing oneself by thinking about them. It would appear from the little we know that William stumbled on something which was highly dangerous to the killer. Though I cannot be certain, I imagine that that is why he was silenced.'

James Martin paused reflectively then echoed Samuel's words. 'I could forgive anyone for murdering Jasper, it would have been a true crime of passion. But the putting down of an innocent child is another matter. It is an act of pure horror, the work of a maniac.'

John nodded gravely. 'Dreadful though the thought is, when one considers the members of the theatre company, I am afraid that you are right.'

Chapter Fourteen

There was to be no sleep for any of them that night. John Fielding having overseen the removal of Will Swithin's body to the mortuary, pending further arrangements to be made shortly by Mr Martin, set a Brave Fellow to guard the theatre and the properties room. He then made his way through the darkness to the home of his friend, David Garrick, before going back to the Public Office. John Rawlings, meanwhile, having been bidden by the Magistrate to go home and change into something suitable for a funeral before returning to Bow Street, took a carriage provided by the Public Office back to his house. Samuel, somewhat exhausted after his exertions but proud to be of service, went with a wretched James Martin to find him a room in The Pillars of Hercules, a commodious coaching inn situated at Hyde Park Corner. Clarice Martin, very deflated and as silent as John had ever seen her, was escorted home by a Beak Runner, having refused to bid farewell to her son, saying that she wanted to remember him as he was. A remark that caused several cynical glances to be exchanged amongst the rest of the company present.

Creeping into the house at almost four o'clock in the morning, John did his very best not to disturb its sleeping occupants. But Sir Gabriel, who he was convinced slept with one ear fully alert, heard him and swept into his son's bedroom, a satin turban upon his head and a gorgeous black nightrail covering his sleeping shirt.

'My dear child,' he said, clearly amazed to see John up and

still in his evening clothes, 'whatever are you doing coming home at this hour?'

'I'm afraid there's been another murder,' the Apothecary answered harshly, and told Sir Gabriel everything while he changed into a suit of sombre black without embroidery.

'Mr Fielding told me to prepare to attend a funeral which, I can only presume, must be Jasper's,' John said by way of explanation, seeing his father's eyebrows rise at his sober garb. 'I don't quite know his reasons, but he no doubt will tell me. I am to return to the Public Office as soon as I am ready. There is a conveyance waiting for me outside.'

Sir Gabriel stroked his chin. 'At what time is this interment?'

'In Kensington, later this morning. Why?'

'I've a strong notion to come and observe. Furthermore, I would like to see the divine Mrs Egleton again. How beautiful that woman once was.'

'And still is in her way.'

'Then I shall prepare myself to be at Kensington church at ten o'clock. The funeral will certainly be no earlier and if it is later, then I shall repair to a hostelry and await events.'

There was no arguing with his parent in this mood and John merely smiled and said, 'Then I shall see you there, for now I must get back. Mr Fielding is opening up the Public Office as soon as he returns, and is calling in all his Fellows. By the time they wake up, every member of the Drury Lane company, including the great names, will have received a notification ordering them to the theatre to make a statement. The Beak is determined to leave nothing to chance.'

Sir Gabriel looked thoughtful. 'The mentality of a child slayer is unique, I believe.'

'How?'

'There is a depravity in it that sets it apart from all other types of killer. You are dealing with someone both cruel and cold-blooded, John.'

'I know.'

'Then tread carefully, my son, tread carefully.'

'I will.'

And they parted, the Apothecary, now looking as gloomy and dark as a professional mourner, into the carriage; Sir Gabriel to his bed to get a few more hours' sleep.

The famous house in Bow Street glowed with light, except for the two upper floors where the females and the servants slept. Though the Public Office on street level was open and manned by a Runner, Mr Fielding had invited everyone else into his salon, where stimulating beverages were being passed round by Joe Jago, with a view to keeping those present awake. The only person to have slipped through this net was Samuel, who lay back in his chair like a becalmed ship, fast asleep and snoring softly.

'Leave him,' said Jago, with a grin, seeing the direction of the Apothecary's eyes. 'Mr Fielding only let him return out of the kindness of his heart. I doubt he'll wake till morning.'

'Is this a full meeting of the Runners?' John whispered.

'Them, plus every peacher in our employ. It's the Beak's intention, with Mr Garrick's connivance, to put them into the theatre as stagehands, that sort of thing.'

John stared round at the motley bunch of individuals, sitting uncomfortably on the upholstered chairs or squatting on the floor. A greater gathering of desperados he had yet to see, for these were the people, petty criminals in the main, who informed against their own class and brought many a thief or murderer to book.

'The crime committed tonight,' the Magistrate was saying, 'would sicken the heart of any who saw it. A defenceless boy was set upon, strung up on a gallows and left to die.'

'Why in Gawd's name?' asked one of the ruffians.

'Well, it may be that the child had inadvertently stumbled across the murderer of Jasper Harcross. There seems to be no other motive that makes any sense.' John Fielding took a mouthful from his coffee cup. 'Gentlemen, I cannot impress upon you too strongly the urgency of finding this killer.'

A peacher spoke up. 'Any whisper whether 'tis cove or dell, Beak?'

'Nothing.'

'Can't be dell, sure, as would kill a kinchen,' said another.

'Don't you believe it,' answered a third. 'I'd soon as face a rum customer as I would a spiteful blower.'

It was difficult to follow but this was cant, the talk of the streets, and John listened intently.

'Be that as it may,' Mr Fielding said forcefully. 'We might yet be looking for two killers. Let us say, for the sake of argument, a jealous woman does away with Harcross, a mad-man with a grudge slays the boy.'

'Then are they working together, these two?'

'On the face of it, no. But who knows in a situation as dark as this one?'

'So what's the plan, Sir?' asked the Apothecary.

'This. Tomorrow, Jago and I will interview everyone connected with that blighted theatre. It is going to be a monstrous task, we can all be sure of it. That is why, Mr Rawlings, when you have returned from Harcross's funeral, which I want you to observe closely then faithfully report back on to me, I would like you to come to Drury Lane. The young and the nervous I shall leave for you to question. You have such a way with them.'

There was a wave of laughter from the rest of the company.

'Then, over the next few days, I shall infiltrate our informers amongst the stage staff.'

'Won't they be noticed?'

'Not if we arrange for several people to leave, giving as their excuse the fact that Drury Lane is an unlucky place.'

'Neat, Beak, neat!' exclaimed a gruff voice.

'Furthermore, I have another little plan, but that is not for public consumption. Now, my friends . . .' He indicated the peachers by waving his hand in the direction of their voices, perfectly accurately, '. . . there's a glass of good brandy waiting for you downstairs. Drink it down and be on your way. We will contact you within the next few days. Meanwhile, stay alert. There's a good reward for the man who nabs this cull and gets him to Tyburn Tree.'

The overwhelming stink in the room diminished as the men trooped downstairs and Joe Jago threw open the windows, ignoring the cold which came just before dawning. Despite the freezing air, Samuel slumbered on, oblivious to all. Then faintly, from upstairs, came the first sound of the servants stirring to get the house prepared for the day.

'A brandy to warm us all,' said Mr Fielding decisively. 'Rudge, would you be so good as to pass the decanter and glasses.'

'Certainly, Sir.'

'And then, my good fellows, I will outline to you the little game I intend to play with our lethal friend.'

The village of Kensington on a cold winter's morning and a stark black cortège winding its way to the church. Hardly the most enlivening sight in the world, John thought dismally as he stepped out of the hackney, doffed his hat as a mark of respect to the departed, and looked about him. As far as the eye could see lay frost covered fields and white roofed houses. The blast of Arctic air that Joe Jago had let into the house in Bow Street to dispel the odour of the peachers had heralded a bitter day to come. And now the icy weather had the land in its grip.

Behind the glass-sided hearse, drawn by black plumed horses, walked one solitary mourner, obviously frozen to the marrow. It would seem that the former Mrs Egleton had come alone to see her murdered husband laid in the earth.

As she walked, a stark, black, veiled figure, she kept her head up and her eyes ahead, looking neither to right nor left but only at the black coffin in its glass carriage weaving a slow and solemn way to the distant church, in the doorway of which the minister already stood, Bible in hand, intoning to himself beneath the sombre sound of a single tolling bell. And then Mrs Harcross slipped, her steadfast gaze not taking account of the frosty ground beneath her feet, and fell onto the rime, as dark as a wounded rook against the white.

A black carriage had been drawn up just beyond the church's gate, a carriage of which John had taken little notice, automatically presuming that another mourner was awaiting the arrival of the cortège. But now its door opened smartly and a postillion ran round to lower the steps for the occupant, who appeared clad in black, his cloak lined with sumptuous jet velvet, a silver button flashing a brilliant, the only point of light in the entire ensemble.

'Father!' John muttered to himself. 'I might have guessed.'

Moving lithely, Sir Gabriel, hardly seeming to need the ebony cane which today was serving as his great stick, hastened towards the unhappy woman attempting to scramble up as best she could and hurting herself in the effort.

'Madam, allow me,' he said, leaning over and raising her to her feet. And then he bowed and offered her his arm, falling into step beside her, so that the funeral procession now consisted of two.

Strangely moved by these solitary figures paying their last respects to a man who obviously did not deserve their pity but, for all that, had answered for his faults with his life, John took his cue from his father and went to walk behind them. At this, a milkmaid, delivering her frozen produce, blue with cold, put down her yoke and buckets and joined the procession. A farmer's boy removed his cap and did likewise. Then came a carter, abandoning his cart as he read the situation. Doors opened, women with shawls and bonnets appeared. And suddenly it seemed as if the entire village of Kensington had come to support the lonely black figure, making its way to church. As Mrs Harcross passed through the lych gate, Sir Gabriel standing back to allow her to go first, a solid mass of citizens went through behind her, united in their desire to help the pathetic creature who had lived in their midst but had been left to face scandal alone.

Standing near the back, the best vantage point of all, John looked round the church. Mrs Harcross sat in the front pew, Sir Gabriel beside her, a place to which she had obviously invited him, as he would have been far too polite to push in. There was an empty row behind her, clearly left out of courtesy, and then came the villagers in a block. There was nobody from the theatre present, not even David Garrick, but then, John remembered, absolutely all of them would be closeted in Drury Lane at this exact moment so they had very little choice in the matter. And it was then that his eye was caught by another figure which had slipped in quietly behind the mourners and now sat in the pew nearest to the door, almost directly behind him.

Whoever she was, she had positioned herself cleverly, because short of turning round and frankly staring, John had very little opportunity to observe her. And then came the moment for a hymn. Pretending that he had no book, the Apothecary circled and took one from the pew at his back. In those few seconds he saw that the cloaked stranger was female and heavily veiled as if in deepest mourning. A memory of something triggered in his brain but refused to come to the fore, and John found himself singing lustily yet not really concentrating on a word he was uttering. Then, with the excuse that the

173

hymn had finished, he turned again to replace the book and saw that the mourner had gone. Determined not to lose sight of her, the Apothecary quietly rose from his place and went outside.

Because of the intense cold, plumes of icy air were rising amongst the graves, curling round the headstones in an eerie, unearthly manner. If ever a place looked haunted and desolate, it was this one and John shivered violently, not envying Jasper Harcross his final resting place. And then he saw the woman again, weaving her way down the path and staring from side to side, as if she were looking for one grave in particular. Not knowing whether to call out or remain silent, John watched, wishing he could remember what it was about her that seemed familiar.

The woman paused, clearly having seen what she was looking for, and the Apothecary realised with a thrill of horror that it was the freshly dug plot awaiting Jasper. As she hurried towards it he began to move quietly after her but the woman must have heard his approach for all his stealth, for she quickly threw something into the grave's yawning mouth, then sped away, almost running, to the far gate at the end of the churchyard which led out to the open fields.

John hovered, not certain whether to go after her at full chase, or to look into the grave and see what it was she had hurled in. Eventually he chose the latter course and was glad he had done so. A waxen image lay on the frozen earth, a pin through its breast, its garb and hair indicating that it was meant to be a woman. Horrified, he knelt beside the yawning chasm and, leaning down, managed to retrieve the hideous puppet from the eager abyss by hooking it up on the knob of his cane. Just as he had suspected, closer inspection showed that it was a crude representation of Mrs Harcross herself. The Apothecary just had sufficient time to conceal it in his pocket as the funeral party came out of church. Not wishing to be discovered kneeling by a grave, John made his way to the far gate and stared out over the fields.

There was no sign of the woman who had obviously doubled back along the path leading round the churchyard, then on into the village street where she could easily disappear into her own carriage, or even onto the stagecoach itself. Sighing with annoyance, the Apothecary stood apart while the interment took place, then quietly went to join his father as he walked away from the graveside.

'Mrs Harcross has prepared a wake. She thought the theatrical profession might honour her husband, you see,' Sir Gabriel informed him.

'Did you explain to her?'

'Yes, I told her there had been another accident at Drury Lane last night and that all concerned were in the theatre with John Fielding. Further, I lied and said that I was here representing David Garrick. The poor woman would have been mortified otherwise.'

'Father, really!'

'I had no choice. *Honi soit qui mal y pense.*'

'And do you expect me to say I am here representing Mr Fielding?'

'Why not? You are, aren't you?'

'Yes, but as an observer, not a mourner.'

'What difference does that make? You will come to the house, won't you?'

'Yes. I need to speak to Mrs Harcross, though this may not be a suitable moment, of course.'

'What has happened?'

John lowered his voice. 'This was thrown into the grave by a strange woman who sat in the back of the church for a while. It is a witchcraft symbol, meant to represent Jasper's widow.'

'What is its significance?'

'That Mrs Harcross will follow her husband into the church-yard within a year, I imagine.'

'God's Holy life! Was it the murderer you saw, then?'

The Apothecary shrugged helplessly. 'That's the infuriating part of this case. I simply don't know. Last night, after I left you, Mr Fielding called together all his Runners and peachers – informers – and held what amounted to a council of war. Out of it came the fact that nobody knows whether the killer is a man or a woman or two people working together, or indeed, separately.' He spread his hands in a gesture of despair.

'Or whether the targets are randomly picked or whether there is a pattern to it,' Sir Gabriel added for good measure.

'Oh, there's a pattern all right,' John answered austerely. 'Mr Fielding thinks that sad Will Swithin confided in the wrong person. But I'm not so sure. Have you heard of the Italian word *vendetta*?'

'Of course.'

'Then that is what I think this is.'

'How very disturbing.' Sir Gabriel's voice changed entirely as Mrs Harcross, who had been walking in front of them with the priest, suddenly drew to a halt and turned. 'Your servant, Ma'am.'

'Ah, Sir Gabriel, my home is just over there . . .' She caught sight of John and paused. 'I don't think I've had the pleasure . . .' And then she recognised him. 'But surely this young man is attached to the Public Office? He visited me in the company of John Fielding.'

'Whom I represent today, Madam.' John bowed. 'He asked me to convey to you his most sincere apologies and to explain that there has been a further development which precludes him from being present.' He bowed again.

Behind him he heard Sir Gabriel mutter, 'John, really!' and grimaced very slightly.

Mrs Harcross flushed. 'Oh, thank you. It was kind of him

to send you. I suppose I should invite you into the house to partake of refreshment.'

'I can vouch for his good character, Madam,' said Sir Gabriel solemnly. 'He is my son.'

'Oh, dear me. How confusing everything is. Then please to step inside. There will be quite a few people at the wake because I have invited the village folk who were kind enough to support me. But that is of no consequence. I had made provision for quite a few. You see, I had rather hoped that . . .'

John interrupted. 'Madam, please don't be disappointed. Try to see the lack of your fellow actors in context. First of all, your whereabouts, indeed the very fact of your existence, are not known to many. Secondly, the casts of *The Beggar's Opera* and the *Merchant of Venice* are acting under instruction from the Public Office. They are being questioned today about a particularly revolting murder that took place at Drury Lane last night. I think my father mentioned it to you.'

She looked nervous. 'He did and I shudder to think about it. But you are right, of course. The wish was father to the thought. Jasper kept me so well hidden during his lifetime he could hardly expect me to be attended by his colleagues in death.'

'I'm afraid that that is very true.' John turned his cane in his hand. 'Mrs Harcross, would it be possible for me to speak to you in confidence a moment?'

'In my home do you mean?'

'No, I would rather it were out here, out of earshot.'

The vicar, looking somewhat irritated, stepped away in company with Sir Gabriel and John drew Mrs Harcross into the sheltered confines of the church porch.

'How much do you know about William Swithin, the murdered boy?'

'Nothing. I had never even heard of him until today.'

The Apothecary had a moment of agonising indecision. Should he tell her the facts regarding Will's antecedents or leave her in blissful ignorance? Rapidly coming to the conclusion that the poor woman had had enough to bear, he simply said, 'Your late husband was fond of the child and it occurs to me forcefully that anyone connected with Jasper could be in danger.'

She looked absolutely astonished. 'Why, in Heaven's name?'

'A bitter hatred in the mind of someone not quite sane can lead to extraordinary events.' He thought of the vile image in his pocket and said, 'Mrs Harcross, I truly think there might be someone with a grudge against you. I beg you to be careful.'

Jasper's widow stared at him blankly. 'But you said yourself that nobody knows about me. So who could possibly wish me ill?'

The slightly ruthless streak that was very much part of the Apothecary's make up came to the forefront.

'Madam, there was a strange woman at the funeral today. She sat at the back of the church, heavily veiled, and slipped out before the end of the service. I followed her and saw her throw something into Jasper's grave. I retrieved it with my stick. It was this.'

And he handed her the puppet, wishing that he had not been forced to take this unscrupulous step.

Mrs Harcross's eyes rolled upwards and she leant against him heavily. 'But this is a representation of myself!'

'I realise that.'

'Whoever could do such a thing?'

'I don't know, but I intend to find out.' He shot her a solemn look. 'Will you take my warning seriously now?'

'Yes, yes I will. Perhaps I could get my maid to sleep in.'

'That at the very least, though a man servant would be better.' The Apothecary paused. 'Mrs Harcross, I have no wish to go over old and upsetting ground but there is one more thing I would like to know.'

'Which is?'

'The name and address of the woman in Chelsea who fostered your two children, that is before the boy went away to his apprenticeship.'

The widow frowned. 'Why do you require this?'

'Because it is a loose strand that needs to be woven into the tapestry.'

'How poetically put. But surely you cannot think they can have any connection with this sorry affair? Remember that I haven't heard from them for years.'

'Mr Fielding believes that in order to solve a crime one must look into the past, all of the past, even though most of it will not be relevant.'

Mrs Harcross sighed. 'She was a Mrs Camber of Jews Row, a house overlooking the Hospital burying ground. I don't know if she is still there. She may be dead for all I am aware.'

'I shall try to trace her.' John took her gloved hand between his. 'You are very cold, Madam, and I believe you should not stand out here any longer. Let us go into your home and rub shoulders with your neighbours. The warmth of their friendship together with a tot or two of brandy, will do you a great deal of good.'

'You are very kind,' Jasper's widow answered and most unexpectedly kissed him on the cheek.

Very proud that he had not flushed, indeed had handled the situation with aplomb, John offered her his arm and together they went down the church path towards her house.

Chapter Fifteen

By the time he got back it was well past midday and tempers were frayed at Drury Lane. David Garrick, he of the magnificent eyes and mellifluous voice, had flown into one of the finest rages ever witnessed, according to the account given by Joe Jago. Declaring that the two murders were obviously aimed at *him* and had clearly been committed by someone who wished his theatre to 'go dark', the technical phrase for shutting down, he had stormed round the place, getting in the way and putting witnesses off their stroke. Only the fact of Mr Fielding growing short-tempered with him had finally calmed the great actor down, and then he had fluttered into a fury again when Dick Weatherby had informed him that three of the stagehands had walked out, declaring that the theatre was cursed.

'I've a mind to cancel tonight's performance,' Garrick had roared.

'No, Sir, you can't do that,' Dick had answered soothingly. 'We've a full house, so think of all the money we would have to return.'

Eventually, peace had been restored, particularly when a trio of hulking characters had appeared to enquire about work, having heard a rumour on the streets that there were jobs going at Drury Lane. Thus, when John returned and sent his compliments to the Blind Beak, three of the peachers were in place, diligently making themselves useful.

'First phase completed?' John said to Jago, casting an eye in their direction.

'Not quite. There are two more to come.'

'And how has this morning's questioning gone?'

'Much as expected. Everyone expressed horror that a child should have been done to death. But nobody was near here, of course. Everyone dutifully went straight home after the performance, or out to friends who can vouch for them. There was one interesting thing, though.'

'What was that?'

'Dick Weatherby came up with the information that he left something behind and returned to the theatre. He thought he heard the murmur of voices and went to investigate, but there was nobody there.'

'What do we presume from that?'

'That Will and his visitor had concealed themselves, I suppose.'

'But why should they?'

'Therein lies the mystery. After all, Will would have nothing to hide from his friend Dick.'

'How strange,' John answered, and would have dwelt on it had not the door to the Green Room been flung open and the Blind Beak appeared, accompanied by Kitty Clive.

'She has been cleared of suspicion, by the way,' Joe murmured. 'There was insufficient time between her leaving the theatre and appearing at the Comtesse de Vignolle's card party for her to have killed the boy. She has been here today, in the main, to assist Mr Fielding as well as to make a statement.'

On an impulse, John asked the clerk, 'What do you think of her sister, Coralie? Could she be a killer?'

Joe shook his foxy head, his wig slipping alarmingly to reveal the tight red curls beneath. 'No, I don't think so. Beneath her theatrical ways she's really a very charming girl, had you not noticed?'

'Oh yes,' said the Apothecary, unable to resist giving the Blind Beak's shrewd assistant a wink. 'I've noticed all right.'

The Magistrate came to join them, Kitty still on his arm. 'Gentlemen, what news?'

'A great deal arising from the funeral, Sir, which will take me a good hour to relate.'

'Then let us postpone it until this evening. You'll take supper at Bow Street?'

'No, Sir,' John answered firmly. 'I know my father will be agog to give you his account of it. He attended, by the way, though there was no need for him to do so. Therefore, if it is not inconvenient and Mrs Fielding will accompany you, I would like to invite you to sup with us.'

'I accept with pleasure.'

'Excellent. Now, who is there left for me to see?'

'Only a couple of people. Two young women were in the theatre last night but unable to attend this morning because of their work commitments.'

'And they are?'

'Adam Verity's sister, Amelia, and Polly Rose, the seamstress. One lives above her shop in New Bond Street, in an apartment she shares with her brother. The other is in Little Earl Street in the Seven Dials. But you'll presently find her in her workroom in Maiden Lane, where she stitches the costumes.'

'Shall I go to her first and then to New Bond Street?'

'A good plan, as long as you remember to send a messenger to warn Sir Gabriel of his forthcoming supper party.'

'I'll have a note delivered by hansom, for I doubt he's even home yet. The last I saw of my father he was reminiscing with Mrs Harcross about the original production of *The Beggar's Opera*. They were deep in conversation.'

Mr Fielding rumbled his wonderful chuckle. 'Perhaps he will learn more in that manner than you or I ever could.'

'Perhaps.' John put his cloak back on. 'Well, I'll be on my way. Until this evening, Sir.'

'Elizabeth and I will join you at eight o'clock.'

John bowed. 'I look forward to it.'

It was as cold as ever and at three in the afternoon there were few hours of daylight left. Hurrying in order to keep warm, John positively sprinted past St Mary's-le-Strand burial ground, thinking he had seen quite enough of those for one day, picked his way down Russell Court, then crossed Bridge Street and made his way through York and Tavistock Streets to Maiden Lane. Here the houses leaned in closely, and the Apothecary always had the feeling of stepping back in time. Indeed, he enjoyed climbing the rickety staircase to the first floor workshop where he discovered Miss Rose sitting cross-legged upon the floor, her mouth full of pins as ever, stitching some elaborate beading onto a costume that appeared, by its rich beauty, to belong to a very famous actress indeed.

John knocked on the open door. 'May I come in, please.'

Miss Rose jumped and practically swallowed the pins. 'Who is it?'

'My name is Rawlings, Ma'am. I am assisting Mr Fielding with the collection of statements regarding the tragic deaths of Jasper Harcross and William Swithin. He said you could not attend the theatre so asked me to come and see you.'

She flushed and then whitened, a pretty little girl with an over-large and interesting mouth. A mouth, John thought, that looked both exciting and passionate.

'I've been so busy, you see. This gown is for Miss Woffington. Mr Garrick plans a production of *Anthony and Cleopatra*, with himself and the lady taking the leading parts. I've had no time to rest, struggling to get all the costumes ready, believe you me. But now, with the boy's death and everything, I reckon the play will be postponed.'

Not quite certain whether to look pleased or sympathetic, John motioned towards a stool. 'May I?'

'Oh yes, of course. Forgive my manners. It's just that I get so involved with my work.'

'Do you sew full-time for Drury Lane?'

'Yes, Sir. Mr Garrick and Mr Cecil design the outfits, of course. I just carry out their instructions.'

'Single handed?'

'No. Madame Ruffe oversees everything but another girl, Marie, and I do all the stitching.'

'That seems like a great deal of work for two young women.'

'It is very hard, Sir, but it's a regular job and wage, which is more than some can say in these bad times.'

'How right you are. Now, tell me, were you in the theatre the night that Jasper Harcross was killed?'

The girl shook her head. 'Definitely not. I only go in if one of the ladies needs help with getting dressed or to do last minute alterations and repairs. I was not called that evening.'

'But I expect you were the night before, as it was dress rehearsal.'

Polly Rose turned the shake to a nod. 'Oh yes, I was there for that.'

'Did you notice anything unusual?'

'No, I was concentrating on the clothes.'

'And were they all in order?'

'Yes, Sir. We pride ourselves on our workmanship.'

She stated this with a certain defiance and John smiled to himself. She really was a lovely thing and that mouth was one of the most interesting he had ever seen. Realising that he was frankly staring, he said, 'You know that the bow from Mrs Delaney's sleeve became detached during the performance.'

She looked uncomfortable. 'Yes, someone did say.'

'Do you think it could have been deliberately severed? As your stitching is so good, I mean.'

Polly's discomfort turned to anger. 'Are you being sarcastic, Sir?'

John adopted an extremely contrite expression. 'Indeed not.

I asked in good faith. It just seemed suspicious that something should drop off a well-made costume.'

The ardent mouth tightened. 'Yes, you are right, of course. It must have been tampered with.'

John's crooked smile lit his face. 'Now, there's a useful piece of information which adds another aspect. Could anybody have done that?'

Polly frowned enchantingly. 'The costumes hang in the dressing rooms on a rail. They are not guarded in any way. I suppose that anyone could damage them if they so desired.'

John produced Coralie's glove from his pocket and handed it to Polly, who stared at it, somewhat startled. 'Do you recognise that?'

'Yes, it's Mrs Delaney's. She wears it in *Love's Last Shift*.'

'Actually, it belongs to Miss Clive, you can smell her perfume on it.'

Polly sniffed cautiously. 'There is certainly a distinctive aroma but all the actresses wear fine scents. I could have sworn that it was Sarah's.'

'Well, there are you wrong. I am an apothecary by profession and make up my own perfumes. My sense of smell is finely attuned. There can be no doubt whatsoever that this is Coralie Clive's.' A thought struck him. 'But if you could make that mistake so might someone else.'

'What do you mean?'

'This glove was found at the scene of the crime when poor Will Swithin was hanged by the neck, which led Mr Fielding to believe that someone was trying to incriminate both the ladies. But supposing the murderer made the same mistake as you and thought it was the property of Mrs Delaney?'

Polly looked bewildered. 'It certainly is a tangled web.'

John stood up. 'And not easy to unravel. But you have been very helpful, Miss Rose. I am grateful to you.'

'Are you finished with me?' she asked, also scrambling to her feet.

'All but for one question, which is your whereabouts last night.'

'Well, I was at the theatre helping Miss Kitty. When the performance was over I hung her costumes up and cleaned the hems, then I hired a linkman and walked home.'

'As simple as that?'

'Yes.'

'Did you see Will at all?'

'Of course, he was round and about as usual.'

'There was nothing in his manner that suggested anything out of the ordinary?'

'No.'

'Ah well,' said John and clapped his hat on his head, then turned in the doorway. 'One final thing, Miss Rose.'

'Yes?'

'Forgive me asking this but as a member of the fair sex, of whom he seemed particularly fond, I would like to know your opinion of Jasper Harcross.'

The fervent lips compressed and Polly shook her head, her features oddly blank. 'I did not like him at all, Mr Rawlings. I found his womanising unbearable and uncouth. He kissed me once, backstage, and when I came home I scrubbed my mouth until it was raw. That was the effect he had upon me.' She laughed thinly. 'I know this is an unusual view of the man but I thought it best to be truthful.'

'I find that very courageous of you, you are not only beautiful but brave,' John answered, then turned to get one last look at her as he went down the spindly staircase and out into the raw November evening.

The note to Sir Gabriel having been written, John hailed a

hansom to take him to New Bond Street then deliver the letter on to Nassau Street. Not wanting to be late home, the Apothecary made good time, for the streets were empty. A freezing fog had settled over London during the late afternoon and most of its citizens had retired indoors, to seek the comfort of their hearths. Looking out of the carriage window, John was particularly struck by how little light could be seen as they bowled down Long Acre, then through a labyrinth of alleys to Leicester Fields, where only the candles in the houses threw tiny points of light to gash the gloom. Finally, though, they were in Piccadilly, where the bulk of Burlington House and its many chandeliers lit the scene before they turned off into Old Bond Street, which ran into New, past Evans Row where John had been apprenticed to Richard Purefoy, Apothecary.

As luck would have it, he caught Miss Amelia Verity shutting up her shop and was, having introduced himself, able to accompany her up the stairs to the very stylish apartment she occupied with her brother. And the style did not end there, John thought. For Miss Verity was as beautifully turned out as any fine lady of the town, and had worked so hard on her face and hair that she appeared lovely though, in fact, she was not naturally blessed. Taking in every aspect, the Apothecary struggled to find a resemblance between her and Mrs Harcross and wondered if there was a faint similarity about the mouth.

It seemed to be the day for mouths, he reflected, for the voluptuous beauty of Miss Rose's lips haunted him still. And though Miss Verity's was very different, a little flower of a thing with a mercurial smile never far away, it was equally arresting in a totally contrasting manner.

Placing him in a comfortable chair by her gleaming fire, Amelia, unexpectedly, took the conversational lead.

'Now I know you have come to ask me questions and I shall do my best to answer them. But, to save time, I have prepared an account of my movements which I thought might be of help to you.' Crossing to her desk, she fetched a piece of paper covered with words written in an elegant flowing hand and passed it to John.

He cast his eyes over it and gleaned that she had not been in the theatre on the night of Jasper's murder but had attended the dress rehearsal for a while. She had come home before her brother and they had then shared a late supper. She had made hats for Mr Harcross and treated him in an entirely professional manner, even though she had little time for him as a person. She had created some new headgear for Kitty Clive, which she had taken to Drury Lane while the performance of *The Merchant of Venice* was still on, but had not stayed until the end. She had seen Will but had not had a conversation with him.

John looked up, somewhat amused by her business-like style. 'This seems very comprehensive. I don't think I have anything left to say.'

'Then would you like a glass of sherry?' she asked, and crossed to a small table which held a decanter and two glasses.

'Very much indeed.' The Apothecary gazed round him. 'May I say how greatly I admire your taste in decor. This apartment really is charming and so beautifully furnished. Don't think me rude, but it seems to me that you and your brother do very well for yourselves.'

'Oh yes,' she answered smilingly, passing him a small crystal glass. 'We make a comfortable living between us.'

'You have always lodged together?'

Amelia's face clouded. 'No, we were separated for a short while when we were children. My brother and I are orphans, you see, and were brought up by a foster mother.'

'Where?' said John, innocently.

'In Chelsea, actually. Why do you ask?'

'Mere idle curiosity. You were saying?'

'Well, he was sent off to be apprenticed – those were the months we were apart – but as he had always longed to go on the stage he ran away to Ipswich to train with Mr Giffard. Happily, he kidnapped me and we went off together into the darkness of night, not telling a soul. It was enormous fun.'

John laughed. 'It must have been. And you have stayed with one another ever since?'

'We are very close as we have shared misfortune from an early age. Now we intend to stay as a unit until one or other or both of us marry.'

'Is there any likelihood of that?'

Amelia smiled delightfully. 'I am a good catch, Mr Rawlings, as is Adam. He is handsome, young, and an actor. In fact he is currently having an *affaire de coeur* with a Duchess, older than he is, of course. Her husband does not know, by the way.'

John laughed again, deciding he enjoyed her company. 'And what about yourself?'

'As I said, I have several suitors, most of them with one eye on my excellent business. This puts me off enormously and I am therefore waiting until I meet someone who can match my professional acumen. When that day comes we shall unite our trades and be very successful.'

'I wish you luck,' said John.

'Another glass of sherry before you go, Mr Rawlings?'

'How very kind of you, I should be delighted.'

And in this pleasant manner John spent another half hour in Miss Verity's presence before a glance at his watch told him it was time to go home.

Even though prepared in haste, Sir Gabriel Kent's supper party proved a great success if somewhat unconventional in fashion. Because of the extreme confidentiality of the subject under discussion, the servants were given the evening to themselves once the main course had been served. Thus, the host and his son waited on table, a task that both of them rather enjoyed.

Also dispensed with was the custom of the ladies retiring while the gentlemen enjoyed their port. As such a vital member of the party, her husband's eyes as it were, Elizabeth Fielding was accompanied to the library by all the rest of the group and took part in the conversation, displaying a lively wit.

John spoke first, telling the Magistrate all that had happened in Kensington, even drawing the puppet from his pocket and passing it round. Mrs Fielding recoiled from it with a look of horror.

'What a gruesome thing. Whoever would want to frighten Mrs Harcross like that? The killer is obviously unhinged.'

'Tormented would be a better word, I think,' her husband replied calmly. 'Taken up with wreaking revenge on Jasper Harcross and all his kin – or so it would appear.'

'I believe there might well be two murderers,' John put in. 'A woman crossed in love and a madman.'

'The missing Egleton children?' asked Sir Gabriel.

'That is one possibility, certainly,' answered the Blind Beak. 'Though the thought could be leading us down the wrong path. However, this strange woman seen in the church is certainly the strongest clue we have so far. You did not recognise her at all, Mr Rawlings?'

'Unfortunately, no. But there's something else. Do you remember that Coralie was visited by a veiled woman announcing herself as Mrs Harcross? Well, it occurs to me that if it was *not* Mrs Harcross, though I am still in two minds about that, it might well have been the woman at the funeral today.'

Mr Fielding looked stern. 'Whether there be one or two killers, crazed or sane, the time has come to flush him or her or them out. I have devised a plan which I have already discussed with your son, Sir Gabriel. *If* I can get it to work – and it calls for the co-operation of several people, all of whom are somewhat temperamental – it should give the killer a sense of false security, so much so that he may feel confident to strike again. But this time, mark my words, we will be prepared for him.'

'What is this scheme?'

'You are aware that a glove found in the room in which Will was murdered belonged to Miss Coralie?'

'Yes.'

'And you are equally aware that that was the murderer's first blunder. Little did he know that Miss Clive's movements could be accounted for entirely that evening.'

John interrupted. 'Excuse me, Sir, but I must just say this. Miss Polly Rose, the seamstress, thought the glove belonged to Mrs Delaney, would have sworn to it in fact. If she could be deceived so could someone else. I believe that it is Sarah they are trying to incriminate.'

'But were she to be accused of murder she could plead her belly,' Elizabeth put in. 'That means transportation once the child is born.'

'A fair way of getting rid of her none the less,' said Sir Gabriel grimly.

'Be that as it may,' answered the Magistrate, taking charge of the conversation once more, 'we cannot let this state of affairs go on. Therefore, I am going to ask Lady Delaney and her doting husband to leave London for their country seat. Then I intend somehow to persuade Miss Coralie to fake a disappearance but actually go and live in Sarah's house, in other words to take her place.'

Sir Gabriel looked blank. 'But why?'

'So that, with Coralie gone, suspected of murder, the killer will strike at Lady Delaney. That is if our theory of a vendetta against Jasper and his progeny is correct.'

'Wouldn't that put Miss Clive in the most terrible danger?'

'No, because all the servants in the house will be replaced by my men. Furthermore, I shall ask Mr Rawlings to move in with her to make doubly sure that all is well.'

The Apothecary felt sweat break out on his brow at the very thought. 'She'll never consent,' he said rapidly. 'It would be like tying her up as a sacrificial goat.'

'I agree with that,' said Elizabeth firmly. 'No woman should be subjected to such peril. Besides, what if either of the two ladies is the killer? After all, your idea of revenge perpetrated by a jilted mistress could still be the correct one.'

'That is a chance I will have to take, though only if she is working with somebody else could Miss Coralie be guilty. The same applies to Lady Delaney, I believe, much slowed down by her increasing size and obviously in no state to commit a violent crime,' Mr Fielding said unyieldingly. He cleared his throat, indicating that the subject was closed. 'And now, let us hear the rest of today's news. What was your impression of Mrs Harcross, Sir Gabriel?'

'I liked her enormously . . .'

'That was obvious!' muttered John.

His father looked at him severely. '. . . and feel it unlikely that she is a criminal. In fact I believe that the very fact she has been given a witchcraft symbol proves her innocence.'

'My dear father,' John said with a sigh, 'please remember that Mrs Harcross was the finest actress of her day. The stricken widow, the terrified woman, could all be part of some calculated act to hide the fact that she is guilty of murder.'

'But you yourself warned her that she might be in peril.'

'Indeed I did – and so she might be. But I am not as convinced by her as you are.'

'For all that,' Sir Gabriel replied coolly, 'it is my intention to move Mrs Harcross to some safe place, where I can also keep my eye on her.'

'Gracious heavens!' exclaimed Elizabeth. 'Will anyone be left in their own home?'

'No one who I think could be endangered by being there,' her husband answered seriously. He turned to John. 'What did you make of the two young ladies I asked you to see?'

'They were both charming in their very different ways. Miss Rose is a tense little thing, obviously overburdened with work. Her evidence was not very useful except for the fact that she detested Jasper Harcross and admitted it. And, as I've already informed you, she believed the glove to be Coralie's.'

'And she has seen and heard nothing of interest?'

'Not that she told me.'

'And Miss Verity?'

'She admitted that she was fostered out in Chelsea, as were the Egleton children.'

'Could she and Adam be one and the same?'

'They certainly could.'

'There is absolutely no proof that Mrs Harcross's children had anything to do with these crimes, you know.'

'Indeed there isn't,' answered John. 'But, never the less, we must consider all possibilities.'

Mr Fielding rose from his chair and loomed magnificently. 'Whoever it is, there is a dangerous killer at large. Tomorrow I shall go and see Coralie Clive and attempt to persuade her to accept my plan.'

'And I shall visit Jew's Row, Chelsea,' the Apothecary answered.

'Are you not going to your shop, my friend?'

'No, I will ask my deputy to do that. If you have no objection, Sir, there is something I would like to check on.'

'When I asked you to help me,' the Magistrate answered, 'I expected you to act as a free agent.' He bowed to Sir Gabriel. 'Good night to you, Sir. An excellent repast, for which I thank you.'

And so saying, his wife led him from the room, leaving both John and his father with the strong impression that even the famous Blind Beak was both baffled and disturbed by these apparently inexplicable theatrical murders.

Chapter Sixteen

Much to John's disappointment his plan to visit Chelsea, where he had hoped to find out more about the children of Mrs Harcross's first marriage, was brought to an abrupt halt. Shortly before breakfast a messenger arrived with a note from the Master of Ned Holby, the apprentice in the last year of his studies who ran John's shop for him when he was about Mr Fielding's business. It said, very simply, that Ned had taken to his bed with a quinsy, and sorry though they were to incommode Mr Rawlings it was a matter beyond their control. They hoped he understood and so on. Reading the note as he finished getting dressed, the Apothecary toyed with the idea of not opening the premises in Shug Lane that day, then decided that it would be extremely bad for business if he did not. And, as is often the way of things, having made that disagreeable choice he was pleased he did so.

First to patronise him, wearing a beaming smile and looking as full of vitality as was possible for a man of his age, came Lord Delaney, bearing another long list.

'My dear young friend, I simply cannot tell you how vigorous your various lotions and potions have made me feel. As for Sarah, she is blooming with health. As you can imagine, though, recent events have upset her and she has decided to retire from the theatre immediately.'

'She knows about William Swithin?'

'Alas, yes. News travels quickly. Melanie Vine called with one of her gentlemen friends and told her everything. They all cried for quite a long while, saying that they had always been fond of the child.' Lord Delaney looked serious. 'Who is doing these terrible things, Mr Rawlings? Is it a person deranged?'

'In a way, yes.' Remembering Mr Fielding's plan, John continued, 'The most common view is that the crimes are being committed by someone who has a grudge against Jasper Harcross which, as far as I can see, amounts to about ninety per cent of the population. In fact the Beak is advising everyone who was connected with the man to leave London, so soon the city will be completely empty!'

Lord Delaney did not smile. 'Zounds, then it is serious indeed. What a relief that Sarah was no more than a working companion to him, so that we can safely stay,' he said, mopping his brow.

Cursing himself for his blunder, John attempted to retrieve the situation. 'None the less, it might be wiser to remove Lady Delaney to your country seat. For all we know, this killer might be attacking people who so much as spoke to the dead man.'

Lord Delaney paled. 'Do you really think so?'

The Apothecary told the truth. 'I don't know what to think, my Lord. Even Mr Fielding admits that he is baffled, there are so many possibilities. All I know is that if I had been even vaguely friendly with the victim I would remove myself as quickly as possible.'

The older man fingered his chin anxiously. 'Can you dine with us soon, my friend? Perhaps tomorrow or the next day, no later. Just send a note round when you would like to come. I know that Sarah respects your judgement and will listen to what you say.'

'Does she not like your country place, then?'

'Not in the winter. She says it's too damnably cold.'

'Better that than cold in the grave,' John said thoughtlessly, then wished he had guarded his tongue as Lord Delaney shot him a stricken and wretched glance. 'Don't worry, Sir,' the

Apothecary continued, realising that his cheery tone was falling flat in the frightened silence. 'I will come tomorrow, and between us we can surely persuade Lady Delaney to leave town until this terrible business is over.'

'I think I'll return to her straight away,' answered his Lordship. 'Can you make this list up and bring it with you?'

'Certainly. Now, my Lord, would you like a quick tonic? Something to restore your spirits?'

The old man nodded feebly, and feeling extremely ashamed of himself for being so tactless, John put a good measure of brandy into the reviving drink.

It was obviously going to be one of those extraordinary mornings, for no sooner had John waved farewell to his elderly visitor than a sedan chair put down outside his shop. Half expecting it to be Coralie, for the simple reason that that was the method of transport she had used when the actress had visited him before, the Apothecary felt a momentary thrill of disappointment when the Comtesse de Vignolle's buckled and brocaded shoe set itself on the cobbles. But this feeling passed instantly and he hurried into the street to help his friend inside.

Today, Serafina looked particularly lovely, her smile captivating, her eyes brimming with gaiety, her elegant racehorse figure showing her clothes to advantage. And yet, John thought, surveying her, there was something different about her. He let his eyes drop rapidly to her abdomen and there, sure enough, was the first sign of waxing. Certain that he was right, the Apothecary kissed her hand. The woman he had once adored was with child.

'My dear,' she said, sweeping into his shop and embracing him. 'How is everything? Are you any nearer reaching a solution?'

It was perfectly obvious that, being outside the theatrical circle, she had not heard about Will Swithin and John hesitated

whether to tell her. She was clearly so happy, so delighted with
the miracle of her child, that to spoil her joy would have been
cruelty itself. And yet she was such a highly respected and
fascinating woman that her views were listened to, particularly
by haughty young ladies like Coralie Clive. John decided to
compromise.

'Unfortunately, Comtesse, there was another murder on the
very night that I supped with you last. A child called Will
Swithin, the theatre boy, was done to death. It was very
shocking and very terrible but good may yet come out of it.
Mr Fielding has formulated some masterly plan by which he can
draw the murderer into the open. You might be able to help.'

'Me?' echoed Serafina, and listened intently as John ex-
plained everything to her. 'But surely,' she said when he had
finished, 'Coralie will not refuse to do this for, if so, I shall be
mightily disappointed in her. Why, I would give my eye teeth
to help thwart such a monster.'

John smiled his irregular smile. 'Comtesse, I rather imagine your days of being the most mysterious and talked-about
woman in London are drawing to a close. I fear you will not
be able to play Coralie's part.' And he winked at her.

She stared at him suspiciously. 'Why, you little devil . . .
How did you know?'

He assumed pomposity. 'Madam, I am an apothecary and
trained to observe the human physique in all its many . . .'

But he got no further. Serafina fell upon him, laughing
joyfully, and tickling him until he admitted defeat. Just for
a moment, though, when she was close, John held her in
his arms and looked into her face. 'I was in love with you
once,' he said. 'Did you know?'

'Of course I did. And I loved you too, for all the good you
did to my morale. It was exciting to be admired, even from
afar, by one of the most attractive young men in town.'

'Are you referring to me?'

'Certainly I am.'

'Then I thank you,' John answered, and kissed her with enthusiasm. Life being what it is, it was into this scene that Coralie Clive decided to walk.

'I am extremely sorry to interrupt,' she stated icily.

The Comtesse turned a radiant smile on her. 'My dear, you are not. John and I are friends of long standing. In fact, I would go so far as to say that had I not been married to Louis, I would seriously have considered him for a lover at one stage in my life. But now, come and join our fun. Today I am announcing to the *beau monde* that I am *enceinte*. Please share my happiness.' And she held out her hand in such a welcoming gesture that Coralie could not resist and was swept into the mutual embrace.

Very conscious of the actress's body close to his, John broke away for the sake of decorum. 'My dear Miss Clive, you called in to see me. How may I help you?'

'Perhaps by explaining this.' And she showed him the letter from Bow Street, requesting her to attend Mr Fielding as quickly as possible about a matter of some urgency which he wished to discuss with her.

Making a lightning quick decision, John decided to plead ignorance. 'I am terribly sorry, Miss Clive, I have no idea why the Beak should ask to see you. I am not privy to all his thoughts. Perhaps he would like your help with something.'

'But how could I possibly assist *him*?'

'Oh come, come. There are so many ways in which a woman could be useful,' put in Serafina, her eyes gleaming. 'After all, you are an actress, my dear.' She paused momentarily, then added, 'I do wish I were closer to it all. How pleased I would be if Mr Fielding asked help of me.'

'Why?' asked Coralie, astonished.

'Because I would like to be the one who sends a child slayer to Tyburn Tree, I mean it truly.'

'Did you know,' said John, 'that the killer left one of your gloves at the scene of Will's murder?'

'Yes, Kitty told me. But for what reason? Is he trying to implicate me?'

'I'm not sure,' the Apothecary answered. 'You see, when I showed that glove to Polly Rose she thought it belonged to Sarah Delaney. It seems to me that she is the one at whom the killer is trying to point the finger.'

'But why?'

'Because she is carrying Jasper Harcross's child, I would imagine.'

'It is all so horrible,' said Coralie, with emotion. 'I no longer feel safe in my bed at night.'

'Then the sooner the murderer is captured the better,' the Comtesse stated firmly. 'If Mr Fielding calls for your assistance then give it my dear, I beg of you.'

'I shall certainly think about it.'

'May I hail you a chair, Miss Clive?' John asked pointedly.

'Thank you, I can manage,' she answered primly.

Overwhelmed by a desire to shake her really hard, the Apothecary for all that pressed a small bottle of perfume into her hand. 'Please accept this as a gift. It is a new fragrance which I have created myself.'

'And what is it called?'

'It does not have a name as yet. Perhaps you can think of one for me.'

'How about Eau de Bow Street?' she replied instantly, and with that turned on her heel and was gone.

'I would like to strangle that girl,' said John forcefully.

Serafina laughed. 'It is only because you are strongly attracted to each other and neither of you knows how to respond – as yet.'

'And what do you mean by that?'

'That there is still such a lot of living left for you to do,

both you and she. You have met too soon. It would have
been better in ten years' time.'

'Yet I feel attracted to others too, that's the devil of it. There's
a funny little seamstress with a mouth that beggars description,
so beautiful and so savage that I long for its touch. Then there's
Amelia Verity who runs a hat shop in New Bond Street. What a
neat and charming girl – with a business to match.' He turned
to the Comtesse in genuine bewilderment. 'What is the matter
with me, Serafina, that I like them all?'

She held his face between her hands. 'You are a perfectly
normal young man, John. That is all that is wrong with you.
If you do not believe me, ask your father.'

'But what of Coralie? Is she the heartless wretch I sometimes
believe?'

'She is probably in exactly the same predicament as yourself,
not knowing which way to turn. Remember that the affair with
Jasper Harcross must have hurt her badly.'

The Apothecary sighed. 'Yes, you are right, of course . . .'

But he could say no more, his next words drowned by
a terrible commotion in the street outside. Wheeling round,
both he and the Comtesse stared in amazement at the scene.
Approaching his shop at great speed, not so much running as
galloping, came Jack Masters of the craggy face and pipe. Right
behind him, loping like a gazelle, came the tall red-headed
figure of Melanie Vine. Bringing up the rear, puffing and
crimson-faced and groaning with the exertion, was the rotund
form of Tom Bowdler, fanning himself with his hat as he ran.
Even while John gazed in astonishment, Jack shot inside.

'You must come at once,' he panted. 'There is not a moment
to lose.'

'What's the matter?' asked John, automatically reaching for
the bag he used when visiting the sick.

'It's Clarice Martin, she's dying. We don't know what to
do.'

'What are her symptoms? You must tell me so that I can bring the right things.'

'She's been poisoned,' gasped Melanie, hurling herself through the door. 'We called round to see her and when we got there she was unconscious on the floor, cold as ice but in a terrible sweat.'

'Has she vomited at all?' John demanded, throwing medicaments into his bag.

'Oh no,' puffed Tom. 'If she had I would have known at once. Can't stand the smell.'

'You should have called a local physician,' John said frantically as they piled into a hansom obtained by Serafina from Piccadilly. 'It's a fair stretch to Portugal Street. She may be dead by the time we get there.'

'We felt no one else should know.'

'God's great wounds! This is no time for sensitivity.' And John groaned in despair as the driver hurled them through Leicester Fields, down Bear Street and through all the back alleys of Covent Garden in order to get them to their destination before a woman's life came to its untimely end.

Chapter Seventeen

Afterwards he never knew how he had saved her. She lay on the floor, billowing like a sail, but as still and white as a ship becalmed. Kneeling down beside Mrs Martin's body, John sniffed her breath and thought he detected, beneath the brandy fumes, the sweet smell of an extract drawn from the unripe seed capsule of a poppy. He, himself, had compounded it many times to help those in pain or who could not sleep. But it seemed that in this case a fatal dose had been administered which, together with the effects of alcohol, had all but done for Clarice Martin. To confirm his diagnosis John raised her slumberous eyelid. The pupil of the eye was minute, a mere pinpoint, while the breathing was so depressed as to be almost non-existent. Desperately, John turned to Melanie Vine, who hovered beside him like an anxious dragonfly.

'She must get rid of the poison, it's the only way. Where is her kitchen?'

'Out there.'

'Then bring me a bowl, a cup and a kettle full of warm water. Go on, hurry!'

He had brought common salt, that great cure-all, with him and now he prepared to make the emetic while poor Melanie, having found the things he wanted, wept nearby.

'It's not so much that I was fond of her, in fact she was really quite terrible at times, but for all that she had a good side, a generous side. Besides, I have known her for years and I don't like to lose my old acquaintances.'

'She's not gone yet,' John replied grimly, administering a feather to the back of Mrs Martin's throat.

'Is this an accident or has the murderer struck again?'

'It may be neither.'

'What do you mean?'

But John could not answer as his wretched patient began to rid herself of the fluids that were killing her, barely conscious though she was.

An hour later it was all over. The contents of her stomach were gone and Mrs Martin had been put to bed by all four of the rescue party, lifting as one. She lay against the white sheets, totally drained of strength, still fighting for survival, for the poisonous combination of brandy and opium would by now have entered her system and there was little further that anyone could do. For all that, John sent Jack Masters, the fastest on foot, to fetch a physician.

'Will she live?' asked Melanie, taking Tom's hand for comfort.

'She might. It really is too soon to say.'

'What exactly were you trying to tell me earlier when you said it might be neither accident nor murder?'

'It could be a suicide attempt, Mrs Vine. I shall know a little more when I have looked at the various bottles and glasses.'

And certainly, John thought, as he examined the brandy decanter, if this had been an attempted murder it was a very clever one. No opium had been added to the brandy, that was clear from the smell. And a patient search of the bedroom revealed an apothecary's bottle which Mrs Martin had obviously purchased in order to help her sleep. Yet another *could* have been present, a person clever enough to pour a dose in Clarice's glass while her back was turned, then wash his own and put it away. Very carefully John put the stopper back in the decanter and, together with the actress's medicine, placed them in a cupboard which he locked, slipping the key into his waistcoat pocket. This done, he awaited the arrival of the physician, who listened to his story gravely, examined the patient, gave instructions that she should be kept warm and that he should be sent for immediately if she either regained consciousness or died, and went.

'What about James?' asked Tom.

'I think he should be sent for,' answered Jack.

'I'm not certain,' said Melanie.

John spoke up. 'Whatever their quarrel he might be deeply upset if you don't at least give him the chance to see her. Why doesn't one of you go to The Hercules Pillars and tell him?'

They could not agree and the Apothecary left the trio of lovers arguing quietly amongst themselves, voices lowered out of respect for the patient, who still lay in that deep unnatural sleep which bodes no good.

'If there is any change in Mrs Martin's condition I'd be obliged if you could let me know,' he said, picking up his bag and hat. 'But for the love of God fetch the physician first this time.'

Jack Masters got to his feet. 'What about your bill, Mr Rawlings?'

'I intend to waive it.'

'I'll hear of no such thing. You're to send it to me, d'ye understand?'

'Very well. It shall be as you say.'

He had left Serafina to lock up his shop for him, then return the keys to Nassau Street. So now, with Bow Street so near by, the most sensible thing seemed to be to call on Mr Fielding and inform him of developments. Aware that the court would be sitting at this time, John squeezed his way into the back of the public gallery in order to listen.

As usual, the courtroom was packed with spectators, it being considered de rigeur by the *beau monde* to visit the Public Office at least once a week and there enjoy the diversion of watching a blind man administer justice. And today was no exception, for there was an exciting case to be heard. The highwayman, William Page, had been apprehended and was about to be sent for trial at the Old Bailey. Rather glad that he had chosen this occasion to make a visit, John crushed into the only space left, a minute gap between two ladies.

William Page was an unusual robber, to say the least of it. Tall, handsome and of impeccable appearance, his game was to drive about in a phaeton and pair posing as a man of fashion. He would then disguise himself with mask and wig, unharness one of the horses, hold people up, and finally return to his other persona of perfect gentleman in order to escape undetected. John had to admit that he had a sneaking admiration for the man's coolness and daring, and in company with the entire assembly rose to his feet to get a better view as Page was led in.

The rogue was attractive enough to enthrall any woman, that was obvious from one quick glance at him, and there were shrieks and moans from the fair sex as he was led to the bar. Acknowledging this with a nod of his head, Page smiled directly at a woman sitting in the front row, near enough to touch him, and at this she grew faint and leant heavily on her male companion. Hoping desperately that no one in his vicinity was going to swoon, John tried to concentrate on Mr Fielding's opening remarks and so was totally unprepared for what happened next.

The Magistrate was just telling the accused to state his name when Page slumped forward, groaning and clutching his chest. Somewhat nonplussed, Mr Fielding, hearing the uproar, leaned over to ask Joe Jago what was going on. Even while the clerk was whispering, Page groaned again and crashed to the floor, apparently unconscious. The like of it had obviously never been seen in the magistrates' court before. Mr Fielding, judging by the uproar all around him and the continued frantic murmurings of his clerk, realised that everything was far from well and called out, 'It would seem that the prisoner is ill. Is there a physician in the court?'

John stood up in his crowded stall. 'I am an apothecary, Sir.'

The black bandage turned sharply in his direction. 'Is that Mr Rawlings's voice I hear?'

'Yes, Sir.'

'Then pray come round and deal with the situation, if you would be so good.'

As John was sitting in the upper gallery, his exit was far from easy. Pushing past an inordinate number of hooped skirts, to the enormous irritation of their inhabitants, he finally managed to extricate himself, sprint down the staircase behind the raised area and enter the court through the lower door. Not hesitating a moment, John ran to the inert figure of William Page and turned him over to start his examination.

Everything that happened after that was so quick that it was difficult to recount the sequence of events. As far as John could recall, one of Page's eyes opened and stared into his. It was a brilliant eye, the colour of farm-brewed Somerset cider. Just for a moment this eye held his own and the Apothecary saw the highwayman mouth the words, 'Thank you.' Then followed a crunch on the jaw that defied belief, apparently being rendered by a fist made of iron. John just had time to say 'What. . . ?' before stars flew before his eyes and the world went dark.

He recovered consciousness in Mr Fielding's private quarters, laid upon a neat white bed with neat white drapery in a room in which it was already growing dusk. Sitting by the bed, staring anxiously into his face, were Joe Jago and Elizabeth Fielding, the Magistrate's wife sponging his brow with a cool cloth.

'Well, that was a rum do,' said the clerk as John's eyes flickered open.

'What happened? Did he escape?'

'Of course he did.' Jago chuckled. 'For all he's a rogue and a rum cove he's a duke padder and no mistake.'

Elizabeth looked at him reproachfully. 'That really is no way to speak of a man who has just eluded the confines of the law.'

The foxy-faced clerk looked as remorseful as was possible for someone with his scampish set of features. 'Beg pardon, Madam. It's just the sheer bravado of the man impresses me.'

John sat up slowly, nursing his aching jaw. 'I'll give him bravado if he ever crosses my path again.'

'Don't speak too soon, Mr Rawlings. He just might for all that.'

'One never knows.' John looked round him, taking in the fact that it was nearly dark. 'Is the court still sitting?'

Jago chuckled again and earned another reproving look from Elizabeth. 'It broke up in disarray, my friend. There were ladies fainting and gentlemen drawing swords wherever one looked. 'Twas like a scene from Hockley Hole, I can assure you. Mr Fielding banged his gavel and called for silence, threatening he would hold them all in contempt. But it was to no avail. As the villain flew out the door and into the street, so those nearest charged after him. I was so afraid you might be crushed to death in the stampede that I jumped down and picked you up myself. It took the Brave Fellows ten minutes to quell the riot.'

'But how did Page escape? Surely he would have been noticed, flying full pelt down Bow Street?'

'The Runner on the door said a coach was drawn up and waiting for him. He hopped in neat as you please. It was all planned, Sir. You just happened to get yourself into the middle of it.'

John smiled painfully. 'I agree, one has to admire the audacity of the chap.'

'Now, that will be enough,' said Mrs Fielding firmly. 'My

husband is downstairs with Miss Clive. Do you feel well enough to join them?'

'I think so,' the Apothecary answered, but was still glad of Joe Jago's arm as they descended the bending staircase.

It was a strange evening, for John, whether through his exertions of that morning or as a result of the fist in his face, felt in an oddly silent mood. Indeed, it was with difficulty that he recounted his story of being summoned to Mrs Martin's side, and his fight to save her life. And even though his audience were all sympathy he longed to be out of their presence, to walk on his own and catch his breath after everything that had taken place that day. Even Coralie's sparkling emerald gaze could not beguile him and, eventually, not knowing whether the actress had agreed to Mr Fielding's plan or not, he begged to take his leave.

'Let me get one of our carriages to take you back,' said the Magistrate, clearly concerned.

'No, I would rather walk, Sir. If Mr Page ever ceased to ride as a highwayman he could certainly make his living as a bare-knuckle fighter.'

Coralie laughed, but sympathetically. 'Poor Mr Rawlings, what a terrible day you have had.'

'The morning was good,' he replied enigmatically, and with those words made his departure.

It was cold again, with the same freezing fog that had pervaded the capital the previous night. Pulling his cloak round him, John hurried along bemoaning the lack of linkmen, then realised that he must have taken the wrong turning off Drury Lane and instead of heading towards Nassau Street was going in the direction of the Seven Dials. Swearing volubly, the Apothecary was just about to change course when a figure that seemed somehow familiar came towards him out of the mist. Compelled by the notion that he must hide, John slunk into a doorway and watched as the woman went by. She had a linkman with her and, as they passed, the light of his lantern lit her features. John gasped audibly in surprise. He was looking at the saddened, but once beautiful face of Mrs Jasper Harcross.

She must have heard him for she paused momentarily and called out, 'Who's there?'

' 'Tis only a rat, Mam,' answered her escort, 'this part of London's heaving with 'em.'

'Oh God help me,' she whispered and continued on her way.

Any idea he might have had of following her was brought to an abrupt halt by a sudden weakness in John's knees. Cursing the name of the debonair Mr Page, the Apothecary had no choice but to get back as best he could to the main thoroughfare, there to seek a hansom cab. But even this scheme was to be thwarted. Suddenly overcome by a feeling of nausea, John clutched at a nearby wall for support and would have fallen to the cobbles had not somebody caught him and set him back on his feet.

'Mr Rawlings,' said a startled voice, 'whatever are you doing out this way? You haven't come to see me, have you?'

It was Dick Weatherby.

Chapter Eighteen

The next hour had passed in something of a blur and John had not come fully to his senses until he had looked around him and seen that he was in his own room, in bed, with Sir Gabriel, *en déshabillé* in gown and turban, sitting in a chair near by. The fire had been lit and a physician hovered beside him, administering a filthy tasting potion which, for all its foul properties, seemed none the less to have restored him to a modicum of normality.

'My dear child,' said his father, 'thank heavens to see you stirring. A message came from Bow Street that you had been involved in fisticuffs with a highwayman. God's truth, whatever next, I ask myself.'

The physician smiled a dry smile, somewhat typical of his profession. 'You have certainly been struck very hard, Master John. Dear me, such pranks.'

Not having the energy to discuss what had happened, the Apothecary simply asked, 'As a matter of interest, what was in the potion?'

The doctor tapped the side of his nose. 'Ah ha! A little secret remedy of my own. Not to be shared with anyone. Now, my boy, it is bed rest for you for at least a day.'

'But I have to go to Chelsea tomorrow,' John insisted. 'It is most urgent that I do.'

'You are quite definitely not to undertake any long and arduous journeys,' and the physician shook his head.

'I really must get up,' John persisted. 'It is imperative that

I visit certain people in town at the very least.'

'He'll fret if you don't say yes,' Sir Gabriel assured the medical man. 'I know him of old.' And he smiled at John the rare and lovely smile which always warmed the Apothecary's heart.

The physician sighed. 'Oh, very well. It will do you twice as much harm to lie in bed worrying as it will to exert yourself. But no visits to Chelsea, mind. You may take a carriage round the centre of town but that is all.'

Sir Gabriel stood up, unfolding his black-clad length from the wing chair. 'You may safely leave him in my charge, Dr Bryant. I shall watch him with an eagle eye.'

At that they left the room and John leant back against the pillow, trying to remember all that had happened after he had left Bow Street. He had taken the wrong turning, that much was certain, and then he had seen Mrs Harcross, he was absolutely positive he had. The Apothecary frowned, wondering whether that unlikely sighting could possibly be an illusion created by the blow he had received earlier. Yet he was sure it had been her, though what she was doing wandering near Drury Lane was a subject almost beyond conjecture.

John thought on. He had reeled away towards the main thoroughfare, too weak to pursue her, and had practically fallen into the arms of Dick Weatherby, who lived in Seven Dials and was returning home to fetch some clean clothes.

'Why?' John remembered asking him stupidly.

'Because I've taken to sleeping in the theatre. There's an atmosphere in the place I don't like at all and I'm determined that nothing sinister will happen there again.'

'So it's your opinion that the murderer is going to strike once more?' John had asked.

'Yes, I believe so,' Dick had answered, then had bundled the Apothecary into a hansom before he could ask any more questions.

The door opened and Sir Gabriel stood there.'How are you

feeling, my boy? Would you like some food?'

'Please, in a moment. But there is something I want to say to you first. Earlier tonight, before Dick put me in a carriage, I saw Mrs Harcross, walking along a deserted street in Seven Dials. I can hardly credit it. What could she possibly have been doing there?'

'Well, anyone can visit London.'

'So soon after her husband's funeral? No, there was something strange about it, I feel utterly convinced.'

Sir Gabriel frowned. 'Perhaps I should go and visit her tomorrow in order to enquire about her health.'

'And if she is not at home?'

'Then we can draw our own conclusions.' His father looked thoughtful. 'Serafina called on me with your keys. She told me that you were summoned out to save a life. Did you succeed in doing so?'

'I don't know, unfortunately. It was Mrs Martin, mother of that wretched boy who was the victim. Someone, possibly herself, had administered her a huge dose of brandy and opium.'

'Then let us hope the poor woman wins her fight, otherwise James Martin will be bereft.'

John shook his head. 'No, he hates her. He told me so himself.'

'Of that,' said Sir Gabriel, smiling a little sadly, 'I wouldn't be quite so certain.'

Despite falling asleep feeling jaded and sick, the Apothecary woke the next morning full of a fierce determination to find answers to all the questions that bothered him. High on the list was the fate of Mrs Martin, whom he had left hovering between life and death. Secondly was the question of whether Coralie Clive had agreed to take part in Mr Fielding's plan to catch a killer. Yet fortunately for John's growing sense of frustration, the solution to the first uncertainty was awaiting him when he went downstairs to breakfast.

'A message has come from Mrs Vine,' said Sir Gabriel without looking up from his newspaper. 'It arrived during the small hours. Apparently Mrs Martin has recovered consciousness, the physician has been called and pronounces that she will live, her husband is at her bedside, and all's well that ends well.' He glanced upwards then looked again. 'Merciful heavens, have you seen your face?'

'Yes,' said John curtly, fingering his jaw.

'It is truly quite spectacular.'

'Thank you.'

Sir Gabriel laughed. 'Actually it makes you look extremely heroic and will no doubt bring a great deal of sympathy from the ladies.'

'How nice.'

'And there is no need to be irritable. I have a letter here from Ned Holby's Master, saying that the lad is feeling much better and will look after your shop for you today.'

'Well, that's one relief, I suppose.'

John's father dropped his bantering tone. 'Are you still not well, my dear?'

'Physically I am in good fettle, other than for this king of all bruises. But my brain will not be easy. What the devil was Mrs Harcross doing in Seven Dials last night? And did someone try to kill Mrs Martin or was her sickness self-inflicted? How can anyone relax with such things on their mind?'

'They can't,' said Sir Gabriel briefly. 'Well, I'm off to play my part. As soon as I am dressed I am going to Kensington to seek out Mrs Harcross, though I do not expect to find her at home. However, I shall leave a note inviting her to contact me.'

'I wonder what she's up to?'

His father shook his head. 'I must say this latest development raises many doubts about her.'

'Indeed it does.'

'But what of you? Where are you going first?'

'To Bow Street, to discover whether Miss Clive has agreed to vanish.'

'And then?'

'To dine with the Delaneys and persuade them to leave London.'

'From what you have told me it will take little persuasion.' Sir Gabriel raised his elegant brows. 'And then you and Miss Clive are to move into the Berkeley Square house, are you not?'

'That is Mr Fielding's plan, yes.'

'Ho hum,' said John's father. He changed the subject. 'As you have been so recently indisposed, you are to take my coach today. I shall travel by hansom.'

'I couldn't possibly . . .'

'There is no point in arguing, my mind is made up,' stated Sir Gabriel, so firmly that there was no purpose in continuing the discussion any further.

Therefore, some three hours later, already dressed for dinner and feeling somewhat conspicuous in his father's smart black equipage with its team of snow white horses, John set forth for Bow Street, only to discover that Mr Fielding had gone out, escorted by Joe Jago.

'He left a letter for you, Sir, in the hope you would come,' said Beak Runner Spink, in charge of the Public Office that day.

'May I read it here in case he wishes a reply?'

'Certainly.'

And John was escorted into the room in which he had first encountered John Fielding, the room once used by the naughty magistrate, Sir Thomas de Veil, to question his lady witnesses.

The note was succinct and to the point. 'Miss Clive has

agreed to my plan and the first stage, namely the announcement that her part will be taken by another actress, will take place before the curtain at Drury Lane tonight. Tomorrow I shall have a full meeting of all concerned to declare that Miss Coralie Clive has vanished but is wanted on suspicion of murder. I shall then put a notice to that effect in the newspapers. I do congratulate you, my friend, on your successful efforts to save the life of Clarice Martin. I shall expect you at Drury Lane at ten o'clock tomorrow morning. Yr. obedient servant, J. Fielding.'

So the game was afoot. The Apothecary felt a thrill of apprehension creep up his spine, as much from the idea of being under the same roof as Coralie Clive as at the thought of the dangerous errand that lay before them.

In the event, the question of persuading Sarah Delaney to leave town simply did not arise. Alarmed by her husband's assertion that the murderer was out to harm anyone connected with Jasper, the visit of the Blind Beak that morning had hardly been necessary. By the time John arrived at three in order to dine, instructions were already under way for the house to be packed up and the servants to prepare for a journey.

'I think we should forgo the entire season and keep Christmas in Suffolk,' Sarah announced as she rose to leave the two gentlemen to their port.

'Why not stay there until the child is born?' asked John.

'Oh no, I should die of boredom. Besides, the murderer is bound to be caught by then, isn't he?'

'I should most certainly hope so,' answered her husband, bowing as she left the room, as did the Apothecary.

Seated once more, Lord Delaney's face changed. 'My dear Mr Rawlings, Mr Fielding has asked my permission to use this house as bait. I hardly know what to think.'

'Did you say yes?'

'Of course I did. I am as honest a citizen as the next man and would do nothing to stand in the way of justice being done. But why should the killer come for Sarah, that is what puzzles me?'

John had a moment of extreme affection for the old man, so delighted at the prospect of having a son, so very deluded about the child's paternity.

'My Lord,' he said gently, 'we cannot be sure that the murderer will strike here. It is just a chance – but one that we really ought to take.'

'I understand that. Tell me, the terrible events concerning Mrs Martin yesterday, was it attempted murder, do you think?'

'I really don't know. As soon as she is well enough she will be questioned by Mr Fielding and then we shall hear her side of it.'

'These are very dangerous times,' said Lord Delaney, shaking his head and downing his port. 'If this plan to lure the killer out goes through, I believe you are to be part of it.'

'I am, yes.'

'Then take care, my friend. I wouldn't like to see you come to any harm.' He frowned. 'I believe that word is going out tonight that Miss Clive has vanished.'

'It is to be a great secret that she is really still in London. You will make quite certain that none of your servants discover it.'

'They are all coming with us. Apparently, the house is to be staffed entirely by Brave Fellows.'

Again, an Arctic wind enveloped the Apothecary. 'Then no harm should come to any of us,' he said stoutly.

'I will drink to that,' answered Lord Delaney, and raised his glass.

It was somewhat drunkenly that John left the house in Berkeley Square some three hours later, and it was inebriatedly indeed that, on a whim, he ordered his father's coachman to drive through the Seven Dials area before going home. Why he did so, he wasn't quite certain. Was it in the hope that he would see Mrs Harcross again? Or was it the fact that Polly Rose lived there somewhere and the thought of kissing that fervent mouth obsessed him? Whatever the case, John positioned himself at the window and stared out into the blackness, watching for the light of the linkmen as they conducted hurrying citizens home. And then, unexpectedly and yet not, he saw her and his heart leapt with pleasure, only to plummet again as he realised that she was not alone. For Polly stood talking to Dick Weatherby, the stage manager, whom she had obviously bumped into on the street corner.

Wondering if there was a *tendresse* between them, John watched. But they seemed to be conversing normally, standing in the glow of Dick's lantern, and the Apothecary was emboldened to lower the window and call out, 'May I drive either of you home?'

They looked up, startled, then John saw that Polly's glorious mouth was curving into a smile. 'I would like that very much, Sir.'

He opened the door and Dick smiled cheerfully. 'Are you feeling better, Mr Rawlings? That was a bad business last night. Good thing I saw you.'

'I'm completely restored now, thank you. Are you on your way to Drury Lane?'

'Yes.'

'Are you sure you want to walk? It's a freezing night.'

There was a suspicion of a wink about Dick's eye. 'No, Sir. You see to young Polly here. I'll be perfectly all right.'

And then there were just the two of them in the darkness and Polly's warmth close to his, and the realisation that her lips were just as wonderful and as ardent as ever they had appeared when he had looked at them.

'I'll take you home,' John whispered close to her ear.

'In time,' she answered dreamily. 'All in good time, Mr Rawlings.'

Chapter Nineteen

As the very first shaft of daybreak splintered the winter sky, John Rawlings crept into his house like a truant-playing schoolboy, got into bed as quickly and quietly as he could, then lay wide awake thinking, not of the two brutal murders in which he had become involved and his part in hunting down their perpetrator, but of Polly Rose and her eager, wonderful mouth. A mouth which revealed the key to her entire personality, lustful and demanding yet giving and generous, all in one.

Yet even though he had discovered things with the little seamstress that he had hardly been aware of before, not only about himself and his needs but about passion in all its aspects, John knew that this was a relationship that he did not dare pursue. For those fervent lips would never be satisfied with a light-hearted lover, a man who toyed and kissed, whereas he was not prepared to be anything more to her, ashamed though he was to admit it.

With these uneasy thoughts uppermost in his mind, the Apothecary waited until it was fully light then rose and washed, carefully shaved round the great bruise left by William Page's forceful fist, then dressed himself in clothes of sober hue. There was much to be done this day and it most certainly was not the occasion for fanciful dressing. Determined that he would miss nothing, from a raised brow to a sigh of relief as Mr Fielding announced to her fellow actors that Coralie Clive had vanished, John went downstairs to breakfast, attempting to put all memories of the last few amorous hours behind him.

Sir Gabriel appeared some half hour later, just as his son was preparing to leave the table, and made a small sound of surprise. 'My dear child, you are up with the lark. Did you not sleep well?'

'Like the dead,' said John, lying cheerfully.

'An unfortunate phrase, to say the least of it. Remind me where you are going. I have seen so little of you in the last twenty-four hours I can scarcely recall.'

'To Drury Lane. This morning Mr Fielding sets his trap.'

'Oh yes, of course. With everyone in place?'

'Hopefully.'

Sir Gabriel drained his coffee cup and looked at John over the brim. 'I did not hear you come in last night. Did you stay late with the Delaneys?'

'Very,' John answered firmly.

'Quite so,' his father responded, and smiled an unnerving smile the meaning of which John did not dare to probe. 'And now to my news,' he continued, his expression bland. 'Much as we had expected, Mrs Harcross was not at home. The maid answered the door and said that her mistress was visiting friends. I enquired when she would be coming back and the girl said she did not know. The poor child seemed quite nervous so I pressed a coin into her hand, at which she appeared more nervous still.'

John let out a shout of laughter.

'I intend to return today and continue my enquiries,' Sir Gabriel added crisply.

'And if the lady is in residence?'

'I shall invite her to dine with me, tell her that Coralie Clive has gone missing and observe her reactions.' Sir Gabriel finished another cup. 'By the way, John, you have a mark upon your neck, no doubt also inflicted by that wretched highwayman. Be good enough to adjust your cravat in order to hide it.'

Somewhat flushed, his son rose from the table. 'I will attend to it straight away.'

'Splendid,' said Sir Gabriel, and waved a languid hand.

Glad to escape, John hurried to his room, made the necessary repairs to his toilette, bade his father a swift farewell then, putting on his thickest cloak, went out into the street.

It was cold again but despite that, having time on his hands, John decided to walk to the theatre, and turned out of Nassau Street towards Long Acre. Behind him, only a stone's throw away, lay that run-down area known as the Seven Dials, but John steadfastly walked onwards and did not look over his shoulder.

Other than for Dick Weatherby, who gave him a quizzical glance which he did not altogether relish, the theatre was empty when John went in. But it was not long before groups of people started arriving, some of whom the Apothecary did not know. An enquiry revealed, however, that this was the cast of *The Merchant of Venice*, who had been at Drury Lane on the night that Will Swithin had met his terrible end.

As well as actors the Principal Magistrate had asked for the stage staff to be present, so that stagehands, many of whom John recognised as peachers, together with painters, milliners, designers and seamstresses packed the place. Polly arrived late, a tremulous smile about her beautiful lips, which lit up as soon as she saw John. Knowing that it would not be honourable to encourage her, yet torn by his violent attraction to the girl, the Apothecary gave her a warm glance then looked away. And at that moment he was saved further embarrassment by the arrival of Samuel, especially invited by the Blind Beak, and full of excitement.

'My dear John, allow me to present you with one of my cards,' he breathed noisily, pumping his friend by the hand.

*   *   *

The Apothecary stared at the card being thrust towards him. 'Samuel Swann, Goldsmith, at the Sign of the Crescent Moon, St Paul's Churchyard,' he read.

'You've started your own business!'

'My father completed the negotiations three days ago. That is why I haven't been able to assist you.'

John, who had hardly noticed his friend's absence, so taken up had he been with events, felt thoroughly guilty. 'Never mind that. This is wonderful news, Samuel. We'll drink a bumper to it later.'

'Anything of interest been happening here?'

'Not a great deal,' answered John, horribly aware of Polly's glance. He lowered his voice. 'Listen, can you have a late supper with me? I'm moving out of Nassau Street in a day or so and may not be able to see you after that.'

'What the devil are you talking about?'

'Don't shout. It's all part of Mr Fielding's plan.'

'Oh, I see. What time did you have in mind?'

'About ten.'

'I'll be there.'

'Good. I'll tell you everything then.'

Further conversation was precluded by the arrival of Joe Jago, who strode onto the stage looking extraordinarily tidy for once. He held up his hand and all voices immediately dropped.

'Ladies and gentlemen, pray silence for Mr Garrick.'

'Fellow actors and colleagues,' said the actor manager, his mighty voice filling the empty theatre. 'This gathering has been convened at the request of Mr John Fielding, the Principal Magistrate. He has an announcement of great importance to make to you. It is an announcement that fills me with much personal woe . . .' He paused sorrowfully and John, well aware that he was privy to the entire plot, thought yet again just how good an actor the man was. 'But though it grieves me to hear

222

anything ill of a member of our company, the truth must be faced,' Garrick continued mournfully. 'Friends, I ask you to pay full attention to Mr Fielding.'

Somebody clapped nervously, then stopped, feeling foolish, and into the ensuing silence came the familiar tap-tap of the Blind Beak's cane. Then, holding Elizabeth's arm for support, the Principal Magistrate appeared, walking majestically, his whole presence suggesting power and strength and the ability to find a wrongdoer and ruthlessly hunt him down.

The Beak found the chair that had been set for him in the centre of the stage but scorned to sit in it. Instead, he stood beside it, one hand lightly resting on the back to give him a sense of where he was.

'Ladies and gentlemen of Drury Lane,' he began, his voice commanding attention. 'As some of you already know, the part usually played by Miss Coralie Clive in last night's performance of *Love's Last Shift* was taken by her sister, Miss Kitty.'

Every eye turned to the elder actress who sat in a stage box looking extremely despondent, another excellent performance.

Mr Fielding continued very quietly, almost in a sinister tone. 'Alas, my friends, this alteration was not brought about by indisposition as was stated at the time. For the truth of the matter is that Miss Coralie has vanished from her home, perhaps even from London.'

There was a murmur of astonished bewilderment and somebody shouted, 'But why?'

'Because, my dear Sir, Miss Clive had been asked to attend me at Bow Street where questions were to be put to her about the murders of Jasper Harcross and William Swithin.' There was a gasp of disbelief above which Mr Fielding continued to speak. 'Certain evidence has been found which can only point one way,' he stated firmly. 'I can say no more at this stage. Acceding to the wishes of David Garrick, I have told you the truth and now must warn you that any attempt by any of you to conceal Miss Clive's whereabouts will be considered a punishable offence.'

This was John's moment, the moment when he must use his eyes and his powers of observation. Slowly and steadily, focussing his pictorial memory so that he could recall the scene later, he looked from face to face.

Lady Delaney, who had been escorted to the theatre by her elderly husband, looked utterly perplexed and bewildered and turned to him with an expression of disbelief on her face, an expression which seemed to declare that she knew Coralie had not committed the crimes. John wondered what made her so certain.

A similar expression was worn by Adam Verity, who stood with his sister, Amelia, both of them staring in amazement. Studying them in detail, John wondered yet again if they were the Egletons for everything, from their physical appearance to their ages, seemed to point in that direction. And yet, would that answer not be too easy? John remembered the Blind Beak telling him that the most simple explanations were often the truest, and conjectured yet again.

James Martin, pale and drained and obviously deeply upset by all the harrowing events he had recently experienced, remained expressionless, his neat little face giving away nothing at all. Whether he had loved Coralie or hated her was impossible to read from the blank features he was currently presenting. And yet, for all his self-control, a muscle twitched involuntarily beside his mouth.

Melanie Vine, on the other hand, looked glowingly triumphant at the turn of events, and John wondered why. What could Coralie possibly have done that a fellow leading lady should react in such a manner? And why Mrs Vine, who had purportedly disliked Jasper Harcross? Or had that been a lie?

At that moment Madame Ruffe, a formidable grey-haired

woman of French extraction, coughed helplessly, so there was a small diversion while Marie, the other young seamstress, patted her on the back and Polly went to fetch a glass of water. Still guilty that he was unable to reciprocate the girl's feelings in full, John gave her a half smile as she returned and looked in his direction, then wondered if some sixth sense had already told the seamstress the truth about him, for he thought he detected a coldness in her glance. Angry with himself for allowing his attention to wander, the Apothecary continued his surveillance.

Jack Masters, blue eyes very glazed but craggy face imperturbable, was giving nothing away. But John noticed that the actor puffed on his pipe as if his life depended on it and the fingers that held the tinder to the tobacco shook. Tom Bowdler, on the other hand, made no secret of the fact that he was deeply shocked. His knees seemed suddenly to give from under him and Dick Weatherby, fortunately standing nearby, was just in time to push a stool beneath the big man's descending weight before it hit the stage. Yet could that sudden collapse have been brought about by relief, John considered? Relief that Coralie had been blamed so that either he, or someone Tom cared for deeply, had escaped attention. As for Dick himself, he was sweating profusely, though whether through the effort of saving Tom or because of the shock about Coralie, no one could tell. He was the man supposed to be above having opinions about the actors yet who had admitted to John that he thought a great deal about them, so this all too human response was only to be expected.

The Apothecary looked round him once more. The identity of the murderer lay concealed beneath one of those faces, a chilling thought indeed, particularly as he knew most of them reasonably well. And then he remembered that baleful figure by Jasper's graveside, the evil symbol it had thrown into the pit, and hardened his heart.

Mr Fielding was drawing the meeting to a close. 'Ladies

Chapter Twenty

It was with a certain amount of reluctance that John rose early, after a late supper with Samuel, during which they had consumed far too much wine. This, in its turn, had loosened their tongues, so that John had found himself telling his friend more than he had intended about his feelings for both Polly and Coralie, and how strangely different those feelings were. Whereas Samuel, for his indiscretion, had expressed a strong desire to meet Amelia Verity, whom he had noticed at Drury Lane and felt irresistibly drawn to.

After only a few hours' sleep it had been a great effort for the Apothecary to go to his shop in Shug Lane, yet again delaying his visit to Chelsea. And it was with a heavy heart that he dusted the bottles and jars and wiped down the counter, wishing that he could follow his intuition instead. For if he had had his way he would have forgotten all about business that day and gone in search of Mrs Camber, hopefully still living in Jews Row in a house overlooking the Hospital Burying Ground, under whose roof had once dwelled George and Lucy Egleton, long since disappeared into obscurity. Or had they?

The Apothecary paused, his duster in one hand, an exotically shaped alembic in the other, his eyes gazing into the middle distance. Into his mind he was projecting the image of that sea of faces, all turned towards John Fielding, as the announcement was made that Coralie Clive was most probably guilty of murder. The Blind Beak's intention had been to lull the killer into a sense of false security, so that, believing himself to be unobserved, he would attempt to strike again at one of Jasper Harcross's intimates. Yet though some present had most certainly evinced signs of relief when Coralie's name had been mentioned, what, the Apothecary thought, did that prove? Never the less, according to Joe Jago, someone, during those vital few seconds, must have given themselves away. If so, John considered, he most certainly had not noticed.

However, not all those involved with the case had been present, among them Mrs Harcross and Mrs Martin, to name the most important. John pursed his lips, considering the two women. Could one have killed two people, including her own child, then tried to take her life in a fit of remorse? And what had the other been doing wandering about in a run-down quarter of London on a bleak winter's night? He shook his head and tried, yet again, to reach some sort of conclusion. And so it was, lost in thought, that John hardly heard the bell which denoted an early customer. It was only when it rang again that he returned to earth, put down the alembic and walked through from the compounding room to the shop to see who had come in.

Polly Rose stood there, looking lovelier than ever, and his heart sank.

She smiled her spectacular smile. 'Good morning, Sir. Or may I call you John?'

'I would hope so after what has passed between us.'

'I thought I should come and see you.'

'I'm very glad you did,' he answered.

'Are you?' she asked earnestly. 'Are you really?'

'Yes,' he said, and catching her wrist, led her round behind the counter. 'I have tea and coffee at the back. Would you like some?'

Her skin was like ice beneath his touch and he was aware that she was trembling. 'Yes, please.'

'Polly,' said John solemnly, 'please don't be afraid, and

please don't be disappointed in me that I am not all that you wanted.'

'How would I know that you are not?' she answered, with a strange little laugh that made him feel thoroughly uneasy.

'Yesterday, when you returned with that glass of water you gave me such a dark look that I felt you had read my heart.'

'And found therein a lack of love?'

'Possibly of the kind you are looking for, yes.'

She metamorphosised before his eyes. The pale cold girl who had come into the shop vanished and in her place stood a lithe wild glittering jewel of a being. Polly laughed again, her eyes taunting him. 'And how do you know what I am looking for, Mr Rawlings? Is passion, then, the prerogative of the male sex? Could it not be that I, too, enjoyed you for what you were and wanted no further commitment?'

John stood speechless, feeling two inches tall. 'But how. . . ?' he managed eventually.

'How did I know all this? You may have read my expression yesterday, but I also read yours. You looked as guilty as a child caught stealing apples. You were a book for any woman worth the name to read.'

'But Polly . . .'

She laughed again, and at that moment the kettle boiled, blowing clouds of steam everywhere.

'My dear,' she went on, 'I may be only a simple seamstress but I have had to fight hard to make my way in the world, humble though my position might be. And during that struggle I learned more about life than many a female twice my age. So feel no guilt that having enjoyed my favours you now do not wish to make an honest woman of me, because I have no wish to be made an honest woman of. As far as I am concerned we can continue to savour passion and leave the situation at that.'

The Apothecary stared aghast, never having heard the like

of it, particularly from anyone as apparently fragile as Polly.

'How strong you are,' he managed to gasp. 'Your appearance belies you.'

And yet did it? he wondered. Perhaps the intense mouth indicated determination as well as sensuality.

'So,' she said teasingly, 'do you wish to remain my lover or is the situation too shocking for you?'

'Not at all,' he answered, rallying. 'I must confess that I have not come across such frankness before, but then I am still young and have a great deal to learn.'

'You most certainly have,' answered Polly Rose, removing the steaming kettle. 'Now, did you not say something about making tea?'

Half an hour later she left his shop, the richer for a bottle of fine perfume. John sat on the chair reserved for customers for a few moments after she had gone, thinking how lucky he was to have encountered such an extraordinary and understanding young female with whom to have a liaison. And then memories of Coralie Clive came into his head and he was forced to concentrate all his energies on compounding and mixing, in order not to feel thoroughly confused.

Though he had not been particularly happy about fulfilling the errand, it had been Mr Fielding's wish, expressed at Drury Lane on the morning of the announcement, that John should call upon Mrs Martin.

'We must find out for sure whether she was attacked or whether she attempted to end her own life,' the Blind Beak had said as he prepared to leave the theatre with Elizabeth and his clerk.

'But surely she would be happier speaking to you,' John had protested.

'Indeed not,' the great man had replied urbanely. 'She owes

her life to you and thus a bond has been forged between you.'

'Do you really think so?' John had replied uncertainly.

'Oh I do, I do,' the Blind Beak answered and had gone on his way.

So now, the hour being three o'clock when most of the *beau monde* sat down to dine and custom was consequently slow, the Apothecary locked up his shop and hailed two chairmen to take him the considerable distance to Portugal Street. He was feeling somewhat too weary to walk after the previous night's drinking, coupled with the shock of Polly's unusual views on love, considerable relief though they had been.

A maid answered John's knock on the Martins' door and kept him waiting a moment in the parlour while she went upstairs to see her mistress. In those few seconds John looked round and thought that though the couple were obviously not rich, the theatre had none the less provided them with a good living. For the house, though small, was furnished in good taste, a great deal of Hugenot furniture being evident, and there being a fine view from the front window over St Clement's Church and its well-kept grounds. John's eye was caught by a portrait of Mrs Martin when young, dressed in costume, and looking stunningly beautiful, a fact which made him reflect bitterly on the cruel toll demanded by the passing years.

The maid appeared in the doorway. 'The Mistress will see you, Sir. But not for long.'

'I shall be brief,' answered John, and followed her up the stairs.

Mrs Martin lay where he had last seen her, almost in exactly the same position. But now there was colour in her cheeks instead of a deathly pallor and her eyes were open, staring at the Apothecary as he came into the room.

'Madam,' he said, and bowed politely.

'They tell me you saved my life,' she said softly, her voice little above a murmur. 'I don't know whether to be grateful or sorry.'

'Why? Did you wish to die?' John asked, taking a seat in the chair by the bed as Mrs Martin indicated.

She made a sad face. 'It seemed to me that I had little to live for. I had lost my husband and my child, to say nothing of the man who was my life's obsession.'

'So you inflicted this suffering on yourself? No one came to call on you and gave you the lethal dosage you consumed?'

She shook her head. 'No, Mr Rawlings, if I had died it would have been by my own hand.'

'I see.' The Apothecary paused, then said, 'I presume that guilt entered the equation somewhere. Or is your heart really made of flint?'

She stared at him, perhaps surprised that he should speak so forcefully to an invalid. 'No, guilt was involved. I realised that if I hadn't abandoned my poor, wretched son to his fate he might still be alive today.'

'And that was all?' John continued mercilessly.

Mrs Martin looked startled. 'All?'

'There was no guilt for having murdered your lover and the child he sired?'

A look of immense cunning crossed the actress's face, a look so sly and strange that John felt himself grow chill.

'Why should I tell you that?' she said in a voice he barely recognised. 'Surely that is for you to find out.'

It occurred to him at once that she had gone slightly insane, that recent experiences had unhinged her.

'Perhaps you could tell me because I saved your life,' he answered with dignity.

She looked chastened, ashamed almost, and John knew with a flash of intuition that her true motive for silence was because she believed James Martin to have murdered Jasper.

'There is one thing I will impart to you,' Clarice answered, speaking so softly that John had to crane forward to hear her. 'It came to me only when I fluttered between life and death and so, I believe, its truth was divinely given.'

'And what is it?' asked John, his voice equally quiet.

'The fact that the killer is not in pursuit of those who loved Jasper. Oh no! His real intention is to wipe the man and his seed from the face of the earth. Don't you see? First Jasper himself, then his bastard, then the attempt to incriminate Sarah Delaney who is carrying his child. Mark my words, she will be next, Mr Rawlings.'

There was a horrid logic to it which the Apothecary could not deny. If Clarice Martin was correct it was a blood feud, not against Jasper and his lovers, but against the actor and his children.

'He wants to make the world as if Jasper never existed in it,' she said again, then closed her eyes and silently wept.

'By *he* do you mean your husband, James?' John asked quietly.

Clarice Martin wept all the more, her eyes lowered so that she would not have to meet his gaze.

'Please leave me,' she whispered pathetically. 'There is nothing further that I have to say to you now.' Then she closed her eyes with such an air of finality that John had no option but to withdraw.

It was dark by the time he came out of the house in Portugal Street, and this time the Apothecary took a hansom back to Shug Lane where he hoped to do another hour's trade before closing for the night. And in the event he was glad he had not gone straight home, for while he had been away a note from Serafina had been dropped through the door.

'My dear friend,' it read. 'I earnestly enjoin you to come to Supper at Hanover Square at six o'clock Tonight. Pray do not Change but come straight from your Shop. There is much of Interest that I would discuss with you. Dear Sir, your Faithful Friend, S. de Vignolles. Post Script: I have written Same to Samuel Swann.'

John took his watch from his pocket and saw that it was already five. Deciding to remain open another half hour, he made a quick toilette in his compounding room, where he kept a jug, bowl and towel, together with a brush and razor, and finally set off at quarter to six to walk the short distance between Shug Lane and Hanover Square.

The quickest way was to go through the narrow confines of Marybone and Glass House Streets, then to turn right into Little Swallow Street which eventually widened out into Great Swallow Street, off which led Hanover Street and the square itself. Not relishing the darkness of these constricted walkways, John none the less took the lantern he kept for such occasions and set off at a brisk pace.

It seemed that the cold had driven everyone indoors for there was hardly a soul to be seen and there was certainly no sign of a linkman. Hurrying through the blackness, his brave light throwing a small circle of radiance around him, John crunched over the cobbles, no doubt getting the most unspeakable things on his shoes as he did so. And it was as he was pausing to avoid just such a puddle of filth, dimly reflected in the lantern's light, that he heard a noise behind him, a noise which stopped as soon as he did, a noise which sounded suspiciously like somebody following him through the darkness.

The Apothecary spun round but could see nothing except a wall of blackness, the outlines of dingy houses just visible on either side of the narrow street.

'Who's there?' he called, his voice echoing down the deserted alleyway.

There was no reply but it seemed to him that something shimmered in the doorway of an empty shop. Raising his stick, John rushed towards it, but its only occupant was a large grey cat which hissed as he approached. And yet he was not alone in that street, he was certain of it.

'I know you're watching,' he shouted again.

Nothing stirred and there was no alternative for him but to set forth once more. With ears straining and every nerve tense, John strode into the darkness, listening for the sound of footsteps behind him. And, sure enough, very faintly but still audible, he heard them. Now the Apothecary panicked, certain that whoever was stalking him was either Jasper Harcross's killer or, at the very least, a foot padder who would rob and probably injure him.

Nearing the junction with Little Swallow Street as he was, John broke into a fast run and headed away from his destination towards the main thoroughfare of Piccadilly where there would be people and linkmen and, with luck, a sedan chair for hire. At his back, his pursuer also broke into a run but gave up when he realised that his quarry was heading fast towards civilisation and, or so it seemed to the Apothecary, turned off into the mean alley of Little Vine Street from where he, or she, could disappear completely into the maze of streets that lay round Golden Square. For all that the sound of the follower had died away, John did not stop running until he reached Piccadilly and had breathlessly secured himself a chair to take him the rest of the way.

Even though he had calmed down by the time he got to Hanover Square, his host must have sensed that all was not well with his supper guest.

'My dear friend,' he said, his French accent somewhat pronounced in his agitation, 'whatever is the matter? You look decidedly pale.'

'It's nothing really,' said John, trying to laugh the matter off. 'Someone followed me in the street, with evil intent I believe, however I managed to lose him so there's no harm done.'

'What's all this?' asked Serafina, sweeping down the graceful stairway.

'John was followed by some villain,' Louis answered. 'Really it is too bad. Why, I swear it is hardly safe to set one's foot out of doors these days.'

Serafina frowned thoughtfully. 'Was it connected with the murders, do you think?'

'It could have been. Who's to tell? Anyway I shook my pursuer off.'

'You must be very careful in future. Perhaps you are drawing nearer to the killer than you imagine.'

'I really don't think so. Neither Mr Fielding nor I can see a gleam of daylight as yet.'

'Well, I have something very interesting to tell you,' said Serafina, linking her arm through his and leading him up the stairs. 'Samuel is already here so let us have some wine and I will recount my story.' She turned to her husband. 'Louis, my darling, even though you've heard what I have to say, will you join us?'

'Just to be in your company is enough,' he answered gallantly, and they exchanged a fleeting kiss.

A huge fire crackled in the hearth of that most exquisite room, throwing scintillating arrows of light onto the walls and the curtains, and gleaming in the rich red wood of the furniture. With only few candles lit and the chandelier dark except for its gleaming reflections, the place at once became mysterious, like some opulent cavern, simultaneously warm, inviting and sensual. Sipping his glass of claret, which shone red as rubies in the glow of the fire, John felt himself grow dreamy as Serafina began to speak.

'Well, my friends, I went to the village of Kensington today to buy some lace. There is a woman there whose craftsmanship is second to none and I often visit her in order to make purchases. Anyway, having completed my transaction, I was walking down the main street towards the inn, where I sought a glass of toddy to warm me for the journey home, when who should I pass, looking mighty furtive I might add, but Miss Amelia Verity.'

'How do you know her?' asked John.

'Very simply. She makes all my hats for me. I wouldn't go to anyone else. She is, beyond doubt, the finest milliner in London. But be that as it may, I could not think what she was doing in Kensington.'

'Perhaps she was visiting a client,' said Samuel, somewhat defensively John thought.

'Perhaps, but the story gets ever more mysterious. She did not see me and hurried into the inn. Naturally, I followed, doing my best to keep out of sight. To cut the story short, there she met with her brother, Adam, and between them ensued a most agitated discussion which, I admit frankly, I did my best to overhear. However, only snatches of conversation came my way, such as, "She's not at home", and "What do I do now?", this last from Adam. Then he said, and I found it chilling, "If the truth comes out I am finished. Should I go to the Public Office?"'

'Good God!' exclaimed John. 'What can they have been talking about?'

'I think it was Mrs Harcross,' said Serafina triumphantly. 'They are, without doubt, her missing children.'

'That doesn't make them murderers,' Louis stated reasonably.

'No, but it certainly draws them into the web. Why should they both be working in the very theatre in which the victim performed regularly? Mere coincidence? I think not.'

'What did Amelia answer to the question about the Public Office?' John continued.

'That I could not hear. Anyway, shortly afterwards they got to their feet, hurriedly paid the bill and left. They did not see me and I presume they went back by public stage. Now, what do you make of that?'

'It's certainly very strange that they should be in Kensington of all places.'

'But they could have been about their normal affairs,' Samuel persisted doggedly.

'If you had seen them you would not have thought so. They were agitated, furtive, and generally acting most oddly. I think you should tell Mr Fielding of it, John.'

'I will certainly.'

Serafina smiled. 'Then hopefully I have been of some use in helping you to solve this terrible case.'

The Apothecary shook his head. 'I cannot say that this leads us any nearer, Serafina. It is just possible that the Veritys were behaving strangely for some entirely different reason.' He finished his wine and looked round the lovely, mellow room. 'My friends,' he went on, 'I must ask you to keep what I say now in confidence, but tonight is the last I shall spend in Nassau Street until this sorry business is resolved, one way or another. The fact is that under cover of darkness, indeed very shortly now, Sarah Delaney and her husband will be removing themselves from Berkeley Square and Coralie Clive and I will taking their places.'

'But why?' asked Louis, spreading his hands and looking delightfully Gallic.

'Because Mr Fielding hopes to lure the murderer into a trap.'

'He thinks that the killer is going to attack Sarah, is that it?' asked the Frenchman.

The Apothecary looked reflective. 'Something was said to me earlier today, something which seemed to make total sense.'

'Namely?'

'That the killer is trying to wipe Jasper Harcross and his

seed off the face of the earth. You see, it all fits into place. The killing of the boy, the careful placing of Sarah's bow, then a glove that was thought to be hers, in the places where murder had been committed.'

Serafina shivered. 'So Coralie, for whom a disappearance has been so cleverly arranged, did agree to assist Mr Fielding after all?'

John smiled in the firelight. 'I think you helped to make that come about, my dear.'

'For that I am delighted, of course. But guard her well, John. I would not like to think that her desire to help brings her face to face with mortal danger.'

'I will do my best,' the Apothecary answered, but even as he spoke his heart plummeted at the thought of the very real menace that lay ahead for both of them.

Neither he nor Samuel wished to be late home so, at ten o'clock punctually, Comte Louis de Vignolle's coach and four came round to the front door of the house in Hanover Square. Much as the friends had insisted that they would be perfectly safe and would find themselves a hansom, both Serafina and her husband, perhaps picking up the dangerous atmosphere that John had brought through the front door with him, had urged their own conveyance upon them. Accordingly, the two of them had climbed into the black coach with the de Vignolles coat of arms emblazoned upon the door, and had gone off in the darkness towards Nassau Street.

'You'll stay with us?' John asked, as the lightly sprung conveyance made its way through the blackness.

'Gladly. I took lodgings in Little Carter Lane today, to be near to my premises. But it's a fair stretch and there's a strange feeling in the air tonight.'

'Things are moving,' John answered, his voice far away.

'I don't know how, or why, but the conclusion is drawing nearer.'

They fell silent, each too full of his own thoughts to speak, and were reaching the point of drowsiness when Comte Louis's coach pulled up before the end house in Nassau Street. Somewhat to John's surprise he saw that the candles were still lit and wondered if Sir Gabriel were entertaining for supper and cards. Yet the house was not alive with conversation as he and Samuel stepped through the front door.

'Is my father still up?' the Apothecary asked the footman who took their cloaks and hats.

'Yes, Master John, he has a guest in the library.'

'Then we shall go and pay our respects.'

And so saying, the two young men made their way down the corridor towards Sir Gabriel's favourite room. John swept open the door with a flourish but his greeting died upon his lips. Sitting in the chair opposite his father's was a familiar figure.

A face once beautiful but still with a loveliness all its own looked towards him. 'Good evening, Mr Rawlings,' said its owner.

'Ah John, my dear,' added Sir Gabriel. 'I have managed to persuade Mrs Harcross to leave Kensington. I know that you will be delighted to hear that she will be staying with us until this present dangerous situation is over.'

Chapter Twenty-One

Breakfast at number two, Nassau Street, the following
morning, had been a somewhat strained occasion. John,
quite convinced that Sir Gabriel was up to some stratagem
of his own, longed to get a private word with his father,
whereas his parent seemed equally intent on not confiding
in him. So it was in a state of considerable irritation that
the Apothecary left the house early, Samuel Swann by his
side, in order at long last to make the fateful visit to Mrs
Camber of Chelsea. But yet again he was to be frustrated.
No sooner had they got to the end of the road than a child
making its way along Gerrard Street was sent flying by
a carthorse and lay senseless amongst the detritus of the
gutters. With no physician available it was up to John to
revive the wretched creature and try to locate her parents,
a task which proved fruitless as the girl turned out to be
living rough. This sad fact immediately tore at Samuel's
heartstrings and he insisted that they took the poor little
being to the Foundling Hospital in a hansom, a task which
occupied the entire morning. Torn between his desire to help
and his longing to track down the Egleton children, John
found himself growing edgy and bad tempered.

'What else could we have done?' said Samuel, sensing his
friend's annoyance and therefore acting defensively. 'We could
hardly leave her wandering round in a daze.'

'But the city is full of children living on the streets.'

'All the more reason to rescue one when it crosses your

path. Come on, John, you wouldn't have left her to die, now would you?'

'No, of course not. It's just that fate seems determined to thwart me at every turn.'

'Go to Chelsea tomorrow.'

'I'm supposed to be in the shop. Which reminds me, why aren't you in yours?'

'The final coats of paint go on over the next few days so I've decided to keep out of the way. Look, I'll take care of Shug Lane for you tomorrow.'

'But you wouldn't be able to prescribe.'

'No, but I could sell medicines for coughs and so on. Oh, let me help, John. I'm as keen to solve the mystery of the Egletons as you are.'

The Apothecary smiled. 'Then I accept. Now, there being nothing further planned, what shall we do with the rest of the daylight hours? For tonight, don't forget, when it is well and truly dark, I am due to move my few possessions into Berkeley Square.'

'I would like to call on Miss Verity,' Samuel answered decisively.

'What? Now? In her shop?'

'Yes.'

'But you can't go and buy a hat.'

'No, but I could pretend to be looking at one for a friend.'

'You are incorrigible,' said John, his grin growing.

And together they made their way through the thronging city to New Bond Street and Miss Amelia Verity's fashionable establishment.

It was crowded with ladies, all trying on elegant items of headgear then staring at themselves fixedly in mirrors. Miss Verity, looking as fashionable as her creations, stood supervising, while a little apprentice milliner, who somehow reminded John of Polly Rose, ran about with feathers and bows and veiling, an extremely harrassed expression on her face. There was a ripple of surprised amusement from this most exquisite of clientele as two gentlemen walked in, and the owner herself came forward to greet them.

'Mr Rawlings, how nice. To what do I owe the pleasure of your visit?'

'Miss Verity, may I present to you Mr Samuel Swann? He is an old and dear friend of mine. I believe he is seeking an item of headwear for an ancient female relative.'

'How do you do,' said Amelia and curtsied neatly.

'Samuel, this is Miss Amelia Verity.'

Mr Swann bowed respectfully, said 'How dee do,' and the introduction was complete.

'Now,' said the milliner, getting back to business, 'have you anything in particular in mind, Sir?'

'No, I'll be guided by you,' Samuel answered.

And they went chattering on, discussing the various merits and demerits of certain hats on the heads of the elderly, leaving John to wonder at the cunning of all human creatures when they are interested in a member of the opposite sex. A half hour passed, then it obviously grew near the dining hour for the shop began to empty of customers, all of whom placed orders as they departed, some very large.

'You have a thriving business here,' Samuel said admiringly.

'Yes, I have been fairly successful,' Amelia answered modestly.

'I suppose you have customers from out of town as well?' he continued.

'Most certainly. From all over the country, in fact. Some people order by post, you see.'

'Do you ever go and visit distant clients?' Samuel ploughed on, in a far from subtle manner.

Miss Verity's expression became slightly guarded. 'Yes. Why?'

Samuel became horribly casual and John cringed. 'Oh, it's only that a friend of mine thought she saw you in Kensington yesterday, but I said it could not possibly have been.'

'I do visit Kensington from time to time. I have customers at Holland House and at the Palace for that matter. I take hats for them to consider.'

'Oh, that would be it, then,' said Samuel, clearly relieved. 'I said that that was what you would be up to.'

Miss Verity looked cold. 'I fail to see what you were doing discussing me in the first place, Mr Swann. Why, I have only just met you. Of what possible interest could I be to you?'

His friend looked so discomfited that John felt he should attempt to retrieve the situation. 'I'm sorry, Miss Verity, your name came up in conversation, that is all. A lady of our acquaintance said you were the finest milliner in town, and was extremely flattering about you. The reference to Kensington was a mere aside.'

'Oh, I see.'

But it was perfectly obvious that Amelia Verity was disconcerted and John guessed that there *had* been something secret about her visit to the village and now she was thoroughly upset that she had been caught out. Had she, he wondered, been calling on Mrs Harcross? Because, if so, the remark made in the inn and overheard by Serafina that *she* was not at home would make perfect sense. Jasper's widow would have been travelling to London in the company of Sir Gabriel at that time. Thinking that he should call at Bow Street and report these latest events, John bowed.

'Thank you so much for letting us take up your valuable time, Miss Verity. I really do appreciate it.'

Samuel recovered amazingly. 'I would like the red hat for my great aunt, Miss Verity,' he said in a grave voice. 'I will come for it within the next few days.'

'Will you not send a servant?'

'I fear that I am only in lodgings. I must wait to see if my goldsmithy succeeds or fails before I can begin to organise a household.'

'Quite so.' She curtsied once more. 'Good day, gentlemen.'

John thought, as he made his way into the street, that it was one of the most delicate dismissals he had ever seen.

It was dark when he and Samuel left Bow Street and parted company. John, aware that he must soon get ready to leave, took a chair to Nassau Street in order to have sufficient time to pack his clothes. The Blind Beak had decided that he and Coralie, who was coming from her sister's house, where she had kept herself concealed for the last few days, should move into Lord Delaney's home during the dead of night, at a time when few people would be about. Meanwhile, several of the Beak Runners and one or two chosen peachers, these being the most trustworthy of that vulpine gang of villains, had taken up residence in the Berkeley Square house disguised as servants.

And yet, the Apothecary thought, there was no guarantee that this highly elaborate plan would work. The murderer might, thinking he was in the clear, merely heave a sigh of relief and let the matter drop. But still the strange words of Mrs Martin continued to haunt him. Was it possible that she could be right? Or was his original idea of the revenge of a jealous mistress or husband the correct one? One thing was clear. Clarice herself believed that James was involved in some way, though surely not as the slayer of the child?

Yet if it truly was the killer's intent to remove all trace of Jasper Harcross, just as if he had never existed, it was only logical that, in time, he would come after Sarah Delaney, who carried in her body the actor's last blood tie.

An announcement had appeared in the *Public Advertiser* that morning. 'It is recommended to all persons having any knowledge of the whereabouts of Miss Coralie Clive, formerly of Drury Lane Theatre, that they come forward to JOHN FIELDING Esq., at his house in Bow Street, Covent Garden. A reward will be paid for any information leading to the capture of Miss Clive, who is wanted for questioning in connection with two recent murders.'

The Magistrate had gone as far as he dared, now he and his associates could only wait to see what would happen.

He had listened most gravely to John's account of his call on Mrs Martin, and also to the story of the Veritys' extraordinary behaviour in Kensington, but had laughed aloud when the Apothecary had told him Mrs Harcross was now living beneath Sir Gabriel's roof.

'What a wily fox your father is. He has brought her to his home in order to keep an eye on her, that's for sure.'

'Do you think so? I thought he might be genuinely worried for her safety?'

'Only if he is convinced that she is not the killer. And I'm not, are you, Mr Rawlings?'

'I was until I saw her skulking about in Seven Dials, now I'm not so certain. Yet, if Mrs Harcross is guilty, who was the woman who threw the witchcraft symbol into Jasper's grave?'

The Blind Beak had shrugged. 'It could have been anyone, even her maid dressed up in order to put you off the scent.'

'Do you really believe that?'

'In the case of an actress as multi-faceted as Mrs Egleton, I am prepared to believe anything.' Mr Fielding had held out his hand to John. 'Let us hope that we don't have to wait too long before the truth comes out. I wish you luck, my brave young friend, though I have no fears for your safety, nor that of Miss Clive. My Brave Fellows won't let a hair of your head be harmed, let me hasten to assure you.'

'Good,' John had answered, but now as he took leave of his father he wished he felt as confident as he had sounded.

They were alone, Mrs Harcross having retired early to bed, yet Sir Gabriel still turned the key in the library door before he crossed to his desk and removed a pair of duelling pistols, both exquisitely made and still in their fine rosewood case.

'My child, I want you to take these with you. I last used them in 1712 when I gave my opponent a choice of weapons and he, being no great swordsman, elected to face my pistols.'

'What happened to him?'

'Sadly, the flash from their muzzles must have been the last thing he saw upon this earth. They are quite deadly, I assure you.'

'Do you think I am going to need them?'

'I pray not. It is my fervent hope that you will be surrounded by a cordon of stout hearts and even stouter arms. I am only lending them to you as a last resort. But if you should need to use them, don't hesitate. Whoever comes creeping into Lord Delaney's house is a vicious killer, you must remember that.'

'You say it as if it is someone I know.'

'I believe it is, my son.'

John shuddered. 'The sooner this is over the better.'

'I quite agree.'

The Apothecary deliberately changed the subject. 'Father, why have you brought Mrs Harcross here? Is it to keep an eye on her as Mr Fielding believes or do you truly think she is in danger?'

Sir Gabriel shrugged his satin-clad shoulders. 'For both those reasons, and another one too.'

'Which is?'

'That I enjoy her company, John. She is a fund of stories

about the great days of theatre and, now that she is freed from the yoke of Harcross, is witty and amusing. In short, I find her a good companion.'

His son smiled unevenly. 'Is this the start of an *affair d'amour*?'

'Most certainly not. We have both reached a sensible age.'

'There is no such thing,' John answered promptly. 'If you had studied the human condition as deeply as I, you would know that.'

'Oh I see,' Sir Gabriel said solemnly. 'So I presume this great knowledge puts you entirely in command of your own emotions? Not for you the foolish mistakes, the nights of passion, the coming home at dawn?'

The Apothecary stared at him suspiciously, wondering how much Sir Gabriel had guessed about Polly. Then saw that his father's eyes were twinkling as brightly as the many diamonds he wore with evening dress.

'Don't tease me,' he said. 'Obtaining information from books is one thing, putting it into practice is another.'

'Quite so,' answered Sir Gabriel, and kissed his son on the cheek before he went out of the room.

An hour later John left Nassau Street in his father's coach, which rolled quietly through the empty streets of London. It was very late, even beyond the hour when the *beau monde* retired to bed or fell down drunk, and only a handful of people, those who had been gambling or whoring the night away, were about. None the less, the conveyance stopped at the entrance to Berkeley Square and John proceeded the rest of the way on foot, gaining admittance to Lord Delaney's house by means of the tradesmen's entrance. Rudge, the Runner with whom he had first gone to Kensington, now smartly dressed as a liveried footman, was up and waiting for him and showed him into the dining room where a very late supper had been prepared.

'May I sit down with you, Mr Rawlings?'

'Yes, of course. We mustn't carry this play acting too far.' The Apothecary took in the fact that only one cover had been laid. 'Is Miss Clive not joining us?'

'The lady presents her compliments, Sir, but asked me to tell you that she has retired for the night.'

'Is she quite comfortable?'

'She seemed so, Sir. As comfortable as anyone could be in this uncertain situation.'

'I wonder how long Mr Fielding wants us to stay here? I mean we can't go on waiting indefinitely for something to happen.'

'I don't think we will have to,' Rudge answered calmly.

'But supposing the murderer decides to strike at someone else?'

'It is a risk we will have to take. However, the Beak seems fairly certain that Sarah Delaney is next.'

'I hope he's right.'

'That remains to be seen. None the less, Mr Fielding has taken the precaution of placing various extra men near the homes of the other members of the Drury Lane company. To be honest we are at full stretch, so much so that the villains of London will have easy pickings.'

John frowned. 'Mr Rudge, I wonder if you can advise me. I work in my shop on alternate days, the others I devote to the Public Office. So obviously I need to be out and about during daylight hours. But will Miss Clive be safe if I leave her? Is it possible that the murderer might strike during the day time?'

'It's possible but unlikely, in my view. I think it is at night that we will have to be most vigilant. And as to your other question, she'll be as safe as anyone can be with a house full of Runners to protect her.'

'Then in that case I shall go to Chelsea early tomorrow morning. Can you tell Miss Clive that I hope to be able to dine with her but that she is to start without me if I do not return.'

'Indeed I will. You'll use the back entrance for going in and out, won't you, Sir. We don't want anyone to know that you are here.'

'I'll be very careful,' John answered.

'Then I'll bid you goodnight, Mr Rawlings. Miss Clive is in Lord and Lady Delaney's room, you are in the bedroom immediately opposite. I am sleeping further along on the same landing.'

'And are you leaving a window open as Mr Fielding suggested?'

'Oh yes, Sir. The trap has been baited and now it is set. Whoever it is who has murder in his heart will not find it too difficult to get in.'

And this said, Rudge left the room, leaving John to listen intently to every sound, however faint, that disturbed the small hours of that chill November night.

Chapter Twenty-Two

Remarkably, the bitter, foggy weather of the last few days had cleared while John slept and he woke feeling refreshed and well, having enjoyed a most comfortable rest in one of Lord Delaney's magnificent beds. In fact the entire room, now that he could see it properly in the dawning light coming through the window, was grand, and John thought that had it not been for the nature of his stay in Berkeley Square he would be about to enjoy himself immensely. For not only was he to live in luxury but was also to have the pleasure of Coralie Clive's company every evening. And then the Apothecary thought of Polly Rose in her drab little room in Seven Dials and felt ashamed.

It was as well for him, with his thoughts going down this disturbing path, that John's wish to find Mrs Camber of Jews Row was now bordering on the obsessional. Briskly shaking off any ideas that might come between him and total concentration on pursuing that course of action, the Apothecary dressed as if the devils of hell were after him, then left the house quietly, using the discreetly hidden back way.

Even though it was so early, a hansom cab plied for hire at the entrance to the square, the horse with its head down as if it were still asleep, the driver stretching and yawning on his box.

'Jews Row, Chelsea,' John called, his foot on the mounting step. 'Do you know it?'

'Not far from Ranelagh, I believe.'

'That would be the one,' and the Apothecary climbed in.

The carriage turned out of the square and down through Curzon Street to Tyburn Lane, then on to Hyde Park Corner, where it turned right and, having passed through the turnpike, proceeded on to the broad sweep of Knight's Bridge. The town had by now been left behind and on either side were green fields and pastoral land, the only sign of civilisation being the occasional glimpse of two parallel roads, The King's Old and The King's New Roads to Kensington. The hansom plodded on, taking its time through the pleasant scenery, then eventually turned left down a narrow path, running through the fields towards a clump of trees. Hoping that the driver knew what he was doing, John stared out of the window at the landscape, bare with winter but for all that glowing in the crisp morning sunshine.

The carriage headed into the trees, their leaves fallen long since, and now the lane twisted serpentine, extraordinarily convoluted, a nightmare for the driver as he urged his horse round ever sharper bends. And then suddenly the path vanished and the conveyance emerged from the trees as they crossed The King's Road, another of His Majesty's private thoroughfares, this one leading him direct to Chelsea. On the far side of the royal highway the narrow lane continued, still twisting though not quite so crazily as before.

'Where are we going?' John called to the driver.

'To Jews Row. It lies just off the path, barely a stone's throw from the Hospital.'

'And if we continued along this winding lane?'

'We'd end up at Ranelagh Gardens.'

'What an ingenious route. I've been to Chelsea many times to visit the Physick Garden but have never come this way.'

'Aye, it's a thoroughfare not known to many.'

'Does the path have a name?'

'Some call it Sloane Lane, after Sir Hans Sloane.'

'Who lived in Chelsea until eighteen months ago, when he

died. There's a statue of him in the middle of the Physick Garden, you know.'

'Aye, so there is,' answered the driver, and concentrated on manoeuvering the animal round the rest of the bends, until they emerged into the outskirts of the village and at long last houses came into view.

'There's Jews Row to the right. What number do you want?'

'I'm not certain. I think it best you drop me here and I'll make a few enquiries. But I shall be needing you for the return journey so can you wait somewhere?'

'I'll be in the Chelsea Bun House just over there, Sir. If you are longer than an hour you will find me in The Seahorse, down by the river.' So saying, the driver went off at walking pace towards the small shop which on Good Fridays was besieged by crowds of many thousands demanding its famous buns. John, for his part, turned away towards the small clean houses of Jews Row.

Despite the coldness of the air, a woman was outside one of them, pushing her baby up and down in a bassinet to stop it crying. The Apothecary, putting on what he thought of as his honest citizen face, hurried towards her.

'Forgive me for troubling you, Madam, but I am seeking a Mrs Camber who used to live here at one time. I wonder if by any chance you might know whether she is still in the neighbourhood.'

The woman's eyes narrowed visibly. 'Why do you ask?'

'I am trying to trace two friends from childhood who were once fostered with her,' John lied glibly.

'Do you mean the Egletons?'

He was shaken to the core. 'Yes. How did you know?'

'Because Mrs Camber is my mother and a very old lady now. And not long since we had another one here asking the same question. Why are those two so popular all of a sudden, that's what I'd like to know?'

'Look,' said John, 'if I could come in a moment I'll tell you everything. It's rather cold out here and the public walkway is not the place in which to exchange confidences.'

The woman gave him a reluctant glance. 'Oh, very well. But I don't want my mother upset, do you understand?'

'Perfectly.'

It was a neat house they entered, bearing all the hallmarks of an old fisherman's cottage. There were heavy beams and whitewashed walls, rugs on the polished floor, and wooden ships collected together on a shelf. In front of the fire an old woman dozed in a rocking chair, a cat upon her lap.

'George and Lucy must have been very happy here,' said John, staring round at the welcoming surroundings.

'They wouldn't have been happy anywhere,' the woman answered surprisingly, removing her cloak. She held out her hand. 'I'm Mrs Atkins. My husband is a soldier and I live in this cottage with my widowed mother, it's easier for all of us. Now, who are you, Sir?'

'John Rawlings, apothecary, presently seeking the whereabouts of the Egleton children. You knew them then?'

'Knew them? I was brought up with them, for all the good it did me. And they had no friends, Sir, so I'm afraid you will have to think of a better story than that.'

John looked official. 'Well, the truth is that I am here representing Mr John Fielding of the Public Office, Bow Street. I cannot tell you why this information is so urgently needed, I'm afraid you will just have to trust me, but to know the whereabouts of the Egletons is of vital importance to us.'

The soldier's wife was no fool. 'May I see your letter of authorisation, Sir?' she asked with a pleasant smile.

Thanking heaven that he had put it in his pocket, the Apothecary sat down in the chair she indicated while she read the Blind Beak's note.

'Well, that seems fairly straightforward. Mr Fielding asks

that full co-operation be given to his representative, and indeed I would gladly do so. But, alas, I cannot help you. The Egletons left here a good fifteen years ago and have not been heard of since.'

John's heart sank. 'Not a word?'

'Nothing.'

He pondered a moment. 'I gather from your tone, Madam, that you did not like the children very much.'

'I detested them,' Mrs Atkins answered shortly.

'In that case would you like to tell me the whole story? It could be of enormous help. I mean, how did Mrs Egleton's offspring come to be here in the first place?'

She sat down opposite him, still rocking the baby gently with one hand. 'Well, many years ago my mother worked in the theatre, only as a costume maker you understand, nothing fancy. Then she married a fisherman and came to live in this cottage. But Mrs Egleton, of whom she was very fond, having been her dresser, had never forgotten her and when that lady wanted to rid herself of her young ones she came straight to my mother and offered her good money to take them.'

'So you were all brought up as one family?'

'In a manner of speaking. Lucy and I were the same age, give or take a year or two. But they weren't the brother and sister to me that my mother had hoped. The little beasts lived only for each other, almost to a strange extent. Do you follow me, Sir?'

'I think so.'

'Anyway, they ignored me completely. I became even more solitary than an only child would normally be. Thus I grew up hating them. Then came the great day when George went off to be a 'prentice. You never heard such goings on from that vile little Lucy. She kicked and screamed and thrashed about. Then she wouldn't eat. How my mother had the patience to bear it I will never know.'

'But what happened after that?' said John, disturbed by what he was learning, even though he had been half expecting it.

'I don't know. Nobody does. George ran away from his Master, then stole here in dead of night and took Lucy out of the house. We never saw either of them again, God be praised, and my mother never had so much as a letter of thanks.'

'So their current whereabouts are completely unknown to you?'

'I couldn't hazard a guess. I presume they went to London but I have no proof of it.'

John leant forward, looking at Mrs Atkins anxiously. 'And the person who came here recently asking the same question as I. Who was that?'

She made a scornful gesture. 'Why, 'twas their mother of course, much aged but still handsome. I had the pleasure of informing her that she was fifteen years too late.'

'And how did she react?'

'She said that she knew her fault and now had to live with the guilt. Then she asked if I had any idea of their present address for she desperately needed to find them.'

The Apothecary's svelte eyebrows rose. 'How very interesting. She actually used the word desperately?'

'She did indeed.'

'I see.'

There was a silence broken only by the splutter of the flames in the hearth, the rhythmic snores of the elderly Mrs Camber and the high, light breathing of her granddaughter. It seemed that the conversation had drawn to its natural conclusion and yet the surging disappointment in John's heart would not let him leave without one final attempt.

'Is there nothing more you can tell me about them? Nothing at all?'

Mrs Atkins shook her head slowly, considering. 'I don't think so.'

'Where did they sleep? Could I see their rooms? It might be of help.'

'George had his bed in the attic, a pleasant enough little place, while Lucy slept on the floor below. Where my daughter now has her cradle.'

'Would you mind?'

Mrs Atkins looked slightly reluctant. 'I won't leave the baby, she might wake at any moment. But you take a look on your own. Lucy's room was to the right of the stair-case, George's up the steep ladder.'

Quite glad that she was not with him, the Apothecary climbed up the stairs, then went to the attic first. The bedroom was minute, with a sloping ceiling and one little window. These days it seemed to be used mainly for storing lumber and, looking round, John thought there were few signs that it had once been occupied by the son of a famous actress. Disconsolately, he went back down the ladder and into what had been Lucy Egleton's room. Nowadays it was very much a nursery, a carved cradle occupying the central position, a few wooden toys scattered round the place. The only decoration was a large and beautiful sampler, hanging just above the crib. John gazed in appreciation, being a particular admirer of this form of needlework.

'In all Misfortunes this Advantage Lies,' he read,
'They Makes us Humble and they Make Us Wise
Lets bear it Calmly Tho' a grievous Woe
And still Adore the Hand that gives the Blow.
Long live the King, Long live the gracious Queen
Our grateful Isle Perpetually shall Sing
Transported See that She can boast Alone
The Happiest Pair Upon the Brightest Throne.'

The sampler ended with the date in which it had been executed,

1691, during the joint reign of William and Mary. And then it gave the name of the child who had so painstakingly stitched it. John read it, and then he read it again before his vision blurred with shock and excitement. A veil lifted and he knew the answer, though not quite all of it. Biting back the cry of triumph that came to his lips, the Apothecary went downstairs to where Mrs Atkins sat feeding her baby, his chest tight with apprehension at the question he still had left to ask her.

'That's a very fine sampler you have in the nursery,' he said. 'Has it always hung there?'

'Oh yes,' she answered, 'it's been on the wall as long as I can remember. My mother stitched it when she was ten years old. I told you she had a talent with her needle.'

John bowed. 'Madam, you have been of enormous help to me. I simply can't thank you enough.'

Mrs Atkins looked mildly surprised. 'But I have done nothing except tell you a few stories from the past.'

'On the contrary,' John answered, bowing once more. 'This house, or should I say its contents, has answered all the questions that I needed to know.'

The Apothecary had found his driver in The Seahorse and in that hostelry had himself consumed several glasses of the best claret in the house in order to celebrate his remarkable discovery. Then, slightly tipsy, he had climbed into the hansom, which had set off in the early afternoon in order to negotiate the bends and twists of the hazardous Sloane Lane during the daylight hours. The driver taking the extra care of one who has had slightly too much to drink, went at a snail's pace, and they arrived back in Berkeley Square past the official hour for dining. Paying him off handsomely and bidding the man a grateful farewell, John hurried into the house through the back entrance and, without ceremony, went to find Coralie Clive.

He had decided during the journey to say nothing to her of his findings, neither wishing to worry nor upset her, but for all his good intentions he was still in a state of some exuberance as he went into the small salon in which Rudge had said she would be found. But there the Apothecary stopped short in the doorway, his mouth opening in surprise at the sight that awaited him.

A perfect facsimile of Sarah Delaney sat upon the sofa, sipping a sherry and reading a book. Gone were Coralie's midnight curls and in their place bounced a lively red wig, as like the hair of her fellow actress as made no difference. The dress Miss Clive wore, if not actually belonging to Lady Delaney, was a perfect imitation of the style she adopted, and Coralie had even gone so far as to pad herself out, so that John had a sudden and overwhelming impression of how she would look if she ever became pregnant.

'My goodness,' he said, and his crooked smile lit his face.

'Mr Rawlings,' Coralie replied in formal tones, then her manner changed and she got up and went towards him, taking hold of one of his hands. 'I am so very pleased to see you back. I have been quite nervous in the house on my own.'

John looked heroic. 'There's no need for that. I'm here now.'

Coralie gave a shimmering smile and he had the nasty feeling she might be suppressing a giggle. 'Have you dined?' she asked, clearly dropping the subject of danger.

'No, have you?'

'I decided to wait.'

'How very kind. Can you give me a few moments while I change?'

'Oh please don't bother, this is hardly the time to be formal.'

'No, it isn't, is it?' And offering her his arm, John led her into the dining room.

It was rather a haphazard meal, obviously cooked by a Runner's wife and served by Rudge with the aid of a peacher.

In fact so strange was it that John was almost glad to rise from the table, hungry though he remained, and retire with Coralie to the safety of Lord Delaney's library, where they sat with a decanter of port and a blazing fire.

'Tell me,' he said, looking at her and thinking how utterly lovely she was, even in her extraordinary disguise, 'why are you dressed as Sarah?'

'Because Mr Fielding asked me to do so. He said to leave the curtains undrawn in those rooms overlooking Berkeley Square and to walk about them in Lady Delaney's attire.'

'And did you?'

'Oh yes. Earlier tonight I sat in the reception room trying to read. The candles were blazing, the windows bare, and I felt like an exhibit at a fair. It was most unnerving.'

'Did anybody see you, do you think?'

'I felt as if I was being watched continuously.'

'You are a very brave woman,' said John. 'Has anybody ever told you that?'

'No, I don't think so.'

'And you are also very beautiful.'

Coralie laughed. 'I *have* been told that.'

John got to his feet. 'Then I'll say no more. I don't want to be classified as yet another of your many admirers.'

'I didn't know that you did admire me.'

'Then why do you think I kissed you that night?'

'Probably because I was being irritating.'

'Yes, that was part of it,' the Apothecary admitted, 'and there was also a great deal more.' He looked brisk. 'But this is neither the time nor the place to discuss it. There'll be no more port for either of us. Lock your door, Coralie, and put this under your pillow.'

And crossing to Lord Delaney's desk, John removed one of Sir Gabriel's duelling pistols from its elaborate box and handed it to her.

'What about you?' she asked.

'I shall be in the room opposite and will be awake, never fear.'

'I do fear,' Coralie answered quietly.

'So do I. But when he – she – they – come for us, I shall be ready and then they'll never know how afraid I was.'

'What a strange philosophy,' she said, kissing him lightly on the cheek, then doing it a second time, and letting her lips linger fractionally longer. 'But then, of course, you are a very unusual man.'

'Thank you,' he replied seriously, and brushed her mouth with his, before he took one of the candelabra and escorted her upstairs, their shadows throwing strange distortions onto the wall and down into the hall beneath them.

Chapter Twenty-Three

He had fully intended to stay awake all night and with this purpose in mind had put more wood on the bedroom fire and drawn up a chair before the flames. Then John had removed his coat and sat down in his shirt, breeches and waistcoat, the duelling pistol on his knees, staring into the glow and wondering what dangers awaited as the darkness grew deep. But the excitements of the day, coupled with the early hour at which he had arisen, to say nothing of the fair amount of wine he had consumed, proved too much to contend with, and the Apothecary's eyelids had drooped then closed.

Almost at once he had experienced an extraordinary dream. He dreamt that he was back in the fisherman's cottage in Jews Row looking at the sampler. This time, however, the name at the bottom was different but, try as he might, John simply could not deciper it. He raised his quizzing glass and peered and peered but all to no avail. The identity of the person who had created this masterly piece of needlework was obscured from his sight. At this point in the dream Mrs Atkins had rushed into the nursery and said that he was to come downstairs at once, her baby had fallen out of its bassinet and was lying unconscious. Filled with a sense of danger, John Rawlings awoke.

The bedroom was almost in darkness, only one candle still burning, the others all having guttered and flickered out, leaving just the solitary flame and the dull embers of the dying fire to throw any light. John strained his ears knowing that anyone coming to attack Coralie would, of necessity, have to climb the stairs. The window which had been deliberately left open led from the area behind the house into the kitchens, so that an intruder would have two squeaking staircases to contend with before he drew near his victim. Silently, John got to his feet and stood facing the door, the pistol in his hand.

There was no sound anywhere except for the low rumble of rhythmic snoring coming from the direction of Rudge's bedroom. So much for the alertness of the Beak Runners, John thought grimly, and wondered what had happened to the man who was meant to prowl the house all night, keeping guard. Then he stiffened, his heart racing with fear, as another noise, faint but distinct and very close at hand, penetrated his consciousness. John cocked the pistol and stood rigid, hardly breathing, as he realised where the sound was coming from. Slowly but surely his bedroom door was opening.

The Apothecary watched in horror and for the first time knew the reality of being frozen to the spot as, inch by inch, the gap grew wider. Then he saw a hand, its knuckles very white in the dimness, insert itself into the space, to be followed by an arm clad in black.

At last he was released from his catalepsy. 'One more step and I'll blow your brains out,' he called, but strangely softly, as if it were wrong to shout in this house of enormous quiet.

The arm drew back, then pushed the door wide, and a figure slipped into the room, almost snake-like in the way it slithered through. 'Don't shoot,' said a voice, and John lowered his gun in astonishment. It was Polly Rose.

He stood staring in utter amazement, quite unable to believe what his eyes were telling him. 'God's wounds!' he managed eventually, his voice grating in this throat. 'What are you doing here?'

'What do you think?' she answered, and threw back the black velvet hood which had been concealing her face.

Trembling with shock, John stared at her speechlessly. 'I can't imagine,' he finally managed to utter.

'Oh come now,' she said, closing the door behind her and advancing into the room with arms outstretched. 'I thought we made an agreement?'

'Agreement?' he echoed stupidly.

'That we could pleasure ourselves with each other whenever we wished. And tonight I wished for you.'

'But how did you know where I was?'

'Very simply. I followed you.'

John shook his head. 'I don't believe this.'

'Why?' said Polly, sitting down on the bed and removing her cloak and shoes.

'Because my whereabouts are meant to be strictly secret, yet you found me without difficulty.'

'Ah, but I *am* your mistress,' the seamstress answered, and with nimble fingers started to unbutton her gown.

Putting down the pistol, John crossed towards her. 'Polly, don't. Not tonight of all nights. We are in great danger in this house. You really must leave at once.'

She lay back on the bed and in the dimness her mouth was a red rose in full bloom, flagrant against the lily of her skin. 'I thought you desired me.'

'For the love of God,' the Apothecary exclaimed angrily, 'do you not hear a word said to you? I am here to guard the life of Coralie Clive, not to indulge in passionate interludes.'

'Except with her, I suppose.'

'I bèg your pardon?'

'I said except with her.'

John stared at Polly incredulously, hardly able to believe the strangeness of the situation, and then, even while he gazed into her face, the most frightening thing happened. Once before, in his shop, she had transmogrified before his eyes, from frightened innocent to worldly woman, and now she changed again. Polly's face contorted and her sensational mouth drew back into a snarl as her body jerked upright, so that she was once more standing before him.

'You worthless bastardly gullion,' she hissed, 'how dare you play fast and loose with me! I know you for what you are, another Jasper Harcross no less. It's your sport to steal a poor girl's heart, treat her body as a bauble, then trample her in the dust. You are beneath contempt, Mr Rawlings.'

'But it was you . . .' he protested.

'Don't add lies to all your other calumnies! You forced your attentions upon me, dishonoured my virtue, and now you want to deny your perfidy. God's life, but you are indeed Jasper Harcross come back to haunt us.'

'And deserve to die like he did, no doubt?' Abruptly, everything had become crystal clear. 'Was that your intention when you followed me in the street that night? Could you not bear it, despite all you said, that I did not love you as you thought I should? Were you going to stab me and leave me to die like a dog in the filth of the gutters?'

The seamstress looked at him, then laughed, suddenly and shockingly, and John saw that on that most glorious of mouths, surely one of the most enchanting ever known, there was a fleck of spittle, like a slug on a rose petal. In the darkness he drew breath in horror, Polly's fatal flaw finally telling him everything he needed to know.

'I perfectly understand, Miss Egleton, that Jasper ruined your early life,' he said calmly. 'However, I think the lengths you went to in order to avenge yourself were excessive. Only a madman kills a child. But then you are very far from sane, I believe.'

She flew at him, clawing and biting, raking her nails over his skin until it bled. 'That wasn't a child we killed. It was his seed, his foul procreation. It had to be put down without mercy.'

'And you did that?'

'No, my brother was the one who saw Will out of the way.'

'You are vile, both of you,' John shouted furiously, then caught her wrists as her hand flew aloft, a glint of steel between her fingers. Yet despite his swift reaction, the lethally sharp scissors raked the side of his neck and he felt the hot blood spurt. And then, from the room across the corridor, Coralie screamed in terror. The Apothecary did not hesitate. Releasing one of Lucy Egleton's hands, he swung a blow to her jaw which rendered her unconscious and, as she fell at his feet like a dead swan, stepped over her inert form and fled to the actress's assistance.

Chapter Twenty-Four

He crossed the corridor in a single jump, at least that is how it felt to him, and went to push down the handle on Coralie's door. It moved but did not give and then John remembered that he had told her to lock herself in.

'Coralie,' he shouted, 'open the door for God's sake. It's John.'

There was no reply but from within could be heard the faint sounds of a struggle. Taking a few steps back, the Apothecary thrust his shoulder into the door and it was only as it swung open that he remembered he had left his pistol in the other room.

At first John could see nothing, for all the candles had blown out in the icy draught coming through the open window, clearly the means of the intruder's entry. Then his eyes grew used to the blackness and he managed to pick out dim shapes. Coralie, in her nightgown, had been half pushed back onto the bed, out of which she had obviously jumped in alarm. A man leant over her with his hands tightly squeezed around her throat, while she flailed and struggled as helplessly as a captured bird. Wishing he were armed, John flung himself at her attacker, dragging him down towards the floor. Very remotely, he became aware of pounding feet and realised that the alarm had been raised at last.

Though he knew, because of the sampler, whom he was fighting, the Apothecary still could not see his adversary, and rolled and grappled and punched blindly, hoping that his fists would make contact with some vital part of the man's anatomy. Then came a roar from the doorway.

'Give yourself up or I fire.' It was Rudge, surrounded by a group of his cohorts, several of whom held candelabra, thus brightly illuminating the scene.

But the attacker hadn't given up the battle yet. Delivering John a blow to the guts which left him winded, he struggled up from beneath the gasping Apothecary and snatched Coralie from the bed, holding her in front of him. John saw that the man had Sir Gabriel's duelling pistol in his hand and that he was pointing it straight at the actress's temple.

'One move from any of you and she gets into her coffin,' he called. 'Now, where's my sister?'

John regained his breath. 'In the other room.'

'One of you fetch her. Then I want a carriage brought round to the front door with four strong horses in the trace.'

'There are no animals here. Lord Delaney took them with him.'

'Don't give it me for nothing! I've been round to the mews. It's packed with beasts.'

There was a shout from the doorway. 'The woman in the other room is unconscious. You'd best let Mr Rawlings look at her.'

'Is this a trick?' snarled the intruder.

'Come and see for yourself,' answered Rudge, his voice full of contempt and loathing. And John thought that the situation was like tinder and just hoped that no one's trigger finger twitched.

The attacker looked at him where he lay on the floor. 'Get to your feet, Apothecary, and go to her. But if you harm one hair of her head I'll blow yours clean off your neck.'

Terribly aware of his predicament, John made his way through the bunch of Runners and peachers, who parted for him like the Red Sea, and went to kneel beside Lucy Egleton's body. Despite the blow he had given her she was breathing normally. Crossing over to the ewer and basin standing on the wash stand, John poured cold water on a towel then applied it to Lucy's forehead, meanwhile holding his salts beneath her nose. Her eyelids flickered and opened and she gazed round her dazedly, then she saw her brother standing in the open doorway, his human shield lolling against him.

They exchanged a look then, a look which only John could see, a look so deep that he knew at once what Mrs Atkins had been talking about. They loved one another; loved with a love that far transcended that normally experienced by brother and sister. Rejected by their mother, fostered out into alien surroundings, spurned by Jasper Harcross, the Egleton children had found comfort only in each other. John supposed that, in the literal meaning of the words, they had fallen in love.

'Are you safe?' she said.

'Perfectly, but what about you?' And her brother unguardedly took a step into the room.

Everything happened. Rudge, seizing the momentary advantage, fired at the intruder who whirled and fired back, winging the Runner in the shoulder. John, seeing his pistol still lying by the chair where he had left it, lunged for it, only for Lucy to claw at him so viciously that he was unable to reach it. At this the ranks of the Runners broke and they charged her brother in a mass. There was a loud explosion followed by a scream and John saw that the man had gone down, dragging Coralie with him. Fighting his way through the heaving mass of bodies, he reached the actress's side and lifted her high, away from all the blood and horror spilling onto the floor beside her.

'Have they killed him?' she whispered as John carried her to the bed.

'Yes,' he answered quietly.

'Poor Dick,' she said, 'poor, poor Dick.'

'Poor? The man was a ruthless killer.'

'But if he was one of the missing Egletons, and I can only

presume he must be, then his fate was decided for him, wasn't it?'

It was no time for argument and after tucking her comfortably into bed the Apothecary momentarily left Coralie Clive while he went to examine the last mortal remains of Dick Weatherby, the wretched soul who had been born into the world George Egleton. Yet just as he bent over the body he was thrust to one side. Lucy had recovered sufficiently to stagger from the bedroom into the corridor, where her brother lay in his own blood and shattered flesh, far beyond the help she so desperately longed to give him.

She fell upon him like a figure from Greek tragedy, covering him with her body and mourning in the manner of a widow. She had put her black cloak back on and she draped it over the two of them for a funeral pall, while from deep within her throat came a sound the like of which John had never heard before. She was neither crying nor moaning but keening, lamenting her dead in a high unearthly wail.

'God's pity, Lucy!' he exclaimed. 'You mustn't agonise like that. You'll break your heart.'

She turned her head to look at him. 'It is already broken, there is no hope for me.' She gave him the faintest smile. 'Do you know, I was fond of you, Mr Rawlings.' Then that beautiful mouth opened and she slipped the muzzle of Sir Gabriel's pistol between her lips – and fired.

Chapter Twenty-five

The room that John always thought of as so light and airy was snug with winter warmth. Despite the earliness of the hour a well established fire burned in the grate of Mr Fielding's salon, in front of which stood a jug of steaming toddy, keeping hot. Seated in chairs on either side of this cheerful conflagration were the Blind Beak himself and John Rawlings who, for the second time in their acquaintanceship, had been drawn into a trail of intrigue and violence and had determinedly followed it through to its ultimate conclusion. Yet though they had been discussing all the terrible events that had taken place for over two hours, in this case there had been a certain amount of personal involvement on the Apothecary's part. And now he needed to talk over this particular aspect with the man whose judgement he respected only second to that of his father.

Yet it was extraordinary really, John thought, looking at the Blind Beak who sat, blissfully unaware of the other's regard, facing the fire, thrusting out his hands to the flames. For John Fielding, despite the awe in which most of society held him, was still only a few days off his thirty-third birthday, young yet to hold a position of such enormous power. However, disregarding the fact that the Magistrate was only ten years older than the Apothecary, the younger man still desperately needed his advice.

'Sir, it is about Polly Rose, née Lucy Egleton, that I am most anxious to talk to you.'

'I guessed as much,' said Mr Fielding, and held out his empty mug that John might refill it with toddy.

'But how?'

'There was something about your voice when you mentioned her to me.'

'Yet I mentioned a dozen other people as well.'

The Blind Beak smiled. 'I told you once before, my friend, that when I lost my sight I gained other compensations. There is scarcely a verbal nuance that escapes me. I gathered from a certain hesitancy in your tone that you and the girl shared a *tendresse*.'

John looked at the Magistrate earnestly, forgetting for a moment that he could not see his face. 'Mr Fielding, I know that in about an hour's time you are due to address the company at Drury Lane and explain to them all that has happened. I also know you will be very frank. So may I just say that I would not like it made public that Lucy Egleton granted me her favours.'

'Naturally you may rely on my discretion. But how terrible for you, my friend, that you became involved with a killer, and that she died in the way she did. It must weigh very heavily upon you.'

'Oh it does, it does,' the Apothecary answered sadly. 'Though to tell the truth it was only a physical infatuation on my part, in my heart I did not love her. Which makes me sound like the biggest rakehell in London, but there it is.'

Mr Fielding actually guffawed out loud. 'My dear Mr Rawlings, you are only doing what most of your fellow humans do. You are learning about life and love. You are no nearer a rakehell than I am a highwayman.'

John sighed, not greatly comforted. 'The puzzling thing is, though, that Lucy let me make love to her at all. I told you of the look she exchanged with her brother. I could almost swear that they regarded one another as husband and wife.'

'Now you are being fanciful,' answered the Blind Beak firmly. 'For all her grievous sin, Lucy was a woman like any other and as free to give herself as the next. If she did love Dick as you say – and that is only your belief, remember – then she was amusing herself with a dalliance, as has done many a married woman before her. You must cease to dwell on it, Mr Rawlings, and realise that your relationship with her was yet another of the innumerable experiences which litter the path to maturity.'

John sighed. 'But I cannot help mourn her.'

'If you did not,' Mr Fielding answered thoughtfully, 'you would not be the young man whom I have grown to respect and trust so well. Now, drain your tankard, my friend, we are due at Drury Lane within the hour.'

It was a strange gathering, this motley collection of theatre people all come together to hear the Principal Magistrate explain to them the link between the violent deaths of Jasper Harcross and William Swithin, and the shootings that had occurred in the fashionable London house belonging to Lord Delaney. By now the fact that Dick Weatherby and Polly Rose were dead was common knowledge, though nobody seemed quite to know why or how. Rumours of foul play had been dismissed in favour of wild talk of suicide pacts, and so it was with enormous interest, if not to say prurience, that Mr Fielding's invitation to meet him once more at Drury Lane had been accepted by all concerned.

This time, David Garrick had set a high chair, used in *King Lear*, on the stage, its back to the auditorium, which was shielded by the drawn curtains. Not to pass unnoticed, the actor-manager himself sat in a somewhat smaller seat, suspiciously like Macbeth's throne of state, beside it. A semi circle of gilt chairs, taken from the boxes, faced it, extra spaces for other people being provided by the boxes themselves.

Coming in through the stage door, following the Magistrate who was being led by Joe Jago, John wondered if it could really have been only a few days before that they were similarly gathered together to hear the announcement that Coralie Clive had gone missing. It seemed more like months, he thought. Without wanting to, he looked round at the places where Polly and Dick had stood and was almost shocked not to see them there.

As if they were going to watch a play, the spectators had arrived early, and there was a buzz of expectancy in the air. Staring about him to find out who was present, John's eyes alighted first on the Clive sisters, sitting together in a box, Coralie wearing a scarf around her throat to hide the ugly bruising caused by the pressure of Dick's fingers. Also there, very pale and subdued and looking a great deal thinner, was Clarice Martin, who sat beside her husband in one of the higher boxes, her face shaded by a large dark hat. Seated side by side on the gilt chairs were Amelia and Adam Verity, he with one leg negligently crossed over the other, she wearing the most stunning headgear in the place. Not to be outdone, the *ménage à trois*, Mrs Vine, Mr Bowdler and Mr Masters, were also dressed exceptionally well, and it briefly occurred to John that most of the theatricals had regarded this meeting as a place at which to be seen as well as to see.

Notably absent from the throng were Sarah Delaney and her husband, he having sent a personal messenger to say that he could not possibly expect his pregnant wife to set foot in their home until all signs of the recent violence had been cleared away. Another face that should have been amongst the crowd, yet no one with any humanity could have expected it to be, was that of Mrs Harcross, that inadvertent bird of ill omen, whose neglect of her children had been the cause of so much suffering. However, one late comer, Samuel, rushed in looking rather red in the face and took a seat beside his friend.

'Sorry to be late,' he panted. 'What a morning! I had intended to close the shop but my father insisted that I get a boy in.' He looked important. 'Now that I have been made Free I am considering getting an apprentice.'

John slanted his brows. 'How very nice for you.'

Samuel looked repentent. 'I'm sorry. I had no desire to be tactless.'

'Be quiet,' his friend hissed in reply. 'Mr Fielding is about to speak.'

And indeed the powerful figure of the Magistrate had risen from his chair while the bandaged sightless eyes appeared to scan the company. Beside him, David Garrick assumed an air of deep gloom and had the occasion not been one of such profound tragedy, John would have laughed.

'Mr Garrick, ladies and gentlemen of the Drury Lane company,' Mr Fielding began. 'The pitiful story which I am about to tell you began and ended in a theatre and thus it is fitting that we are gathered here today in order that I may recount it. As ever, my well trusted friend Mr Rawlings will fill in those parts of the tale that are relevant to him. I shall outline the rest.' He paused momentarily, then went on.

'I think it was a shock to many present to discover at the time of Jasper Harcross's murder that he was a married man. I am not repeating cheap tittle-tattle but stating a fact when I tell you that he loved the ladies well. Indeed in many instances in this strange account you will see that art mirrored life, and no more so than in the similarity between Captain Macheath and Jasper Harcross. However, despite his amours, it is now known that Jasper had contracted a marriage many years before, when he was struggling to make his way in the theatre, and with no less a personage than the great Mrs Egleton, the actress who created the part of Lucy Lockit in the original production of *The Beggar's Opera*.'

There was a loud murmur of surprise from several people present and somebody coughed nervously. The Magistrate waited for the hubbub to die down, then continued.

'At the time of the marriage Mrs Egleton was a beautiful widow in her thirties, probably at the height of her career. However, this same career had not been achieved without a certain amount of sacrifice. By her first husband the actress had borne two children, a boy and a girl, to whom their father, being considerably older than their mother, devoted himself. However, on his death she put them out to a foster mother, a Mrs Camber of Chelsea, and in that sowed the seeds of destruction. What it was about these particular children we shall never know, but let me say, very simply, that they could not have been of a robust mental disposition. In other words, whereas some young people would have made the best of this twist of fate, these two appear to have turned in on themselves and to one another for their salvation.

'It now appears that after some years, when she had remarried, Mrs Egleton offered them a ray of hope and invited them to come home once more. To actors like yourselves, used to envisaging the emotions of others, it cannot be difficult to picture their excitement and joy. But this was to be dashed, for Jasper Harcross refused to have then under the same roof, and once again these children were cast aside. It must have been at this time that a loathing for the man, so violent that it could only have come from very tortured beings, was born. It was this loathing that brought about the two violent deaths in this theatre. You may be wondering at this point why William Swithin should have been a victim of their hatred and I will ask Mr Rawlings to explain that to you.'

Acutely aware that Mrs Martin was sitting in a stage box only a few yards away from him, John got to his feet.

'The reason why the boy should also have been killed puzzled me enormously. At first I thought it might be because he knew something that the killer did not want him to repeat, and indeed that may have been partly true. Sleeping in the theatre as he did, the poor child might well have seen the person who sawed through the planking of the mobile and yet have been reluctant to say who it was. In fact he came to my shop to tell me something but was thwarted in the attempt. Because of that I could not let the matter rest. I already knew that someone from Drury Lane was acting as patron to a poor orphan boy, but at that stage had made no connection. However, a visit to the Foundling Hospital revealed some new evidence. I feel I should spare the feelings of certain people present and simply say that William Swithin was the son of persons connected with this theatre.'

Once again there was a gasp of amazement which grew to a crescendo as Mrs Martin stood up in her box. Her face may have been shadowed by her sweeping hat but her voice was clear for all that.

'Friends – I hope I may still call you that – I was the mother of William Swithin and Jasper Harcross was his father. My dear husband who, since my recent illness, I have grown to love and respect more than any other being upon this earth, wanted me to keep the baby, knowing full well that it was not his. It was I, selfish, shallow creature that I was, who insisted that the boy be left at the gates of the Foundling Hospital. James took him there, even though it must have broken his heart to act thus, but dropped an embroidered initialled handkerchief as he did so. In this way Mr Fielding and Mr Rawlings arrived at the truth about the boy's parentage.'

There was a stunned silence, as if nobody could believe what they had just heard. Mrs Martin sat down again, turning her face away behind its concealing cover, and John noticed that James had put his arm around her shoulders in a comforting gesture. Then the voice of Adam Verity broke the silence, 'I admire you for saying that,' he called, and another person cried, 'Hear, hear.'

'Pray continue, Mr Rawlings,' said the Blind Beak as soon as silence was restored.

'I was obviously not the only one to discover the truth about Will. The Egletons must have found out too, and in their fevered brains their quest became to erase Jasper and his progeny as if they never had been. Thus they concluded that the theatre boy must be done away with. You know the rest. He was hanged by the neck until he suffocated on the same gallows on which his father had perished.'

Now there was the silence of pure horror as that imaginative collection of people considered the wretched child's fate. During this pause, John sat down again. Responding to the lightest tap on his arm from Joe Jago, Mr Fielding took up the tale once more.

'It was Mr Rawlings who first began to query the whereabouts of Mrs Egleton's two children. When he had asked her about them she had told him they had vanished when the boy had been sixteen, the girl ten. Mr Rawlings added to this the fact that a mysterious young woman, heavily veiled, warned Coralie Clive to break her association with Jasper Harcross. Then saw another, answering the same description, throw a witchcraft symbol into Jasper's grave. This made him wonder whether someone from Mrs Harcross's past hated her enough to wish her dead within the year.'

Coralie's voice interrupted the proceedings. 'May I ask a question please?'

'Certainly.'

'Why was I warned off? Why did one of the killers come to see me? Surely I could just have been left to play my dangerous game and take the consequences?'

Mr Fielding paused. 'We shall probably never know the

answer to that but I wish to think that one or other of the pair – indeed perhaps even both – liked you well enough to try and turn you away from Jasper Harcross.'

'Do you mean that they did not want me to conceive a child by him and thus put myself in mortal danger at their hands? In other words they had no wish for me to die but would have murdered me if I was carrying his baby?' Coralie asked boldly, though her lips trembled with the strain of actually saying the words.

'Yes, that is just what I do mean. Now, let us leave the matter. After the two appearances of this veiled woman, Mr Rawlings concluded Mrs Harcross's missing daughter might fit that bill very well. I think it was at this stage we both realised something very frightening was afoot. Mr Rawlings, would you care to continue?'

John stood up again. 'It was something my father said to me that made me decide to follow their trail. He used words to the effect to watch out for the young Egletons. So I made up my mind to locate them. Then slowly I became convinced that they had been under my nose all along, right here in Drury Lane. My suspicions fell on various people, none of whom seemed quite right. But I did not know for certain who the boy was until I finally managed to visit Mrs Camber in Chelsea. There I had a conversation with her daughter, who could tell me little except how close the two children had been. And then I saw a sampler stitched by Mrs Camber when she was a young girl. It was signed with the name Emma Weatherby. At that moment I realised that when George Egleton, whom I have subsequently learned was baptised George *Richard*, absconded from his apprenticeship and took his sister with him, he adopted the first name that came into his head, the one that he had seen on the wall for so many years of his childhood. However, this still left me with the mystery of the identity of the missing girl.'

Mr Fielding spoke once more. 'While Mr Rawlings sought

the Egletons, I became convinced that the killer would strike again and felt certain the intended victim was Sarah Delaney. An effort had been made to incriminate her by dropping Lucy Lockit's bow at the scene of the first killing. Then a glove appeared at the second. But in that the murderers made their first mistake. The glove belonged to Coralie Clive, though they obviously did not think so. And Miss Clive's whereabouts at the time of Will's murder could be fully accounted for. Thus to lead them into a trap – though please remember that at this time we were not certain that there were two of them – we announced that Miss Clive had vanished but was wanted for questioning in connection with Will Swithin's murder. Lord Delaney co-operated fully and removed Sarah from harm's way and Miss Coralie, with great bravery and courage, took her place.'

Simultaneously, both Jack Masters and Tom Bowdler called out, 'Bravo,' and 'Well done,' smiling broadly in the direction of Coralie's box. At this Melanie Vine let out an audible clucking sound and John, staring at her, suddenly realised that the older actress was jealous of the high esteem in which both her lovers held the younger. At last understanding her look of triumph on hearing that Coralie was suspected of murder and had disappeared from the scene, he grinned to himself.

There was a long pause, then Adam Verity asked, 'But what made you suspect Polly Rose?'

Mr Fielding's face became unreadable. 'I think Mr Rawlings can tell us that.'

John looked into the middle distance, afraid that his eyes might reveal the truth. 'I regret that I didn't suspect her, Adam. Not until the very night she and her brother came to kill who they believed to be Sarah Delaney. I knew Polly, of course. Had interviewed her about the murders. But I simply couldn't believe that . . .' His voice trailed away and there was a slightly uncomfortable silence.

Help came from an unexpected source as Coralie spoke.

'Dick broke into the house by climbing the wisteria on the outside wall, then smashing the glass of my bedroom window. At first he thought I was Sarah but when he recognised me knew that I would be able to identify him so therefore had to die. But I do not hate him for attacking me. Dick Weatherby will always be the stage manager to me. As far as I am concerned George Egleton was the evil part of him, and that is how I intend to think of the situation.'

Her sister, Kitty, applauded and remarked, 'Well said!' and there were murmurs of agreement.

Mr Fielding rose to his feet. 'And that I believe is a fitting epitaph for this tragic pair, as doomed as Romeo and Juliet. Though the murder of a child is beyond forgiveness, let us remember them simply as Dick and Polly, so helpful about this theatre. It was their other sad, neglected lives which finally led them to commit so atrocious and terrible a crime.'

'It is Mrs Harcross I blame,' said Jack Masters, lighting his pipe.

John shook his head. 'No, Sir, she is as pathetic as her offspring. A silly feckless woman, though for all that talented and witty, retribution came to her when she married Jasper. She loved him to distraction and he gave her a life of misery. But finally, after I had set her wondering about them, she went to see Mrs Camber to find out about her children, and presumably followed the same path as I. She must have seen the sampler, recognised the name as that of the stage manager, and come in search of the missing pair. For one bitter night I saw her in Seven Dials, where she must have heard they lived, frozen with cold and obviously near to tears.'

'Will she be told all this?' asked Amelia Verity.

'No doubt she will discover it,' John answered heavily, 'but I for one intend to remain silent.'

Again there was a murmur of agreement, sufficiently strong to give him hope that the terrible truth about Mrs Harcross's children would not come from the people of Drury Lane.

Somebody unseen asked the inevitable question. 'How did Dick and Polly die?'

The Blind Beak's voice sounded amazingly matter-of-fact. 'Dick wounded a Runner and, in turn, was shot himself. Polly chose suicide and put a pistol to her head. She obviously could not face Tyburn Tree.'

Coralie spoke again. 'And you really had no idea about her, John?'

He hesitated, then said, 'Mr Jago, the Magistrate's clerk, swore that I would know the identity of the murderer after the announcement that you had disappeared. And, strangely, I did intercept a look Polly gave me. It was dark and black, unreadable. But I thought she was annoyed with me over some trivial matter and did not interpret it for what it actually was. In other words I closed my mind to the idea that she could be guilty, even though the evidence was there all along.'

'I see,' said Coralie, and John thought, Oh God, she does!

Mr Fielding broke in. 'Are there any more questions?'

David Garrick spoke for the first time. 'Fellow members of the company, I believe that we owe a great debt of gratitude to John Fielding, whose brilliant brother contributed so much to the literary splendour of this fair realm. And also, of course, we must give thanks to John Rawlings, the young apothecary who first tended both Jasper and Will, and who has helped so much in bringing their slayers to book.'

There was a round of mild applause which died away, it obviously being considered a tasteless way of expressing appreciation. The Blind Beak got to his feet. 'Ladies and gentlemen, I hope one day to meet you again in more pleasant circumstances,' and with that he tapped his way across the stage and vanished from view.

Everyone stood up, all looking slightly stunned, and though John was longing to stare round at Coralie, he felt it wiser not to do so. Then the Veritys came towards him, smiling broadly, and his attention was distracted elsewhere.

'Mr Rawlings,' said Amelia, holding out a hand which he kissed, much to the annoyance of Samuel. 'I do vow and declare you thought Adam and I were the Egletons at one stage. Am I right?'

'You most certainly are. Particularly after the Comtesse de Vignolles saw you behaving somewhat strangely in Kensington, a fact which she reported back to me.'

Adam's bright eyes flashed. 'Ah, yes. Well . . . er . . . there is an explanation for that.'

John gleamed. 'I wouldn't dream of asking for it.'

''Zounds, but you'll hear it none the less, my dear fellow. The truth is that I have been indulging in a liaison with a married lady of some renown, titled in fact. Well, not to mince words, my fancy has recently strayed elsewhere, you know the way it does?'

'Only too well,' said the Apothecary, and sighed.

'Anyway, she cut up damnably awkward and said she would tell her husband all if I did not stay with her. She got so savage about the whole thing that I had a mind to tell the Public Office of her blackmailing threats. Amelia, who is a damn fine woman as well as being my sister, came with me to Kensington, where the lady in question has a country place, and we attempted to see her to beg her to be lenient. But she was out and there was an end to it.'

'How did it all resolve?' asked Samuel, open-mouthed at such frank revelations.

'Amelia conceived the brilliant notion of introducing her to a friend of ours, another actor from the Haymarket, much better looking than I. The stratagem worked and Madam has decamped with my supposed rival.' He burst out laughing.

The Goldsmith, who was obviously longing to say something, could be seen adopting a bold stance before he asked,

'Mr Verity, if you are agreeable, I would like to invite Miss Verity to accompany me to a ridotto at Ranelagh Gardens on this forthcoming Friday.'

Adam grinned. 'That depends entirely on my sister's wishes.'

Samuel whirled, windmill like, to face Amelia. 'Madam, it would give me great pleasure if you would allow me to escort you.'

'How could I refuse so charming an invitation,' she replied, and curtsied.

Samuel lit up like a beacon and John suddenly felt rather saddened and alone, memories of poor dead Lucy, completely crazy though she clearly had been, filling his thoughts.

'Gentlemen,' said Adam, sensing something of the Apothecary's unhappy feelings and trying to put things right. 'May I invite you to New Bond Street to sink a bumper or two? There'll be no more work for me today.'

'Nor me,' said Amelia spiritedly. 'I'll put the shop in the hands of my head girl.' She turned to look at John. 'Anyway, my dears, sad though it is, I feel we should drink to the safe passing of troubled spirits. May they rest in peace.'

'Yes,' answered the Apothecary quietly, 'may they all rest in peace.'

Chapter Twenty-Six

That Christmas of 1754, Sarah Delaney, large with child and glowing with triumph, gave a ball in order to show off her new house to all her friends. She had returned from the country, once assured that danger was past, and immediately announced to her adoring husband that she could never set foot in the Berkeley Square home again. Having spent one night there and thrown into the argument a pale ghost with a peony red mouth who roamed the place crying out and weeping, her doting spouse, thinking of his unborn son, had given way and had bought his vivacious wife a splendid new establishment.

Situated in a prime position in Pall Mall, its elegant exterior decorated with a frieze depicting classical figures, its interior sumptuously filled with crystal chandeliers and alabaster pillars, Lady Delaney's residence was considered one of the most beautiful places in London, and invitations to the house warming had been fought over by members of the *beau monde*. But despite the smattering of Princes and Dukes amongst the guests, Sarah had not forgotten her old friends, and everyone from Drury Lane theatre had received one of the highly-prized gilt-edged cards, together with all those who had been involved in the tragic circumstances surrounding the death of Jasper Harcross.

An orchestra played music for dancing in the first-floor circular saloon, reputedly one of the finest rooms in England, its walls made up of sparkling mirrors in which the lovely clothes worn by the guests were most splendidly reflected.

Tables had been set for supper in the drawing and dining rooms, and card tables put up in the library and music room. In this last John Fielding sat, his wife beside him whispering the denominations of the cards he held, playing whist with the Duke of Marlborough, the Duchess of Bedford and Sir Gabriel Kent, one of the most exquisitely dressed men present, his usual garb of silver and black heightened by a great flurry of diamonds. Not to be outdone, his son, so very highly regarded by the host, was wearing a new suit of deep purple figured silk embroidered with clusters of glittering rhinestones, shiny black shoes with fancy buckles upon his feet, and a lilac coloured silk ribbon tying the queue of his wig.

In order to celebrate the Yuletide, the incomparable house had been decorated throughout with trails of greenery, and yule logs spluttered in every fireplace. A huge silver punch bowl, constantly topped up by servants with steaming jugs of potent spicy brew, stood amongst festoons of holly and ivy, scarlet ribbons tied to its handles and to the great ladle that lay beside it. One glass having a very powerful effect yet being utterly delicious and demanding a second be consumed, there was consequently a good deal of merriment, and conversation flowed easily, particularly amongst the younger people.

Standing near the bowl, glass in hand, talking to Samuel and the Veritys, John, noticing the effects of the punch give him a slightly heady feeling, found himself constantly glancing into the great overmantel mirror above the fireplace, looking to see whether Coralie Clive had come into the room. She was in the house somewhere, he knew, having watched her arrive in company with her sister and the celebrated actress Peg Woffington, David Garrick's mistress. But after a charming smile in his direction, she had disappeared to join the dancers, and he had not been brave enough to follow her.

After the double tragedy in the house in Berkeley Square they had drawn close to one another for an enjoyable few days, comrades in misfortune. Then, when Coralie had recovered sufficiently to return home, a noticeable distance had grown between them. Of course, John had to admit, the actress's coolness had coincided with his admission to the Drury Lane company that he had been unable to accept Polly Rose, born Lucy Egleton, as a murderer. An admission which anyone with any knowledge of the world must surely have been able to see through.

'You're very quiet,' said Amelia, breaking in on his train of thought.

The milliner wore the most interesting headdress in the entire gathering, a swirl of flowers and butterflies, shimmering and iridescent, and all made up of rainbow hues. An excellent advertisement for her own establishment.

John smiled at the clever little business woman. 'I was thinking.'

Amelia exchanged a glance with Samuel with whom, it was perfectly obvious, she now enjoyed a certain degree of intimacy.

'Mr Swann, our friend is in a fit of gloom. What are we going to do with him?'

'I suggest we all dance,' her escort answered gallantly.

'An excellent thought! Let's find some partners,' put in Adam, grabbing John by the arm. 'Look, there's Melanie Vine without either of her lovers. I'll ask her.' And he bowed low before his fellow thespian, who graciously extended her hand.

The Apothecary looked round, seeing whom he might lead into the ballroom, and there was Elizabeth Fielding, released from her duties at the card table, heading towards the punch bowl.

'Madam,' he said, with a flamboyant salute, 'will you do me the great honour of joining me in a dance?'

She smiled delightedly. 'Mr Rawlings, it would be a pleasure,' and Elizabeth put her arm through his.

The saloon glittered with a hundred extra candles, the reflections of which shimmered and sparkled in the gilded mirrors and in the jewels of the dancers. Everyone was there, jolly Tom Bowdler puffing round the room with Peg Woffington, while Garrick himself danced with his legal wife, Madame Violetta. Jack Masters was leading out Madame Ruffe, who had once employed poor Polly, while Clarice and James Martin danced together, John was much touched and gladdened to see. Even Sir Gabriel had come into the room, his son observed, his partner none other than the Comtesse de Vignolles, now noticeably rounding, while Comte Louis danced with Kitty Clive. Of the girl John wanted most to see, there was no sign at all.

The music, *Bonny Dundee*, came to an end and the orchestra struck up a new refrain, a longways dance, *Would You Have a Young Virgin*. Everyone led their partners into position and it was then that the Apothecary saw Coralie Clive, flushed and laughing, and dancing with none other than that celebrated young rake, the Duke of Richmond. Jealous yet torn, because Richmond was someone whom John held in high regard and deep affection, he turned all his attention onto Elizabeth Fielding, who was obviously enjoying the rare pleasure of being able to dance.

The music changed again, this time to *Maid in the Moon*, a round for six. There was a general shuffle about and the Apothecary found that his immediate partner had gone to join a circle of others and he was now standing with Sir Gabriel Kent, Serafina de Vignolles, Samuel Swann, Amelia Verity and Coralie Clive.

'Well,' said Serafina, slanting her eyes at the others, 'this could be a reflection of our situation, do you not think?'

Amelia looked blank. 'What do you mean, Comtesse?'

'Why, that this dance reflects our lives. When I first met Sir Gabriel, Samuel and John, we formed a quadrille as we slowly discovered the truth, each about the other. Now here we are, six of us, who no doubt will meet again and continue to dance round one another as time goes by.'

Sir Gabriel spoke, looking down at his fellow guests from his commanding height, his heavily powdered nine-storey wig making him seem taller than ever. 'My dear Serafina, what a pretty conceit. Is it your contention that the weaving threads of fate are, then, but a dance?'

'And that life is a series of steps, some of which might make us fall over, whilst others send us leaping on?' asked Samuel. Then, not waiting for an answer, added, 'I think it is a splendid notion, don't you, Amelia?'

The milliner smiled happily and nodded, the faintest hint of deepening colour appearing in her cheeks as the fiddle struck the opening chords.

Emboldened by the punch and the brilliant surroundings and the generally heightened atmosphere, John took Coralie's hand in his.

'And what about you, Miss Clive? Will you continue to dance in our circle of friends or, indeed, in my circle? Or will you seek other partners?'

Her green eyes were as bright as the mistletoe berries which garlanded the mirrors and cascaded down from the chandeliers.

'That remains to be seen, does it not?'

'And what do those words mean exactly?'

'That we are both young yet and have a great deal of living to do.'

'I see.'

The music was starting up and John glanced quickly round the room. The Martins were still together, as were the Delaneys, sitting out the dance but surveying their guests with obvious pleasure. Melanie Vine, standing in her circle, had Jack Masters and Tom Bowdler on either side of her, Mr Garrick doing likewise with Madame Violetta and Peg Woffington. That loveable fox, Joe Jago, had appeared from nowhere and was now partnering Mrs Fielding. While sitting in a high chair besides his hosts, the Blind Beak was tapping his foot and had turned his bandaged eyes towards the musicians, obviously enjoying their lively sound.

There was only one missing face in all that bright company; the beautiful, haunted countenance of Elizabeth Harcross. John had never questioned his parent, not feeling it his right to do so, about what had happened when the terrible news concerning her children had finally reached her, as inevitably it must. All the Apothecary knew was that she had been missing for several days from the downstairs rooms in Nassau Street, confined to her bedroom, and that his father had spent a great deal of time talking to and comforting her. Finally, though, the unhappy woman had moved back to Kensington, leaving Sir Gabriel strangely quiet and pensive.

John was aware that a tactful interval had elapsed before his father had gone to call, only to find the house empty, all the furnishings gone. And then a letter from Mrs Harcross had arrived from Italy telling Sir Gabriel that she had gone to live with an invalid cousin, whom she was intending to nurse for the rest of his days in order to atone for all her past wickedness.

'A ruined life! How sad,' said John, remembering both her and her daughter with a desperate sense of pity.

'What do you mean? Your life is ruined because we are both still young?' Coralie exclaimed, astonished.

He seized her round the waist and executed the initial sequence of steps. 'No, just for a moment I was thinking about something else.' He smiled down at her. 'Do you know, it suddenly occurs to me that at long last we are even.'

'Even?' she repeated, looking still more puzzled.

'You saved my life once and I, though somewhat clumsily I admit, also saved yours.'

'Then are we not supposed to be responsible for one another? Is that not the superstition?'

John shook his head. 'I really don't know.' He paused, then drew her closer still, ignoring the others who by now were dancing in the centre. 'But perhaps when we have done all this living you talk about we might be able to find out,' he said softly.

Coralie Clive regarded him with a quizzical expression. 'Perhaps,' she said as, with the music gathering momentum and the lights from the chandelier glistening in their eyes, the two of them started to dance.

Historical Note

John Rawlings, Apothecary, was born circa 1731, though his actual parentage is somewhat shrouded in mystery. However, by 1754 he had emerged from obscurity when on 22 August he applied to be made Free of the Worshipful Society of Apothecaries. After two unsuccessful attempts to be made Free, he eventually became a Yeoman of the Society in March, 1755, giving his address as number two Nassau Street. His house still stands and can be found in Gerrard Place in Chinatown. Well over a hundred years later, this was the address of H. D. Rawlings Ltd., Soda Water Manufacturers, proving conclusively that John Rawlings was probably the first apothecary to manufacture carbonated waters in this country. After some early research on him, his ebullient personality continued to haunt me, and I brought him into the spotlight in the first book in this series, *Death in the Dark Walk*.